Enna
Burning

Enna Burning

Shannon Hale

BLOOMSBURY

Published by Bloomsbury, New York and London
Distributed to the trade by Holtzbrinck Publishers

Library of Congress Cataloging-in-Publication Data
Hale, Shannon.
Enna burning / by Shannon Hale.
p. cm.
Sequel to: The goose girl.
Summary: Enna hopes that her new knowledge of how to wield fire will help
protect her good friend Isi—the Princess Anidori—and all of Bayern against
their enemies, but the need to burn is uncontrollable and puts Enna and
her loved ones in grave danger.
ISBN 1-58234-889-8 (alk. paper)
[1. Fairy tales. 2. Fire—Fiction. 3. Nature—Effect of human beings on—
Fiction.] I. Title.
PZ8.H134En 2004
[Fic]—dc22
2003065817

First U.S. Edition 2004
Printed in the U.S.A. by Quebecor World
1 3 5 7 9 10 8 6 4 2

Bloomsbury USA Children's Books
175 Fifth Avenue
New York, NY 10010

For the Bryner sisters

(perhaps you've heard of us)
Melissa, Katie & Jessica

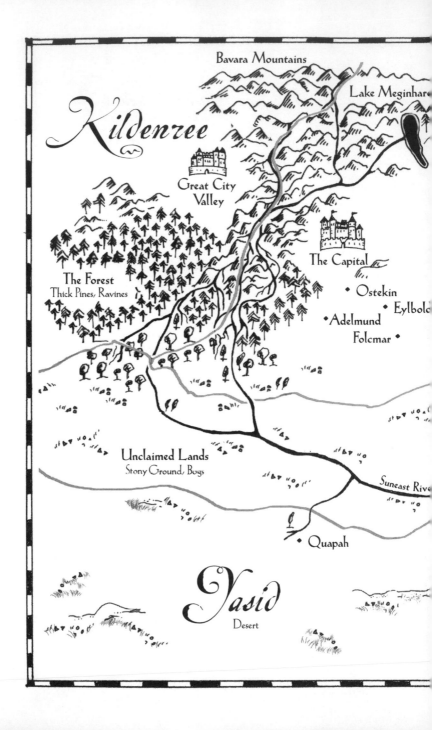

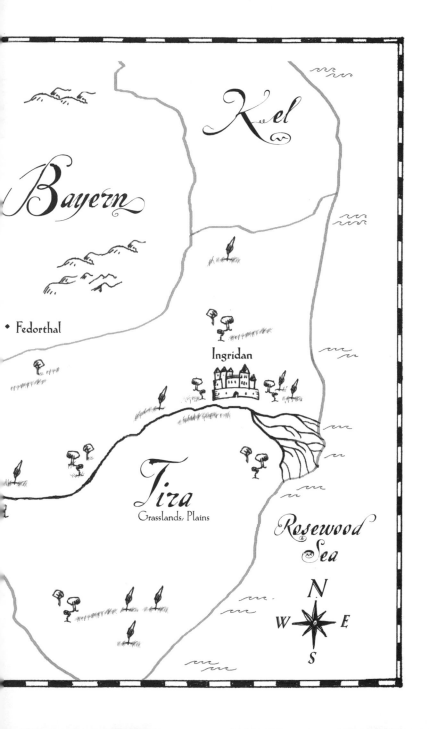

Prologue

he woman bore a scorch mark from her chin to her brow. The vision in her left eye was still blurry, as though she were looking through a scratched pane. She had been walking away from the burning for a few weeks by now and so supposed the eye would never heal, even if she lived long enough to give it time. Closing her bad eye, she squinted to see where she was going. There was a patch of greenness on the horizon that stretched into the east. A forest. Perhaps that would be far enough away.

As the woman walked, she leaked fire unawares, and the dead river wood occasionally smoked beside her or crackled into flame. Once or twice, to ease the burning, the woman threw herself into the stream beside her path, choking on the water and weeping as the stream took away her heat. It was hard to get back up after that, but memory of the horrors she left behind drove her on.

Her skin twitched to remember hot ash falling;

her eyes roved as though watching again and again the village in flames. She clutched the sack containing the vellum tighter to her chest, remembered her purpose, and walked faster.

She walked until the wet forest air enclosed her and washed the scorched smell from her hair. She walked until she fell. Then she dug where she fell, pulling away handfuls of soil from under a young fir tree.

"Here," she said, talking to the fir, "keep this."

The woman unrolled the oiled cloth and took out the vellum, looking again at the writing that had started the end of her everything. It was still in beautiful condition, though the vellum had been made from lambskin in her mother's time. Tight, delicate writing filled its face, each black stroke bleeding tiny lines thin as spiders' legs, each word stitched together in a lacework of ink. Glancing over it again, she sobbed once at the beauty of the knowledge it held. Her eyes stung, and the fever burned away any tears.

She loved the fire, loved it more than her own flesh now. Destroying the vellum and the truth it held seemed a hopeless gesture. Deep inside, behind her scorched eye, she knew she probably should. But no, she would hide it to prevent destruction like the kind she had caused. And she would hide it so that perhaps one day someone with the talent to learn could read it and know its goodness. She prayed it might be someone stronger than she.

She wrapped the vellum back in its cloth, then slipped

both into the slim clay pot she had used for water, burying the tiny coffin beneath the pine.

The woman lay down and let herself relax, deep inside, where for so long she had trembled to hold the fire at bay. Her control broke like a tree limb under too much weight, and the snap made her cry out. Heat poured from her chest and pressed out against her skin, burning her as she had burned others. Her blurred eye went dark, her good eye saw gold, and the forest pulsed with life, then stilled under a winding breeze.

She rested her head on the ground. The pine needles pressing into her cheek began to crackle. Smoke rose in fragile tendrils, and she watched them rise until she could at last give in fully and die.

Part One

Sister

nna let the fire burn out.

She was not used to this duty. For the three years she had lived and worked in the city, the hearth had been the hall mistress's responsibility. And when Enna had returned to the Forest a year ago at the onset of her mother's illness, her mother had continued to tend the fire. After her mother's death in the spring, Enna had become the mistress of this little Forest house, but with a garden to tend, wood to chop, and a brother, a goat, and chickens to feed, she often forgot the fire.

It was not hard to do. A fire in a kitchen hearth was a quiet beast.

Of course, Enna thought, she *would* overlook the coals on a night when her brother and, more important, the flint in the kindling box were out wandering in the deep woods. So she walked to the house of her nearest neighbor, Doda, and borrowed a spade's worth of embers in her milking pail. She struggled home, gripping the hot handle with a rag and the end of her skirt.

The embers drew her eyes. They were beautiful, pulsing red in the bottom of the dark pail like the heart of a living thing. She looked away, and the orange coals stayed before her eyes, burning its image over the night. She tripped on a tree root.

"Ah, ah," she said, trying to regain her balance and keep the hot pail from touching her or spilling to the ground. She cursed herself for the hundredth time that night for being so careless, sought out the dark outline of her house, and headed for it.

"Strange," said Enna, blinking hard to clear her vision. There appeared to be a light in her window, and it was getting brighter. Enna ran through the yard and looked into the open window.

First she noticed the hearth fire blazing. She was about to exclaim when she saw her brother, Leifer, sitting beside it, his pack on his lap, his attention taken up by something in his hands. Enna thought he looked handsome like this, his face still and thoughtful. He shared with Enna the black hair and dark eyes that had marked their mother. At age eighteen he was two years older than Enna, though unlike her he had never left the Forest even so far as to visit Bayern's capital, just two days' travel from their home.

Leifer unrolled the thing in his hands, and the firelight illuminated it from behind so that it glowed like a lamp. Enna could see it was a piece of vellum with writing on one side. Leifer could read a little, as could she—unusual for Forest-born, but their mother was from the city and had taught them. Parchment was rare in the Forest, and Enna had no notion where he had found such a thing.

A slow, burning pain in her hands reminded her what she held, and she tottered onto the porch and through the door. She caught sight of Leifer hastily rolling up the vellum and stuffing it in his pack.

"Hot," said Enna at a near run. She put the pail by the hearth and brushed off her hands. "Ow, but that rag grew thinner the farther I walked. Greatness, Leifer, I thought the house aflame from a distance."

Leifer closed up his pack and shoved it into the darkness under his bed. "Well, had you kept the fire going . . ."

"Yes, yes," said Enna, shooing away his protest with a wave of her hand. "No need to remind me I'm as good as a fish when it comes to the cookfire. Really, you're good to get a full blaze going in a dead hearth in just the time it took me to get a pail of embers from Doda. You did spook me coming up out of nowhere, though. Why're you back a day early?"

Leifer shrugged. "We were done." He looked out the window, though the night was so dark that it opened only to a view of blackness. He seemed thoughtful, but Enna would not have the silence. He had been gone for six days, and she had driven the chickens to ceaseless squawking in a vain quest for conversation.

"So," said Enna, her voice expressing exaggerated impatience, "what'd you find?"

"Oh, you know. Gebi found settling places with fresh springs about an hour's walk from here. We found another pasturing place, brought back some berry bushes and onions for planting, and . . . " He paused, then rose to close the shutters on the night. He stood a moment, his hand splayed on the wood. "And I found a lightning-dead fir in the deep Forest. We, we pulled it up by the roots, dragged it to the spring for settlers to use."

His voice hinted at more.

She cleared her throat. "And?"

"Something curious . . . " He looked back at her, and his voice was edged with excitement. "There were some shards of pottery wrapped right up in its roots, like something, maybe a bowl or jar, had been buried there before the fir took deep root. I counted the rings, and I think the tree was near a hundred years old."

"Hm. You find anything else?" *The vellum*, she thought. She knew if Leifer did not bring it up on his own, all the cajoling in the world could not squeeze a secret out of him. When he did not speak, she grabbed a boot and threw it at his backside.

"Ow," he said with a laugh, and rubbed the spot.

"Why're you so quiet?" said Enna.

Leifer snorted. "You know, Enna, you're like a baby who needs to be constantly cuddled and cooed at."

Scowling, she scooped up the remains of an apple-and-oat stew and shoved the bowl into his hands. "Would a baby serve you supper?"

Leifer smiled at his bowl. "Thanks," he said.

He eyed her to see if she was actually angry, so she scowled again and ignored him for her knitting.

"I mean it," said Leifer. "Thanks for—"

"Swallow, then talk."

Leifer swallowed hastily. "Thanks for sticking around all year, after Ma . . . and everything. I mean it. You know . . . I can tell . . . I see how you look. You're not always happy here."

Enna shrugged.

"The Forest isn't exciting for you, after living in the city, I guess." The corners of Leifer's mouth twitched. "Stay a while longer. I think it'll liven up soon."

"What, pine nut season?" Enna smirked. "You Forest boys have heads stuffed with fir needles. There are other things in this world besides trees."

"I know." Leifer finished his bowl and then stared at the bottom. A crease formed between his eyebrows.

"What does that look mean?" Enna asked.

"I was just remembering something Gebi told me. When he was in the city at marketday, a city butcher called him a squatter. The more I think about it, the madder I get."

"Hmph," said Enna, knitting more emphatically, "you never step out of the canopy's shade, what do you care what some city butcher thinks about you?"

"I don't know." He rubbed at the tight spot on his brow. "I don't know, but it bothers me now. Our people have been living for over a hundred years on land the city folk thought was too rough. And still, they call us squatters."

"There are some ignorant people in the city, I won't argue that, but you know that things're changing for us."

"Yes, I've heard you go on before, and I don't want to hear it now."

"Well, you're going to," said Enna, her heart beating harder at the prospect of a good quarrel. "In the city, when I kept chickens for the king's house, all the animal workers were Forest folk like us, living there because our parents couldn't afford to feed us out here. Dozens of us huddled together in our animal keeper quarters, not permitted to mingle with the city folk."

"I know, Enna, but—"

"No, you listen. You weren't there. It was hard. Our boys couldn't buy a drink in a tavern or court a city girl or earn a coin any other way but tending animals. We've got rights now. I saw with my own eyes the king bestow Forest boys with javelins and shields, just like the city boys and village boys get when they come of age. We're citizens. Just look at how we're clearing our own market centers and acting like proper villages."

"But don't you care? They call us squatters, and I'm not going to just take that."

"Of course you will, because—"

"I'm not!" Leifer bolted out of his chair and hurled his clay bowl against the wall, shattering it to bits. Enna stood, dropping the yarn. The ball rolled until it hit his boot.

"Leifer, what . . . ?"

Leifer kicked the yarn and scowled, and for a moment Enna thought he might break something else. Then his breath heaved and his face softened.

"I'm sorry, I—" He shook his head, grabbed his pack from beneath his cot, and ran outside.

Enna followed him into the yard and watched him disappear into the night forest. "What's the matter?" she shouted after him. "You sick or something?"

She stood a while in the yard, expecting him to mope back and apologize, but he did not return.

"Leifer?" she called again. He was gone. Enna shook her head. "Wonders."

It was late summer. The air felt thicker at night, the darkness full of unspent action. The house stood in a clearing just big enough for the animals and the kitchen garden, and then the yard was stopped by towering evergreens—thick trunked, spiny armed, their heads blocking the view to the stars. Sometimes, especially at night, those trees felt like a wall.

She walked to the edge of the yard, leaned against a dark fir, and felt her chest stretch against that familiar feeling, that yawning bit of panic. It felt as though something were missing, but she did not know what she was mourning.

Maybe Leifer was feeling the same way, that the Forest was not enough anymore, that he had to find something bigger to fill his life. But just going to the city to tend the king's animals was not the answer now, not for either of them.

You're not always happy here, he had said. He could *see* that. Enna wondered what had happened to the girl who was content just walking the deer paths padded with needles, her feet sticky with sap and her pockets full of pine nuts. She pressed herself against the coarse trunk and felt again how much she loved the Forest and remembered a time when she had never wanted to leave.

And then there had been the city, and her best friend, Isi, who had been an animal worker just like herself. Enna sighed homesickness, missing her friend whom she had not been able to visit since her mother took ill. Isi was wonderful. She had stopped a war, honored her friends, married her love, discovered a great power. Enna could not be content now that she had seen all Isi had done. *There could be something like that for me*, thought Enna again, *if I knew where to look.*

A hunting owl passed so close that she felt the air from his wings brush her face. Then he was gone, as he had come, in silence.

Leifer did return the next morning, though not quite apologetic enough to satisfy Enna. She found herself glaring at him regularly. The glowers did not work. Leifer's easy laugh seemed hard to come by. Once he yelled at her over some unswept ashes.

"What's the matter with you?" she yelled back. "Why're you acting like an injured boar? Has this got something to do with that vellum?"

Leifer gave her such a hateful look that Enna found herself wishing for her mother. Then she grabbed a broom and pushed him out of the house.

"You can come back when you can be nice!" she shouted after him.

Enna spent the morning glad to have him gone, then bored, then so lonely that she wished he would come back and glare at her some more so she could have a nice interesting fight or at least have another try at dragging information out of him. She was thinking on Leifer and kneading bread dough so vigorously, she did not know anyone had approached until she happened to look out the window. Someone was watching her from the yard—a boy of sixteen with longish black hair, large eyes, and a mouth fixed in a pleased grin.

"Good crows, Finn, how long've you been standing there?"

He shrugged.

"Well, come in. Don't stand out there like a stranger," said Enna. "Why didn't you speak up?"

"I was just watching you." Finn set his pack on the floor, washed his hands in a water pail, and grabbed a lump of dough. "Didn't want to interrupt."

"Don't be trying to help me, Finn. Sit. You must've been walking since daybreak."

She tried to snatch the dough away from him, and he side-stepped her.

"What're going to do, wrestle it from me?"

Enna laughed. "Well, thanks, then, and good to see you, Finn. How's your mother?"

Finn nodded. "Good. I'm—we're ready early for market-day, and she said I could take a couple of days to come see you."

She said I could. Enna sometimes thought it was good for Finn to get away from his mother for a time. If not for her, undoubtedly he would have gone to live in the city with other Forest folk like herself. Through their friend Isi, he had made many friends among the animal keepers there and often went to visit when in town for marketday. Since Enna had returned to the Forest, he had become a regular guest at her house as well.

"Well, Finn, you came just in time to save me from screaming craziness. Leifer's gone mad, that's all there is to it."

Finn looked concerned. "What, he didn't hurt you?"

"Oh, no, just woke up with a case of grumpiness that would scare off any nanny goat. And I swear he's got a secret, something he found off in the woods. What with his strangeness, I haven't spoken to a sensible person in days."

Enna peeled the dough off the table and threw it down

again. "Look at me, Finn. When we met in the city two years ago, did you see me in this kind of life? Kneading this dough, living out here like my ma, tending the house and animals, and talking to myself for company? She was married at my age, but that doesn't fit me, does it, Finn?"

"Somehow, I can't think of anything you could do that would surprise me," he said. Enna pushed him playfully with her shoulder. He took a couple of off-balance steps, but she suspected he did it on purpose to make her feel tough. "What do you think you'll do?"

"About Leifer? Knock his head and listen for the hollow thunk."

"No, about you."

Enna paused. "I don't know, Finn. I need to do something." She flexed her hand and watched the sinews stretch. "I feel like I'm homesick for something, maybe for Isi and the old days in the city. When I was an animal keeper, it was hard work, but I loved the winter nights or rain days when all us Forest-born would hole up in the workers' hall, Isi and Razo and the rest, and play games and hear tales and watch the fire." She smiled. "And later, too, when stuff was happening, and we helped Isi from the louts who tried to kill her, and she married the prince. What a wedding, huh? You in fine cloth and holding a javelin and all? And the nights up in the palace when you came to visit, and Isi would have a picnic on the throne room floor and invite all the animal workers."

Finn nodded. "Times I thought I could stay there forever, and I thought you'd never leave."

"Me too, once." Enna stopped pounding the dough and watched it rise. "But later, I don't know, I felt different, like I was just a guest, you know? With all the courtiers and ladies-in-waiting and guards and everything, after a while, it didn't seem like Isi needed me anymore."

"But you had to leave, for your ma," he said.

Enna nodded. "I know, and I stayed because I thought Leifer needed me. But lately . . . it seems like all he really needs is a good kick to the head."

"I'd miss you, Enna, if you left the Forest . . . if I couldn't see you much."

"Well, thanks for that."

The ease of the moment made Enna realize just how many times they had stood together in such an exchange, Enna talking about whatever was on her mind, Finn listening. She thought that perhaps he had heard more of her thoughts than any other person. She turned to look him over. He noticed and glanced away.

"Huh, what a patient person you are, Finn," she said. "I should be more like you."

Finn shook his head. "No. If I'm patient, then you don't have to be, because one of us already is."

Enna did not argue. To Finn, the point seemed to make perfect sense.

They worked together until the house was clean and bread

hot to eat, then sat outside to watch the night come on. The tree shadows merged into a general darkness, broken only by pale splatterings of moonlight. The crackle of a pinecone underfoot startled Enna upright in her chair. Leifer emerged from the Forest blackness.

"Oh," she said, leaning back. "It's just you."

He came up behind her and rested his forehead on the crown of her head.

"I'm sorry," he said.

"That's the first bit of sense I've heard from you in days." She hoped Leifer might be all right after all and gave a friendly tug to the back of his hair. "Say hello to Finn."

"Hello, Finn. I can barely see your face. Dark, isn't it?"

Leifer walked over to the yard fire pit, his back to them. Enna saw an orange spark, then the pit was blazing. He turned to her, his smile lit by the orange glow.

"How'd you . . . That was a fast fire," said Enna. "What did you put in there besides wood?"

Leifer ignored her question. "Finn, I'm glad you're here. I was just thinking I needed to talk to someone like me who's always been Forest blood to bones, someone who never ran off to live in the city."

"I've been in the city many times," said Finn.

Leifer waved off his comment. "Yes, to marketday, and to visit your old friend the *princess.*" He hit that word with a touch of mockery that immediately put Enna on her guard. "But it's clear where your allegiance lies."

Finn glanced at Enna for a hint of how to respond, but Leifer did not give him time.

"Just listen a moment—don't interrupt, Enna—because I've been thinking. We've done all right in the Forest, haven't we? Now the borders of Bayern have tossed a noose around the Forest and claimed it a boon. I don't trust them, Finn, touting their cobblestones and saddled horses and all the while enslaving Forest girls and boys."

"Enslaving?" said Finn. "I don't think—"

"There are others who see like we do, Finn, others who would join a fight if we decided to rebel."

Enna felt her jaw lower in awe, and she waited for Leifer to laugh and admit he was joking. But there was a hardness in his voice she had never noted before, and he flexed and unflexed his hands as though he meant action.

"Leifer," Enna began.

"Hush, Enna," he said. "You know, Finn, lately I can't stop thinking about Bayern over there, eyeing our lands and trees and using our people—and it all started with that meddling, foreign princess."

Enna croaked a dry laugh. "Oh, you wouldn't dare start belittling Isi with me sitting right here."

Leifer turned his back to the fire, and she could see only the glint of one eye. His voice was thin. "I know she's your friend, and I'm supposed to be scared of her because of the rumors she can summon birds and wind. I say there's something bad about her, and when I get the fight going, she'll be the first to burn."

"Leifer!" Enna stood. "How dare you talk like that?"

"I'm talking to Finn, Enna. I knew you wouldn't understand."

"You think I'll stand by while you threaten the princess?" said Enna. "You know I won't."

"Hush, I said." Leifer crossed to the fire and threw pinecones into its heart. They hissed and popped.

"I can't believe what I've put up from you this week. Poor Finn has sat patiently through your crazy talk, but when you start mouthing off on Isi, well, you'd be half a horse not to think either one of us would knock you down flat before we'd allow you to say another word."

"I said shut up!" Leifer turned. Enna could see his face caught up in the fire's shivering orange glow. His shoulders and arms trembled, and his expression was so foreign, she could scarcely believe he was her brother.

"Leifer," she said, suddenly afraid, though she did not know what she expected would happen.

Leifer grimaced as though fighting pain, then cried out. Enna felt a rush of heat and a sudden sting. She looked down to see her skirt on fire.

Enna screamed and dropped to the ground, trying to kick off the blazing skirt. Finn tore off his coat and beat at the flames. He extinguished them, and Enna lay still, breathing hard.

"Are you all right?" said Finn. He knelt beside her, his

anxious hands hovering over her legs, afraid to touch them. "Enna, are you all right?"

Enna nodded, too stunned to speak. She looked up to where Leifer stood, his hands covering his mouth. Finn arose, putting himself between Enna and her brother.

"Leifer," said Finn, like a challenge.

The fire at Leifer's feet died down, feeding leisurely on the wood. The low yellow light lit his features from below, exaggerating the creases in his forehead and under his eyes so that he looked like a very old man. He stared at Enna, and he seemed his old self, her brother, the little boy who had put beetles in her bed, the young man who brought her a bucket of mushrooms as proudly as if he had found gold. There was a sad horror in his face as he seemed to realize what he had done.

"Enna. I'm sorry. I, I didn't mean . . . " He turned and ran into the trees.

"Leifer!" He did not turn back. Enna exhaled slowly and felt her chest shudder. "What just happened?"

"I didn't see, it was so fast," said Finn. "Do you think he's got fire, you know, like Isi has wind, and he can control it? But why would he hurt you?"

"I don't know."

Finn helped Enna into the house and looked at her red ankles, humming to himself as though to ease her worry. He would not leave her alone long enough to fetch her neighbor Doda, so he himself applied soothing lard to her legs and wrapped them in clean rags. His natural calmness made the strange night and the biting pain feel easier to bear.

"I'd best stay with you for a time, make sure he doesn't try . . . whatever it is he did."

Enna stared at the hearth fire. "All those bedtime tales were preparing me for this. Isi once said that hearing and telling unbelievable stories make it easier to believe when strange things happen." She found she could believe what Leifer had done, but what frightened her was the unknown of what he would do next.

They both were silent, watching the hearth coals throb orange in the ashes. Even the sight of fire made Enna's ankles feel worse. Just then, she thought burns the cruelest wound. Enna's mother used to call the ache from cuts and bone breaks "the feeling of healing," but the burn kept on burning as though the fire were still in her skin, using her body as fuel.

A lump of blackened wood crumbled in the hearth, and a yellow flame rose higher for just a moment before pulling back inside the embers. Enna closed her eyes against it, heard Finn creaking in the rocking chair to the pulse of her blood in her wounds, and knew she could not wait for Leifer to act again. She needed help, and there was only one person to ask.

nna sent Finn home the next morning, though he
protested valiantly.

"I'll be fine, Finn," she said. "Leifer won't show
his face here for a time, I think. I'll ride out with Doda
tomorrow for marketday, and we'll pick you up along
the way."

She had saved a number of eggs in the cool root cel-
lar, and they would fetch a better price in the city than
at the Forest marketday. Though after several months'
absence from the capital, she had more important reasons for wanting to return than the prospect of some
extra coin. If anyone could counsel her on Leifer's
situation, it was Isi.

A day later, Enna left her house for Doda's. She
checked her pack to make sure she had flint and kindling, and when she looked up again, Leifer stood
before her. She tried not to flinch. His clothes carried
evidence of the Forest floor, the red indentation of fir
needles still marking one of his cheeks.

"Been by yourself for two days?" asked Enna.

"Yes." His eyes looked haunted, wide open, like someone who has had too much sleep and awake still seems to dream.

"Da used to say, 'There're smarts in Leifer's head like there's fire in flint,'" said Enna, "'but you have to knock the flint to get to the flame.'"

Leifer bowed his head. She thought the memory might make him laugh, then was glad he did not. He had no right to laugh yet.

"I'll expect you to keep an eye on things while I'm gone," she said, "and I'd better not find any roasted chickens waiting for me."

He nodded solemnly.

She felt a bit annoyed by the lack of confrontation, and her voice hardened. "And maybe you could give me any coin you've saved so I can buy myself a new skirt."

Leifer covered his face with a hand and cried. Enna stood beside him, her hands on her hips, and felt a little more satisfied.

"I'm sorry, Enna. I swear I'll never burn you again," he said.

Enna whistled long and low. "A brother should never get to a point where he has to make that kind of a promise. 'I'll never burn you again.' That's just sad, Leifer."

Leifer laughed ruefully.

"And where've you been?" she asked. "What you do with the fire—can you just get rid of it?"

"I can't." His voice was raspy from crying or thirst. "You don't understand if you ask me that question. I have to use it."

"Why?"

"I can't . . . "

"Just tell me why, Leifer."

"Look," he said gently, "it's different than you imagine. It's . . . there's a need, and . . . it's not a bad thing, Enna. I don't know what happened the other night. I lost control. You were trying to stop me, like you were my enemy, and I had to . . . I'm sorry. But I believe that I'm learning to control it."

"Then teach me the fire, too, so I can help you," she said, feeling suddenly bold, but a little afraid, like balancing on the edge of a precipice just for the thrill. But she felt confident, too, that she could handle it better than Leifer. For all he was older, Enna had taught a young Leifer to use a slingshot, and Enna had been the first to climb a tall tree. Enna had trained him to set up his kindling and send the flint's spark into pine shavings.

"Teach me, and together we can figure this out," she said.

His lips twitched, a hint at a smile. "It would be nice, I think . . . but I can't. I don't think I should." He paced away from her. "I want to figure this out for myself. It's my chance to make everything better."

"Everything what? And since when did you care about anything but the four seasons and salt on your porridge?"

"Since I . . . since I learned about the fire."

Enna hefted her pack on one shoulder. "Then I'd best go. While I'm gone, don't be rash, all right?"

She shook her head at herself as she walked away. It was almost funny, telling a boy who set his sister on fire not to be rash.

It was a relief to settle in the back of Doda's small wagon and feel the productive motion of the donkey's step and the uneven road. The trees jolted by, and she imagined they, not the wagon, were jumping and tilting like dizzy children.

The wagon was crowded with Doda's carved wood bowls, as well as two Forest girls Enna knew casually. Enna took care to keep her legs isolated, but the occasional bumps knocked her crate against her ankles, and she winced.

"What happened to your legs?" asked one of the other riders.

"Nothing," said Enna. She refused to let Leifer become a bit of Forest gossip.

Doda picked up Finn and his bag of home-knit pullovers an hour into their journey. He was quiet, occasionally passing a worried glance over Enna's legs or face. She wanted to talk to him about Leifer, but not in front of the other travelers. He seemed to understand, so they rode in silence.

The party camped that night, and by afternoon of the next day, Doda's wagon was one of hundreds heading down the main road to the city. The land was open there, stripped of trees and striped with farms that rolled where the earth rose and fell. The city itself was built on the tallest hill, completely ensconced in an ancient stone wall five men high. The lines of the city led the eye to look up, where the three- and four-story buildings grew and dozens of towers and turrets ascended, red tile roofs topped with iron spears. Up the sloping streets, at the highest point in the city, the palace blazed, pale stone washed orange in the setting sun.

The guards at the gates had tripled since Enna had last been through them, and the line of wagons moved painfully slowly. When Doda's wagon finally passed the gates, night had fallen. They set up their camp on the stones of the market-square, back to back with many other Forest dwellers and merchants of other towns here to make their monthly profit.

Enna sighed as she finally sat down while Finn prepared a quick meal. Sidi, one of the girls from their wagon, was gushing to the others about her imminent wedding.

"Embo's got a plot out by his da's, and we've got enough coin saved up to buy a goat next spring. And Embo's been cutting and storing wood for our house for a year. . . . "

Finn glanced at Enna, and she rolled her eyes at him and smiled. *Embo's been storing wood*, she thought mockingly. *He sounds duller than winter.*

Sidi was still singing Embo's praises when Doda returned from stabling the donkey, sat beside Enna, and shook her shoulder teasingly.

"Mercy, Enna," said Doda, "you shouldn't let your face show how jealous you are of that Sidi."

"Ha," said Enna.

"So what about it, girl? When're we going to see you secure your own Embo?"

"You'll never see me with an Embo," said Enna. "For one thing, our names would sound horrible together."

"Excuse me," said Finn, stepping around Doda to leave their camp and walk out into the market. Enna wondered what friends he was seeking out so late at night.

Doda thumbed in the direction Finn had gone. "What about . . . ?"

"Finn?" Enna smiled and looked down. "When we were younger, our friends teased that we'd end up together, but it was all nonsense."

"Was it?" Doda raised her brows. "I wonder. Seems to me the boy might be fond of you."

Enna shook her head. "We've been friends for years and he's never said a thing. He's a nice boy. Truly the nicest boy I've ever known. How does one person get to be so nice, Doda? Did his ma nurse him on honey milk?"

Doda nudged Enna with her boot and laughed. "Nice? Seems like you might like nice."

Enna straightened and sighed with exhaustion. "He's just Finn. We've been friends too long and I know him too well, you know? And he's still a boy, Doda. If I ever find a man, he'll have to be a man, really a man, to handle me."

Doda shrugged and crawled into her bedroll. Enna lay down carefully, arranging the blankets around her ankles, and turned on her side. There, sitting against the wall, was Finn.

"Oh," she said, "I didn't know you'd come back."

He did not answer. In the light of the crescent moon, she could not see where he was looking.

"Finn, did . . . " She started to ask him if he had heard her speaking to Doda, then decided that she did not want to know. What had she said, anyway? She could not remember exactly, just that she and Finn were not a couple, surely something he already knew. *No harm done*, she thought—she hoped. She bade him good night and uneasily tried to fall asleep.

Enna woke in the bruised-eye blue of predawn to the creaking of wagons and scratching of dragged barrels. Finn slung his sack of knitted goods on his shoulder and wandered off to sell elsewhere, a halfhearted smile on his lips as he nodded farewell to Enna. She did not know if she had hurt his feelings the night before, and she realized that if she had, Finn would never say a word.

Enna set up her crate of eggs next to Doda's wood bowls, and as soon as marketday crowds wandered in, she began to pitch lower prices than normal. It would be nice to make some extra coin, but her gaze kept wandering to the rising streets, up to the wind-fingered orange flags on the palace turrets.

Across the market-square, Enna thought she eyed a small group of palace guards, and she strained on tiptoe to spot any familiar faces. They were lost in the crowd. A woman purchased a dozen eggs, and when Enna had filled her basket, she blinked at what was revealed. Inside her crate, in the middle of her cream and pale yellow supply, sat one orange chicken egg, the color bright as a poisonous berry.

Enna peered covertly at the crowd. There, walking steadily but quickly away, she was sure she spotted an all-too-familiar figure. A boy of fifteen, slight, unremarkable but for a shaggy head of hair that stood nearly straight up. Razo. He had been an animal worker in the city as well, and Enna remembered often wondering with Isi and the other girls if his hair naturally stood on end or if he encouraged it up to compensate for his short stature.

Enna put a hand over her mouth to hide a smile as her thoughts turned mischievous. When she had kept the king's chickens in the city, Razo had spent a week slipping brightly painted eggs under one of her hens and had Enna convinced that the creature was suffering some horrible ailment. There had been pranks to get back at him in the past, but it seemed the gauntlet had been thrown yet again.

Enna held up the odd egg, threw back her shoulders, and shouted.

"The orange egg! I have it, the orange egg of the omen!"

A bent woman stared at her suspiciously. "What are you gabbing about, girl?"

"Haven't you heard of the orange egg that guarantees the finder fortune and long life?" Enna turned slightly to the gaping Doda and winked. "It's a treasure. And to celebrate my luck, I'm selling all my eggs for half the price!"

No one seemed to have heard of a portentous orange egg, but Enna's exclamations and prices brought in a small crowd. Enna glanced slyly to where Razo had gone. She could see him standing among his brothers and their wooden goods for sale. His gaze was directed at her, and he seemed completely stunned.

It did not take Enna long to empty her stock of eggs and attract curious bystanders as well. People walked away, muttering about the special egg to their companions. Razo soon stood a few paces away, staring at Enna and looking fretful.

"Razo," she said, and smiled at him. "I haven't seen you since my last trip to the city. How've you been?"

Razo nodded in answer and shuffled closer. "Wh-what you got there, Enna-girl?"

"Don't you see?" she said with high enthusiasm. "It's the orange egg of the omen."

Razo groaned. "Oh, Enna, there's no orange egg . . . "

"How can you say that? Look!" She held the thing up close to his face and barely kept from laughing.

"Enna, shh." He looked around uncomfortably. "I feel bad now. I only meant it as a joke, really, a kind of 'hello, I'm here, too,' you know? I was sure you'd know it was me. I didn't think you'd get so worked up—"

"There she is!"

Three palace guards with iron-tipped javelins interrupted Razo's confession. Enna started and nearly dropped the egg. She did not recognize any of them.

The tallest one saluted her with his javelin. "We heard of you, miss, from across the market-square, the finder of the long-searched-for orange egg."

"Uh . . . ," said Enna.

The sound of the hard wings of pigeons was suddenly loud in her ears, and in a moment she was covered in the birds, as they perched on her shoulders and arms and one proudly on her head.

"You see, even the birds recognize the egg," said another soldier.

"Er . . . ," said Enna, suspiciously watching the birds flit away.

"We should take you before the king. This is a great day for all of Bayern."

Enna glanced at Razo and thought that he must look even more astonished than she did. "Uh, yes, of course, let's go."

"Are you a friend of hers, then?" the tall guard asked Razo. "Lucky lad." He thumped Razo's shoulder and turned to escort Enna through the crowd.

As soon as they were out of sight of Razo, a young woman with her hair wrapped up in a scarf like a Forest woman's walked in step beside Enna.

"I just wanted to congratulate you, miss, on your remarkable find."

She turned her face, and Enna stopped midstride to laugh, at once understanding that Isi had sent the guards. And even the pigeons, no doubt prodded by Isi's gift with bird speech, had been part of the ploy.

"Oh, Isi, that was brilliant!"

"Razo will never recover, I think," said Isi, smiling broadly.

"Nor will I, you rascal. You should feel my heart thumping. When the birds landed on me, what a fright! And I saw myself before the king trying to explain. . . . I'm so glad it's you."

They flung their arms around each other and laughed and hugged. Enna held her friend at arm's length and looked her over.

"But what are you doing out here, and in . . . ?"

"In the old goose girl disguise? I like to go out occasionally without the fanfare, you know, just walk around and feel like a normal person. If I don't hide my hair, I can't go two steps from the palace without being recognized as the princess."

Enna nodded. Isi's hair was yellow, a novelty in a land of black and brown hair, and when uncovered it hung to her hips. Even though Isi was from another kingdom, her accent sounded truly Bayern, one word bleeding into the next, with short vowels and deep consonants. Enna noted that today the princess sounded like a city woman, though she often slipped into the rougher tones of a Forest dweller. Enna smiled, remembering that if there was one thing her friend did well, it was imitating sounds.

But something seemed different in Isi, in her expression, as though she were pained and trying to hide it. Enna tried to guess what might be amiss. "So, any news? I've been hoping to hear that you're expecting a, you know . . ."

Isi sighed. "Yes, you and half the court. Everyone wants an heir to the throne. It's been two years, and a touch of desperation has crept into the ministers' eyes. Look at you. Whenever I see you again after some time apart, I have to remember how pretty you are. And how about me?" Isi turned sideways with a serious face, as though she posed for a portrait.

"You still look like the goose girl to me."

"Good," said Isi.

They continued to stroll through the market. Enna glanced at the guards to see if they looked confused by their talk. She did not know how much the people of the palace knew, as she and Razo and Finn knew, of the way this foreigner came to marry their prince Geric. She was certain they knew pieces of the story—how a princess of the neighboring western kingdom had been betrothed to the prince, but the treacherous lady-in-waiting rode into the city instead, bearing the name Princess Anidori-Kiladra Talianna Isilee. And how the true princess, aided by a group of animal workers, confronted the false bride in front of the king and prince before the marriage took place.

But did they know of the months when their princess hid her yellow hair in a Forest woman's headscarf, donned a Forest accent, called herself Isi, and tended the king's geese? Did they know that she was largely responsible for the Forest dwellers gaining citizenship? And did they believe the rumors of her power with wind and birds?

"I like to see what friends the Forest lets loose on marketday, but I didn't expect to be so lucky as to have my Enna back," said Isi. She purchased small bags of roasted nuts and gave them to the guards and Enna. "This outing is often my only time away from the palace. Seems like I don't leave much lately."

"Why not?"

Isi shrugged, and Enna could read in her manner that she would rather talk about it when they were alone.

"I'm glad I made it here today," said Enna, "if only for the Razo trick."

"Whenever you come back—"

"It's like I never left." Then Enna remembered. "Leifer," she said heavily. "Isi, I've got to talk to you privately."

Isi nodded and without any questions gestured her guards toward the palace.

hey did not speak of Leifer as they left the market-square and climbed the narrow, cobbled streets. Enna had not seen Isi since her mother took sick. She was shocked to hear now that the young prince, Geric's brother, had passed away from a fever in early summer.

"I would've come see you," said Isi, "but Geric was stricken, and things here were . . . " She paused and looked around distractedly. "Watch that cartwheel."

"What?" said Enna.

"Oh, nothing." Isi seemed embarrassed and did not explain.

The farther they walked, the more distant Isi seemed, and sometimes she did not respond at all to what Enna said. Enna watched her silently, worry creeping over her like a chill.

When at last they reached the hilltop and the palace courtyard, Isi dismissed the guards and took Enna to a side entrance. The door was partly ajar, but before

Enna could push it open, a breeze did so for her. Isi tugged at her headscarf to loosen it, then another breeze unwound it from her head and laid it in Isi's hands. Her long yellow hair fell free.

"Isi, your skill with the wind is much better than I remember," said Enna.

Isi tilted her head and whispered something about a palace page in a hurry.

"What was that?" said Enna.

Isi scrunched her eyes closed and batted the air before her face. "Being out in the crowd, it affects me so much faster than it used to. Let's go somewhere—quieter."

Isi took Enna's hand and led her deeper into the palace, farther in and farther down. Isi nodded to a sentry standing beside a stone door, and he grunted as he pulled it open. There were no windows. The guard lit a rush torch on the wall, and thin smoke crept along the ceiling. Enna could make out a small room, shelves loaded with armor, lances, javelins, axes, golden boxes, ivory statuettes.

"A treasury," said Isi. She sat on a blanket that lay on the floor, and Enna followed. The sentry shut the door, and there was a hollow thunk as it sealed. The light in the room was low and yellow. Trembling shadows moved over Isi's face.

Isi sighed. Her face smoothed as she relaxed. "Geric found this place for me a few months ago, just after it started to get worse. He says he can't talk to me anywhere else. He says it sadly."

"What is it?"

"The wind."

"Oh," said Enna, beginning to understand.

"You know, when I first learned to understand its language, I could feel only the bigger winds. I'd sit in the goose pasture, and when a breeze rose off the stream I could hear, or rather sense, where it had been, what else it had recently touched—wet stones, a sparrow, a lost goose. And when I was indoors, I rarely felt anything, just a draft from the hall, a slip of air from an open window. Now, Enna, it's everywhere. I've come to realize that air is made up of tiny parts, and wind is a lot of them moving fast. Right now, even in a still room, I can feel the air. I hear it constantly.

"That's why Geric likes to trap us in here like a couple of worms in the earth. We can shut out most of the movements. And I can have a few moments of . . . quiet." Isi smiled. "So now that I can hear you, tell me about Leifer."

Enna took a breath. "I was wondering if there's such a thing as fire speech, like how you know bird and wind speech. Leifer, I think he's learned to control fire somehow, but he . . . can't seem to control it very well."

"Oh," said Isi, a soft, birdlike sound, and gently lifted the edge of Enna's skirt from her ankles. "You're hurt. I wonder why I didn't hear the wind whisper of it before. There was so much going on outside, I guess, and that bit got lost. I can have a physician look at it later. Enna, did Leifer do that?"

Enna shrugged off the concern and jumped into the story

of Leifer's trip to the deep wood, the vellum, and his behavior up to the night when he set her on fire. "You see why I need to know what I can, now, before he does something else, something worse."

Isi looked at her a long moment, still and unblinking, as though she were a robin waiting for a predator to pass. When she spoke, it was in her softer voice that Enna remembered from evenings around the hearth when Isi would tell stories to the animal workers. "Fire. It must have a language, though I never learned it. According to the old tales, most everything has a language.

"The story I know says that the Creator first spoke the word to make the world, and then all things could speak to one another, but each thing multiplied and withdrew into its own kind and forgot the languages of the others. Once snail and stone spoke, wind and tree, frog and water." She took Enna's hand and looked at her fingers as though for comfort. "Once, people could speak to all things, and that means to me that it's possible for us to learn all those languages again."

"Anyone can?" asked Enna.

"Some people have more of a knack for it than others, it seems, just like a good wheelwright can burn bread and a good baker might miss a nail. Once, before knowing wind speech gave me any trouble, I tried to teach Geric, but he just couldn't learn it. Fortunately.

"There are three different gifts—people-speaking, animal-speaking, and nature-speaking. Some people are born with the ability to learn one. I knew others from my home kingdom who had people-speaking from birth, and all their lives they knew how to talk to people just so, to encourage love and loyalty. I wasn't born with wind speech—I was sixteen when I first understood its words, so who knows when and how a person can learn?

"Even for people with the knack, I think most languages are too difficult for us to figure out on our own. When I was little, my aunt taught me how to hear birds speaking to one another, and I had a skill for imitating the sounds back. Even with natural talent, I needed her help to understand in the beginning."

"But no one taught you to hear the wind," said Enna.

"No," said Isi, "that was different. I was ready to hear it, I guess, and seeking it. With the wind, all it took was one word to get the sense of it. After wind gave me a first word, I began to hear many more, and then I began to be able to suggest a breeze go this way or that."

"Well, I don't know who would've taught Leifer to understand fire speech, unless that vellum gives him power," said Enna.

"I doubt it," said Isi. Enna smiled and remembered that for someone with such uncanny abilities, Isi was remarkably unbelieving when it came to superstitions or reports of magic. "Maybe the vellum contains writing about fire-speaking, and he's learned it on his own."

"That blasted vellum. You know, it makes me mighty

uneasy, Isi, that my brother is chest-deep in something sticky and I can't haul him out."

"Fire." Isi's eyes looked unfocused, as though she were seeing something far away. "It must be extraordinary and . . . and terrible. I don't know what it would feel like to understand it."

"Well, it's bound to be something like wind, right?"

"I wonder." Isi rubbed her forehead and looked down. "Wind is unique. Its very existence is a language, and it can't help but carry the images of where it's been. Every air movement that touches my skin tells me of what else it's touched. But fire doesn't move like wind, and it's so much more intense. I don't know what to do for him."

"So, you don't know of a way to, I don't know, erase it? Maybe if I could learn the fire tongue myself, I could figure out how it works and help him."

Isi blinked. "Erase it? I read once, somewhere in that old library, accounts of a desert kingdom called Yasid, to the south. Travelers from there reported of a people who had some kind of relationship with fire. Maybe they would have an answer to that, but I don't."

Enna looked at the orange heart of the smoky torch on the wall and was surprised to feel hopeful. "So, maybe the best thing after all would be for me to—"

"No," said Isi. "No, don't, Enna. Please don't try to learn fire."

"Why, Isi? I thought, being who you are, you'd be at

least curious to try."

"There are consequences to learning to speak with any part of creation. I'm learning that at last."

Enna pressed her lips together. "Consequences, like your distraction."

"Yes, for the wind it's the constant howling. It took time for that to affect me, but the nature of fire is so severe, maybe what's happening to me with the wind is happening to Leifer with the fire, but much more rapidly."

Isi stood and walked to a shelf, fingering some small ornament there. "And the distraction isn't the only change. You know my horse, Avlado? I had one before I met you— Falada. My aunt taught me to attend a horse's birth and, when he emerged, to listen for him to say his first word—his name—and repeat it back. That was the beginning of our communication, and we grew to be able to speak together silently. He's dead now. We were . . . separated, and he went mad. I missed him so much, I made the same connection later with Avlado, but now I think I was reckless. Maybe Falada never would've gone mad if it hadn't been for me. Maybe speech between us was . . . unbalanced. As much as I love Avlado, I'll never be so careless again."

"Isi, you can't blame yourself for Falada."

"Can't I?" said Isi. "Are you sure? Look at me with the wind. It used to be a peaceful thing. But now it presses on me with its language, overcoming me. Is that what happened to Falada?" Her chin quivered. "And will I go mad, too?"

Enna stood to comfort her, but Isi shook her off.

"At first, the wind was difficult for me to hear and harder for me to control. No longer. Not just its voice has grown stronger."

Enna sensed a finger of wind brush her cheek and flinched.

"When I first learned to ask wind to change its course," said Isi, "I could only take an existing breeze and suggest a new path, and it didn't always respond. Not now."

The breeze licked Enna's cheek again and then began to spin around her, growing larger and stronger, whipping her hair so that Enna had to close her eyes.

"I can always feel the air vibrating around me, Enna," she said in a strangely calm voice. "I can make a wind from nothing, and it always obeys."

The wind blew sharp around Enna's head, gusting into her ears, tugging on her clothes. She hugged herself against its force. This was not what she was expecting from Isi, once so quiet and careful, now making a delirious windstorm in the belly of the palace. The weapons and armor rattled on the shelves like chattering teeth, and the torchlight sputtered madly. In the center of the wind, Enna felt pushed and pulled, barely able to keep her feet. The loss of control was frustrating, then alarming.

Isi gripped Enna's hand. "Frightening, isn't it?"

"Enough!" Enna shouted.

Abruptly the wind died. The room was still. Enna heard

the stone door scrape open.

"Is everything all right, Princess?" said the sentry.

"Yes." Enna could see Isi's face more clearly now. Her cheeks were pink, and she bit her lip and look ashamed.

He shut the door, and Isi looked away. She seemed a bit shaken, blinking more than usual, her breath quick. "I'm sorry. I meant to just show you how things've changed since you've been gone. And maybe to show you what might be going on in Leifer's mind. But you see now, right? You see how easy it is to lose control, and why it's better that you leave the fire alone."

Enna blinked and found her legs felt weak. She sat down, and Isi sat beside her.

"I see," said Enna.

"I've gone through three waiting women in two years. It's trying for me and disturbing to others, but in the end it's only wind. But Leifer . . ."

"Yes," said Enna, her thoughts as dark and dancing as the treasure room shadows, "fire's another matter altogether."

Isi looked up. "The old tales say once a person could speak all the languages. Maybe it's just because I know so few, just some bird, and wind, and the bond with my horse. But if I could speak everything, then I wouldn't be overwhelmed by wind. The knowledge would be balanced.

"If that's so, can you imagine what it's like for Leifer to just know fire? A thing that can't exist without destroying something else? Leifer must be so lost in fire speech that he can't see the light for the flame. I think it must be too much for any person to balance being human and hearing fire. Flame and flesh can't live together."

The stone door rasped against the ground, and a broad, handsome man could be seen calming a sentry. Enna could hear the sentry whispering, " . . . noise . . . rattling and howling . . . said she was all right." The young man nodded to the sentry and then stepped into the torch-lit gloom.

"Drat these internal windstorms," he said with a smile. "I can't imagine what might be the cause."

Isi smiled and heaved a blissful sigh. "Oh, hello there."

He stooped and kissed Isi on the forehead. "I thought you might be here when I heard tell of a certain visitor. Good summer to you, Enna. Found this little room a bit drafty, have you?" Enna laughed. "If the road conditions are what keep you away so long, I'll attack my father with the improvement issue today."

"It has been a time. I was sorry, Geric, to hear of your little brother."

Geric bowed his head and nodded.

"Enna's brother has made an unnerving discovery," said Isi, changing the subject.

Enna explained Leifer's fire-speaking, his attack, and his sudden antagonism against Bayern.

"We don't need division right now," said Geric. "Do others in the Forest feel as Leifer does, that they really don't belong to Bayern?"

"I wouldn't take it too seriously," said Enna. "It's very odd for him to suddenly be so resentful."

"Is it?" Isi looked thoughtful and newly worried.

"All the same, I'd like to have the Forest behind us right now," said Geric. "It could be war, Enna."

"War? I wouldn't've even mentioned what Leifer said if I thought it would worry you. Honestly, the few people who feel disloyal are no threat."

"Not the Forest. It's Tira, the kingdom to the southeast. You may have noticed more soldiers in the city. There have been rumors all spring, and Tira has begun to harass our borders. Forest dwellers are citizens now, and I'll expect them to join and defend Bayern. Will they answer the call, do you think?"

Enna waved a dismissive hand. "Oh, yes. For every big-talking boy, there're fifty Forest lads who are aching to belong to the whole of Bayern. I think it'd make a difference, though, if someone high in rank courted our loyalty. We'd like to believe that we really are important to you."

Geric nodded, his eyes distant as though already making plans. Enna met Isi's look.

"War," Enna said. "Soon?"

"Soon," said Isi, tilting her head as though she heard the tidings on the wind.

Chapter 4

eric sent out messengers calling all Forest javelin bearers to meet at Sprucegrove in three days. Enna left the capital ahead of Geric and Isi to find Leifer. When she came home, she saw the chickens were fed and watered, but the house was empty, the hearth cold. That night she slept fitfully, starting awake every time she thought she smelled smoke. Disappointed, in the morning she freshened her pack and set off alone.

An empty house was a lonely thing, but solitude in the Forest felt right. There was too much life bursting beneath her feet and in the canopy over her head to need human companionship. As she neared the campsite midway to Sprucegrove, other travelers began to fall in beside her. Like her, they seemed silenced by their long walk alone in the woods, and the sounds of their breathing and bootfalls were just a part of the groaning, beating, swaying, and creaking voice of the Forest. They were all Forest boys, most younger than her, nearly all carrying a javelin and painted shield.

She slept that night in a clearing, hedged in by snoring bodies. She listened to the crackle of the campfire until deep night and, half-asleep, wondered if its pops and bursts were words. There was a silent, shared breakfast, and then the informal group continued on. Several among the boys had also been animal keepers, though most had now returned to their families in the Forest or taken other occupation in the city. They walked together, engaged in the slow, halting talk that grows out of travel and plenty of time.

"Move aside," said one, jogging up from behind. "I've got a word to give Enna-girl."

"Razo." Enna could not say his name without adding a laugh. Razo pressed his mouth shut and looked at her as they walked. He had the most expressive face of any person she knew.

"It was Isi who sent the guards, wasn't it?" he said finally. Enna laughed again.

"And the birds, I suppose, weren't acting on their own. Huh. Well, all right, that was good." He pulled himself a little straighter, walking as though he thought himself quite tall and not two hands shorter than Enna. "Orange egg of the omen. I'll probably laugh about that soon, any moment now."

They arrived at Sprucegrove in the golden heat of late afternoon. The prince's yellow tent stood in the center of the small market-square and was surrounded by smaller tents, wagons loaded with supplies, and a line of horses. The assembly implied he intended to stay several days.

Dozens of boys and men milled around the square or sat together in anxious groups. The hushed conversation and trembling mood chilled Enna's stomach. She could see three distinct shield designs and so knew there must be some, if not all, of the members of the Forest's three separate hundred-bands. In Bayern, each village maintained a group of one hundred soldiers for defense and for times of war. Larger villages and towns were represented by several hundred-bands. The Forest's three hundred-bands had never gathered together before. Enna thought how the word had certainly spread quickly.

Isi stood beside Geric at the mouth of their tent, her wringing hands expressing what her face did not. Enna left Razo and ran up to Isi's side.

"A word, Your Highness," said Enna.

Isi smirked and punched her arm. "Oh, stop it, Enna."

"Well, what should I call you? You look so . . . I don't know, official."

Isi closed her eyes, and Enna thought she might be trying to shut out the many voices of the wind. "We've had news."

"What is it?"

Isi glanced up at Geric, who was mounting his horse. Two mounted guards hit swords against shields above their heads. The conversations hushed immediately, and nearly three hundred faces turned to their prince. Geric drew himself up and looked out at the crowd. It had always seemed to Enna that Geric's face was made for smiling—the corners of his lips curled slightly even at rest. But just then, Geric's severe expression made her wonder how she had ever thought so before.

"My brothers and sisters of the Forest," he began, "I think you've waited long enough to hear what I've come to say. Let those who continue to arrive learn from your mouths the news of this day.

"Until recently I was unaware that many of you still questioned your place in the kingdom of Bayern. I had planned to come here and assure you of Bayern's need and desire to count the Forest dwellers among our own. There have been unsettling rumors of war coming from the south all summer, and I knew that before long the crown would be calling to all her citizens to raise the javelin in defense of her borders.

"Time has already overtaken us. Not three hours ago a messenger from the capital overtook my party here in the Forest. His news was grim. Tira has struck."

"Oh," Enna said softly. She heard similar gasps of disbelief and anger simmering throughout the camp.

Isi took Enna's hand. "It's bad, Enna. This is bad."

"Our borders are already broken," Geric said. His voice commanded attention, and the murmuring stopped. "We know they've taken Folcmar and Adelmund, and perhaps other towns closer to their border. They were moving north toward Eylbold and Ostekin, and by now those towns may have fallen victim to their invasion.

"The king set out with his army today to defend our land from further conquest on the fields of Ostekin. I'm called to meet him there and to bring my own army, gathered as I may. I'll not command you, Forest kin, as this will be your first service in the name of Bayern. But I will ask you in all boldness to offer your javelins, your swords, and, if necessary, your lives to stop the assault of the Tiran armies.

"Will you join us? Will those javelins given to you by your king rise to fight beside him? Will you be Bayern?"

The Forest boys banged javelins on shields, raised their fists in the air, hollered their affirmation, and swore to fight to the death. The quickness of the response tightened Enna's throat.

"So ready to die," she said. "I hadn't a doubt that Forest boys'd be quick to be loyal, but I never imagined they'd also be quick to offer death."

"They don't know death yet," said Isi. "They don't know what it is they offer." Her eyes were wet, and she rubbed her face as though to reach a deep headache. "I need to get out of the wind." She gestured around her randomly. "It's all so much."

Enna nodded and led her to the tent, then stopped when she caught a glimpse of Leifer. He was standing at the edge of the camp, his eyes on the prince.

"Go on in, Isi. I'll be right back."

Geric called the captains of the hundred-bands to him for

counsel, and Leifer headed that way as well. Enna caught his
arm and pulled him to her.

"Leifer, you're here."

"Enna." He smiled at her, so honest and open that she was
tempted to throw her arms around his neck and get a big-
brother hug. "I was with Gebi when we heard. I almost didn't
come, but now . . . "

"I'm glad you came. This isn't what I expected, either. I
thought he'd just give some rousing speech to win your
allegiance, you know, make you feel all cozy and Bayern."

"So did I." His gaze hopped to the southeast horizon, and
she could feel his arm tighten. "This's better."

"Are you going, then?"

"Of course. You think I'd leave my friends to follow our
king without me?"

Enna laughed. "*Our* king. You'd think the boy from a few
days ago wasn't ranting about gathering a Forest army for
rebellion."

"I want to be Bayern. I want to be loyal to the king.
Before, I was just angry, and now, I don't know, that's all
gone, and instead there's Tira. They're the enemy. It's like the
fire's just been waiting for them, and now it's time to burn. I
should tell the prince."

She pulled his sleeve to stop him. "He knows. I told him
about you." She studied his face. "I don't understand, Leifer.
A fortnight past I'd've said you were as constant as a walnut
tree, but first you get all riled up about Bayern, and then just

as quickly you're ready to fight Tira. Is it the fire doing this to you?"

"I don't know." He frowned, then shook it off. "I don't want to think about it. Right now, everything is so clear, Enna, it all feels right. I'm going to pledge myself to the prince so I can help fight Tira."

"But, Leifer . . . "

He held her shoulders and looked at her with a small, hopeful smile. "You'll be proud of me, little sister. And that makes me happy."

Enna watched him approach the prince and explain something with his hands, his brow wrinkled in earnestness. The movement of his lips made Enna think he was probably stuttering. She smiled sadly. He could rage against the kingdom on a Forest night, but when it came to addressing the prince, he became a little boy.

Enna hurried back to Isi's tent. Geric entered just before her, speaking low with one of his counselors. Isi was sitting on a floor cushion, her face in her hands. Enna sat beside her and began to plait one of Isi's locks, as she used to do in the palace on cold evenings. The attention seemed to soothe her.

"Well, my lady, what's my part in all this?" said Enna.

"I hope you'll go."

"But as what? I need something to do, Isi. My arms are itching as though I've been idling an afternoon lying on wool. I'd like to help, but not like"—she hesitated—"not like before, when I lived at the palace with you. I can't just be the princess's friend, the girl who sits around while the princess does important things."

"I'm sorry, Enna," said Isi, "I didn't realize."

"Of course not. And I was happy just to be there, before. But now I need a place, Isi, a mission. I'm chewing at my bit just to go somewhere and run."

"Come as my maiden," Isi said brightly. "A maiden usually serves a queen, but I'd rather call you that than my lady-in-waiting. I want you by me, Enna. I need your clear sight."

"Princess's maiden. Fine. That's me."

"So, you'll go?"

"Yes," said Enna. "Of course, yes. You have to ask? You're going, I'm going."

"You're not going, Isi," said Geric. His counselor left, eyes averted as though he did not want to witness to an unpleasant argument.

"I'd like to go," said Isi.

"No." Geric rolled up the maps. She stood beside him, but he would not look at her.

"Bayern women go with their men to war, to inspire courage and, and to remind them of what they would lose."

Geric winced. "You're not Bayern."

"Geric, I could help. I could read the wind and give you numbers and locations, and I could push them back, confuse them."

"I said no!" He slammed his fist on the table.

Enna held her breath so she would not say a word. She

was tempted to step in, but this was Geric. She had never seen him lose his temper.

"I don't need to be reminded what I would lose." He looked at Isi. "I'm a terrible prince. I should put my kingdom first and everything else second, but you're first. I want you by my side every second, but I know I would crumble if I lost you."

She stepped closer and he gripped her in his arms, burying his face in her neck.

"But I will go." Isi stroked his hair, and his shoulders began to shake.

Enna slipped out, quietly lowering the tent flap behind her. She looked up to see Finn standing in the shadows, his arms flat against his sides as though he were already practicing at being a soldier.

"Finn," she said, surprised. She tried to keep her face relaxed, pretending not to remember their last uncomfortable confrontation in the market-square. "I didn't realize that you were here."

"Seems that's happening a lot lately," he said.

From anyone else, Enna thought, that statement would have been biting, but from Finn's mouth it was just the truth.

"I'm going to fight." His face was smooth, almost without emotion. She had never seen him look so old. "I just wanted you to know, so if I go missing, someone would know I was here and could tell my ma."

Enna nodded. Finn returned the nod, smiled briefly, and

walked back to his hundred-band. She stayed behind, leaning against a pine for comfort. Before her, the market-square and surrounding woods were dotted with cookfires, points of light mirroring the randomness of the stars. There was no singing. The general hush of many low voices drawn together swept to her on a Forest breeze, as though the Forest sighed disquiet and warning. Enna pressed her cheek against the bark and breathed in the grounding smell of pine. Everything had suddenly become quite serious.

eric's bands marched south. *Four days,* he had said. *Four days,* the Forest boys muttered to one another. Each night they practiced swordplay around the fires, grunting and slicing and laughing. Enna watched, disturbed by their levity. Two years before, when Isi and her friends exposed the false princess before Bayern's king, her treacherous country-men had drawn their swords and fought the king's guards. Enna had stood in the midst of that battle, had heard the rush of a thrown javelin, had seen soldiers cut other men down. She could not now forget that the products of fighting were corpses, as well as the haunted looks and shifting hands of the surviving boys who had learned to kill.

Mostly she watched Leifer. He lit the fires each night, and soon all the prince's camp knew of his talent. A boy of fourteen years, eager, always armed, sat beside Leifer and begged to be taught. "I'm a warrior like my grandfather," he said. "I want to light my enemies on fire and please the king."

Leifer glanced up at Enna, who stood by a neighboring fire, frying bread. He shook his head. "I can't teach you. Go on back to your own camp."

The boy left, angry. For a moment, Enna thought she could see a pale corner of vellum peeking from beneath Leifer's overtunic before he pulled it closed. The hand on his chest thrummed eagerly.

"You did right," said Enna, sitting beside him.

"You see," he said, "I'm making you proud already. And you thought all I was good for was chopping wood and finding the nastiest bugs to put on your pillow."

Enna slapped a too hot piece of bread in his hand and laughed at how gingerly he held and cooled it. "Tell me more about the fire, Leifer. Did the talent just happen? Or did you learn something from that vellum you found?"

Leifer's expression hardened. "I don't think we should talk about this."

Enna did not respond, eating her supper and listening to the angry sounds of the campfire biting into a log.

After a time, Leifer sighed, sounding resigned. "You're my sister, my whole family, and the smartest person I know. What you said before . . . if you want me to try to teach you, I will."

Enna hesitated. "No. I think it's dangerous, and I wish you hadn't gotten tangled in it yourself. I mean, think what fire does. It eats things up. It destroys."

Leifer considered. "It does so much more than that."

"And makes smoke that clouds your brain," she said.

"And makes heat and light, and makes the night beautiful and meat taste good, and makes me feel . . . "

"Scorched," said Enna.

"Alive," Leifer said with conviction.

Alive, she thought. His eyes did seem brighter, his skin healthy and pink, not pale from languishing in the Forest shadow. Enna shrugged. Such a gift offered so many opportunities to do good things. Isi had warned her, and she trusted her friend's instinct in this, but perhaps Leifer knew more than she guessed.

Enna threw some sticks into the fire's heart, and they sat in silence and watched them blacken and burn. She had always been drawn to a fire in the night, but she had never considered before that there were things to know about fire, that there was a hidden way it worked, and that holding that knowledge imparted power. And she found herself dwelling on something Isi had said before, how learning animal speech or nature speech was a talent and that some people showed more capacity for it than others.

Does that mean, she thought, *since my brother is one of those, that maybe I am, too?*

The thought felt right. Each time she contemplated fire, she felt surer that she *could* learn it and felt a place inside her, a place in her chest, yawn eagerly.

✻   ✻   ✻

From sunup to sundown, the company marched. They marched on the broad, rocky road, sometimes spilling onto harvested fields. Farming women stood in doorways, their arms around their children, and stared with little hope at the prince's small Forest army, only three hundred strong.

Enna and Isi rode in a supply wagon with two other Forest women. Normally, Isi would have ridden Avlado, but she said she did not want to take her horse near a battle, and Enna wanted her close so she could care for her when the wind became too much. The Forest women were talking of Tira. Isi did not know all of the history between the two countries, so the women told her of Bayern's belligerent past, up until the current king, of how former Bayern armies had raided and harassed Tira. Now Bayern's new peace seemed a weakness.

"And it is," said Enna. "For here we're caught unprepared, marching south to a war that's begun without us."

Isi nodded. "The king underestimated hate's memory."

"Yes," said a Forest woman, her hair wrapped up in a yellow scarf, "the Tiran remember us brutal, and so we were. They'll not give up until they feel we've bled twice for every Tiran ever killed and paid two bushels of wheat for every bushel ever burned."

The Forest women grew silent, and Isi was anxious. Winds fluttered her hair and clothes, and she looked to Enna as a person might before submitting to water and drowning. Though the day was warm, Enna covered her in a thick blanket, so the only place of contact with the wind would be her face. It seemed to help some. After a time she drifted into sleep, and Enna hopped out of the wagon to walk a bit. Finn marched nearby, and she fell in step with him.

"Good morning to you, soldier," she said.

He nodded and kept his eyes straight ahead.

"Finn, why're you going? You don't have to—"

"I'm going because the king gave me my javelin and shield two years ago, and I want to show I'm grateful and protect things and do some good."

Enna laughed. "You interrupted me. You've never interrupted me before."

Finn did not respond.

"All I meant was, good for you."

They walked in silence for a time. Enna found herself wishing she could talk to him about everything she was thinking, worries for Leifer and the strangeness of sudden war and feelings on fire. She was used to Finn's silences, but this kind did not seem to welcome discussion.

When Enna broke away to return to the wagon, Finn said, "Good-bye, Enna," with real sorrow in his voice.

He thinks he's going to die, she thought. The realization made him seem stronger to her than the brave, foolish boys who believed they were invulnerable. She watched him march on, his face resolute, his hand resting on the hilt of the loaned sword at his hip.

On the morning of the fourth day, Geric called a halt on the breast of a hill.

"They're close enough that the wind knows them." Isi stood on a wagon seat, her arms out, fingers splayed, as though she were a weather vane reaching for every hint of which way the wind blew. "The king's there and a Tiran army. Vast. Men like trees in a forest, swords, the whisk of arrows, the thud of arrows against shields, the soft entry of arrows in flesh, bodies on the ground . . . " She stopped. Enna could only imagine how vividly Isi saw the battle, and her skin ached at the thought of what was to come.

Geric mounted and led the army forward, his horse stepping high as though wishing to canter. The march became swifter. Of the women, Isi and Enna alone did not leave the army for an encampment, choosing to remain in the wagon that would go to the threshold of the battle.

They could hear the noise of battle first—a cacophony of human voices that did not converse and beating metal like a thousand blacksmiths at work. The little army climbed a hill toward the noise. Enna sat on the wall of the wagon and held on to the sides. The wood squeaked under her hand in the uphill strain. The donkey moaned once. Enna looked at a sky masked by clouds, the air softly wet from recent rain, and observed how the air smelled rich and sweet. *It shouldn't be so sweet on a battle day,* she thought. *It should pour.*

The wagon crested the hill, and the noise was suddenly real. Geric called a halt. The captains of the three hundred-bands, also on horseback, drew next to him and looked down. The two armies congregated on a withering wheat field, three thousand on the north side, perhaps five on the other. They saw the king leading his Bayern army, their backs to the north. Geric said something to the captains that Enna could not hear.

The four men began to shout the words of a battle song. As they sang, the men behind them gathered on the crown of the hill and joined in. They raised their shields to their mouths and sang into the rounded metal so the sound of the song reverberated and swelled into the valley. The pulsing metal made an eerie call: *Tear down the borders, tear down the shores, tear down the walls, tear down the doors, the king to victory, we cry, the king to victory.*

The captains called forward, and the Forest bands marched down the hill, still shouting the battle song, their shields lowered now. The action in the valley slowed briefly as faces looked to the new players. The battle was thick. Archers had already dropped their bows for swords, so there was no line of arrows to slow the Forest bands' approach.

Abruptly the song dropped and shouts began. Enna watched three Forest boys cut down before javelins left their hands, and she turned away.

Enna looked at her trembling hands and said, "How is it, Isi?"

Isi closed her eyes. She seemed eerily calm. "The Forest bands, they give our men new hope, surely, but the Tiran forces are greater. For now we're standing our ground."

"The king should've waited to muster more troops before fighting."

Isi nodded. "He was hurrying to protect the people. In addition to four towns, Tira has already taken ten villages."

Enna stood in the wagon to see if she could spot Leifer, but his was one dark-haired, leather-helmeted head among hundreds. Then she saw flames.

Isi's eyes opened wide. "Fire. It's Leifer."

Enna spotted him a little apart, just east of the battlefield, south of his own band. Two Tiran near him were on fire. Her ankles throbbed in memory, and she thought of rushing the field and telling him to stop. Then another fire started, and another.

"He'll draw attention to himself, Isi," she said. "And I don't know that he can control it. Maybe I should—"

A cry burst from below, followed by a wailing and screams of fury. Something was wrong. The Tiran were cheering and the Bayern stumbling back.

"What is it, what is it?" Enna asked anxiously, her eyes scanning the scene. A moment later Isi cried out, her face white.

"Oh, the king," said Isi, "the king has fallen."

Enna could not see his gray mount, his metal helmet, or the ensign of the Bayern sun. The army of Bayern looked smaller. "Fallen? But he isn't . . . is he killed?"

"He tried all his life to avoid war," said Isi, "and to die

now, on a battlefield—" Her voice caught in a sob.

The Bayern were screaming savagely and rushing the enemy. The armies of Tira seemed to move forward with confidence. Enna spotted Geric in the crowd, still mounted, still leading the Forest bands from the side. They appeared to have lost some men.

"Geric." Enna felt panic pull her tight like a rope. "Geric's out there, and, and you! They could wipe out the entire royal family in one day. Isi, I've got to get you away."

Enna hesitated, looking out again where Leifer burned, but Isi's danger felt more critical. She hopped onto the bench, searching frantically for the reins. She had never driven a wagon before. "Go, go!" she shouted to the mule, slapping his backside. He shifted his weight but did not move.

A burst of light. And then screams.

Both girls stood in the wagon and looked out on the scene with a mix of horror and relief. One corner of the field was boiling with flame. Entire groups of Tiran soldiers were burning.

"Oh, Leifer," said Enna.

She could not see him in the bedlam, she could see only explosions of fire. Even from the hilltop Enna could hear the burning men scream. New fires flamed up, again, again, again. The tide of Bayern soldiers stood their ground and slowly, slowly, began to push forward.

"The battle's changing," said Isi, exhaustion and disbelief heavy in her voice.

"How can he keep it up?"

Isi shook her head. "He's out there, right in the middle. Leifer himself is burning. Not on fire, exactly, but burning, somehow."

Below, a Tiran leader was shouting. He pointed his sword up the hill at the two girls and then began to climb.

"They think we're the cause," said Isi.

"Well, let's not tell them differently. It'll allow Leifer more time." Enna grabbed a spare javelin and shook it at the soldier. "We'll never stop, you devils!"

Some forty men broke off from the fighting and followed the Tiran leader. One shouted, "Fire-witch!" and pointed his sword at Enna.

"Oh," said Enna. She gripped the javelin and felt very tiny. "Isi, can you?"

Isi closed her eyes and nodded. The wind gusts suddenly had purpose. Enna could feel them circling the wagon like a great finger making rings in a pool. Bits of grass and dirt picked up, and the wind became a nearly visible barrier. One of the Tiran soldiers aimed at Isi and let loose an arrow. It hit the wind barrier and flew wild. Isi did not flinch.

"Ha, ha!" Enna brandished the javelin and smiled. "Go back or die!"

The Tiran closed their eyes and raised their hands against the thrash of dirt and pebbles but still pressed forward. Their helmets flew off, their clothes whipped about their body. Sometimes a finger of wind pushed out of the circle and knocked a soldier off his feet. Two tumbled back down the hill. The others kept on.

"Is it going to be enough?" asked Enna.

Isi shook her head. The leader slowly lifted his sword against the force of wind, getting closer and closer. The mule eyed him and the windstorm uncomfortably, lifting its front hooves and bawling. With great exertion, the soldier slapped the mule's rump with the flat of his sword.

The wagon rocked, the mule wailed. Enna dropped the javelin, grabbed Isi, and pulled her out of the lurching wagon. As they landed on the hilltop, the wagon tipped, and the mule and its load slid backward down the slope. The wind grew softer.

"Isi, don't let it go, don't."

"It's getting so hard, so many people . . . " Isi kept her eyes closed, and her concentration appeared to cause her pain. Enna stood in front of her as the men neared.

"You harm her and—and the entire field goes up in flames! You fools, you kill her and you die with her."

The Tiran seemed unconvinced. The wind burst again and pushed several men to the ground, but the others still advanced.

"Forest band, to me!"

A beating of hooves, a responding shout, and Geric crested the hill. His sword downed the farthest soldier. The leader turned away from the girls and called his men around him, rallying to take down the prince. But behind him a hundred-band of Forest men ran up the hill, hollering and throwing javelins.

The prince led the charge, and the Forest men fell in beside him. Enna spotted Razo and Finn among those still alive and fighting. The swordplay was quick and bloody. From this close, Enna could hear the men scream when metal ripped open their middles, could hear them whimper when a finishing blow stopped their hearts. In a few moments, Enna and Isi's attackers lay in heaps at their feet. The protecting wind dispersed into random breezes. Isi slumped on the ground.

Geric dismounted and took Isi in his arms. "Are you hurt? Are you all right?"

Isi put her face against his chest and breathed out. "I am now. Geric, your father . . ."

Geric nodded and cleared his throat, as if trying to dislodge emotion caught there. His eyes were wet.

A new noise from below caught their attention. Enna and Geric, holding his wife, stood and looked out. The Bayern were cheering. The Tiran soldiers retreated, some fighting as they left, most running for the woods south of the field, toward the villages they had captured and their reinforcements and supplies. Enna could not see Leifer, and amid the shouts of victory, she felt her stomach chill.

"We won this battle," said Geric, his voice disbelieving. "They won't take Ostekin now. We wouldn't have . . . but the fire, Leifer, he changed everything."

"Geric," said Enna, "shouldn't you . . . " She gestured to the fleeing Tiran and the cheering Bayern, who lacked a king to lead them forward to catch and kill their foes before they could regroup.

"I . . . " Geric hesitated. The Tiran entered the woods. "We'll finish it another day."

Enna thought perhaps it was for the best, looking over the field of slain bodies and wounded, the exhausted men of the king's army who had been fighting since dawn, and the body of the king himself, slumped over his downed mount, the Bayern banner thrown over his body.

Enna saw Geric's gaze reach the spot on the field where his father lay slain. His face hardened, and he suddenly looked less like a concerned husband and more like a king. Geric asked Razo and Finn to take Isi to the encampment of women, then raised his sword and shouted atop the hill.

"Bayern, you are victorious! This is just the first battle of this war, so stand together and save the injured. I, Geric-Sinath of Gerhard, king of Bayern, declare this day doesn't end until every acre of our soil is cleared of the Tiran."

"How long'll this day last, then?" asked Enna.

"It feels like forever." He straightened his shoulders and marched down the hill.

Enna left him and ran into the battlefield. The sky growled with thunder, and when rain began to fall it felt only right. Smoke rose as the rain doused the burning corpses. The wounded moaned and wept. A broad-faced Bayern soldier was wading through the bodies and delivering quick deathblows to the gravely injured Tiran. Enna looked away.

"Leifer," she called, loudly at first, urging herself to believe that he was all right somewhere, that he could answer her call. *Leifer himself is burning*, Isi had said. *Not on fire, exactly, but burning, somehow.*

She found him too quickly, before she had prepared herself, before she had allowed herself to actually think, *Leifer died today.*

She recognized his long, lanky body, the way he let the laces of his boots dangle, the cut of his tunic, though there was nothing else to identify. He looked as though he had burned from the inside out, for his body was worse than his clothing. His skin was charred black and stiff—not a quick death like the others with burned bodies who suffocated on smoke, their skin patchy red and black or just gone. He must have burned slowly, evenly, like a roasted pig.

Enna knelt before him and cursed herself for not stopping him. He had won the battle, she reminded herself, but she felt no consolation. She did not understand what bade him start the fires and make them ever bigger even while the action gutted him of life. But she knew he would never lace his boots again or shell walnuts or push his hair out of his eyes. He would never marry a Forest girl. He would never breathe again. She put a hand on his chest. It was still warm, but not with life.

Enna shouted at the sky. She had done this. She had not

talked him out of using the fire on the battlefield, and she had pretended to be the fire-witch to distract the Tiran instead of rushing out to stop him. When she pulled her hand away from his chest, she brushed across something round and long. The vellum.

She jerked the thing free from his tunic. The oiled cloth wrapped around it was blackened and warm, and it smelled greasy and dirty like a garbage fire. Her throat constricted against a sob, and her fist tightened around the cloth. The parchment inside crackled a little, the noise of a secret.

None of it made sense, why he would burn his sister, and suddenly hate the city dwellers, and just as suddenly join with the king to fight Tira. And then to burn with such abandon, even to his death. The cloth trembled in her hand. Would it explain why Leifer had changed? Whatever intelligence was inside had helped turn back the invaders today, but did it also demand the wielder's life? Did Leifer really have to die?

Enna peeled back the cloth. The vellum was white as bone, rolled tightly, and tied with a string. She lifted it out carefully, but the string had burned, and it dropped away in pieces. The vellum unrolled before her eyes.

She jerked back, afraid to have such a thing open to her. Then she took a breath and nodded to herself. She had to know what had happened to Leifer, why he had ended this way. She read carefully at first, trying to make out the many unfamiliar words and understand the tight, sloping script and bleeding ink. Then she read fast, too fast to understand it all at once.

I, a woman of the River, keep brief record of the greatest power our people have seen—how to shape fire from the heat of the living, how to pull heat from the air and give it life inside fuel. How to hear the heat, how to bring it inside myself, form it into flame, and set it free . . .

Enna closed her eyes, and she could see the black ink strokes of the text flaming orange against her lids, as though the letters were branded behind her eyes. The idea of the knowledge burned impatiently against the strikes of raindrops on her neck and hands. She opened her eyes and the world seemed different, the colors brighter, everything pulsing with heat and life.

"Fire," she said.

The tip of her tongue warmed. Beside her, a stalk of downed wheat smoked in the rain.

Part Two

Warrior

hat night the rain stopped suddenly, leaving behind low, sluggish clouds to mix with the smoke. After the sun fell, the sky was black.

Enna sat on the ground beside Leifer's body far into the evening. Men patrolled the field, searching for wounded to take to nearby Ostekin. They glanced at Leifer's scorched remains and quickly passed on. Enna wrapped the vellum back in its cloth and slipped it inside her tunic. Her thoughts hunted after the words she had read, sought to catch them, cut them open, and understand.

Every living thing gives off heat, the vellum had said. *That is the key. I believe I was born with the ability to be a fire-speaker, though I did not know it until I was taught to feel that heat. Now it is so real, I wonder if I can see the pale yellow heat that trails from animals, people, plants, I wonder if I can hear the heat find me, tap against my skin, beg to be made into fire. Before it is pulled apart in the cruel, cold air, heat remembers that it was once a part of something living, and it seeks to be so again.*

After nightfall, men began to place the bodies of the slain into piles. Dumbly, Enna still sat on the ground and watched, her hand on Leifer's chest. When men tried to take Leifer, Enna roused.

"He's my brother," she said. "I will."

She grabbed his ankles and dragged him to the nearest heap of corpses. He was so blackened, Enna was afraid at first that he might break apart like a burned-out log and collapse into ash. But he was still strong.

"Enna." Isi stood by, her face barely recognizable in the night. "Leifer should be buried in honor. He was a hero today."

Behind her, Geric and three captains lifted the king's body into the back of the wagon, to be taken to the royal tombs in the capital. She could hear Isi's uneven breath, torn from sobbing for the king and the day. Enna felt the vellum scratch under her tunic, and she put a self-conscious hand to her chest. Standing before Isi, the words of the vellum churning in her mind, reminded her she had acted rashly. Perhaps Isi would not approve. Now was not the time to tell her. She looked at her brother's body sprawled on the ground.

"Leifer wouldn't want to be in cold earth," said Enna. "He should be burned."

Isi squeezed her shoulder and returned to Geric.

Once you are aware of the heat loose in the air, the vellum had said, *it becomes aware of you. Take it, form it into flame, send the flame*

*into something dead so that it, too, can live again. Trees grow in the heat
of life. Deadwood remembers that life. Make heat flame, send it into the
deadwood, let what once was tree live again as fire.*

Men in a wagon brought wood from Ostekin. Everything
under the sky was soaked and miserable. They stacked the
wood around the mound of bodies and, hunching over flint
and kindling, began to try to coax a flame.

Enna closed her eyes. The air was damp and clung to her
lungs as she drew it in. On the skin of her face and hands,
she thought she felt the air a little heavier, a little more profound. A little warmer. Focusing on the touch of that air,
she followed it back to its source—the men. She opened her
eyes. Yes, there, she had known the men were there by the
heat that had left them, slithered through the air, and found
her skin. The more she focused on the heat, the more sensitive her skin was to its touch. And the strands of heat that
found her stayed near.

*To make heat into fire, you must draw it inside you. I was never
aware of that small, hollow place inside my chest until I was taught to
feel it, expand it, fill it with heat. If you are one who might have the
ability, you can feel that place, too. Gather the heat touching your skin, then
draw it in. Inside a living person, heat can become flame. Do not let it
stay and burn you. Send it out into something dead, and the heat becomes
live fire.*

Enna felt the warmth on her skin and listened to all
around her. She heard a man curse. The rustling of shaved
wood. The snap of rubbing flint. A hiss, a flash, a sigh. She

could almost feel the first word of fire sitting inside her, behind her eyes, on her tongue, while the man struggled to ignite even a tiny flame. She knew she could help the men light their fires, she could bestow all the dead piled there with the brief life of fire. This last gift for Leifer. The heat near her began to move as if in anticipation.

"Just this once," she whispered, "for Leifer."

With a thought, she gathered in the heat she had been feeling, the lost heat from the frustrated men crouched over their kindling, the drifting heat from the wet, green grasses and the roots of wheat stalks. She was afraid the next part would prove too difficult, but as soon as she willed it to enter, the heat came into her, into a place in her chest. She felt the place expand. Her eyes lifted open with the rush of life and the sting of heat. *Get it out*, was the immediate need. Quickly, she sent the transformed heat tearing through the air and into the nearest fuel.

A little heap of wood shavings burst into flame. The soldier working at it wiped his brow, relieved. Others left their own piles and went to him, patting him on the back, saying, "Well done, you got it. Didn't think we'd get anything going in this damp."

Enna looked over all the stacked wood, at the clothes of the dead soldiers, at all the fuel that she could inject with heat and bring back into a brief, blazing life. But she did not have to look far for reasons not to. There on the mound, one arm flung over his face, lay Leifer.

Enna whispered, "That's all, Leifer. I'll never burn again."

Soldiers gathered, lighting sticks in the fire Enna had begun, distributing the flames to the stacked wood around that mound and other mounds. The fires grew taller, and the men stepped back. No one wanted to smell the burning-meat odor of their dead. Someone started to sing, and the living men gathered in to one another and joined with dissonant voices. As the fire bit into the rough wood and ate up the clothing, it growled and crackled and breathed, so that Enna imagined it sang harmony to the men's voices.

"Up, up, up with your glass," they sang, "the man has fallen down. Lift up, up, up your last glass, lift up for the downed, downed man."

It was a rough tavern song, but one they all knew. Enna liked it more the more they sang. The rhythm clipped, the words rolled over each sound, and some men pumped their arms as though they toasted the dead. It reminded her that there was still living to be done.

She watched the flames, but her focus slipped past them to the dead bodies, an arm tucked there, a face blackened in smoke, a tunic eaten through. The last of Leifer in this world, made brilliantly hot and bright and alive. She walked away before the fire burned out, before all that was left was ash.

Two weeks after the battle of Ostekin Fields, Enna walked back to the Forest. She felt uneasy, as though Leifer were at home waiting for her, hungry, unable to make a stew without her help. She knew it was not true, but she told Isi, "I just have to go see that he's not there, and make sure the chickens are all right."

She traveled in the company of a dozen Forest boys, most of whom were needed more at home than on the battlefront and some of whom now stared about with wide eyes and wizened brows, unready as they were to have seen what a war really was. Enna had thought Finn would be one of the returning, but he surprised her.

"Send a message to my ma, if you can—I'm staying with the prince," and he walked swiftly back to his hundred-band camp.

Enna thought how Finn was changing, how everything was.

Faintly, she could feel the heat of her traveling companions as they walked beside her and the living plants beneath her feet. A few days into the journey, her sense of their heat was unmistakable. At night she felt uncomfortable around the fires, instead sleeping several paces beyond the others on the edge of the firelight. Even from there, she could sense its delicate heat weave through air to touch her skin.

When they passed under the Forest canopy, she was surprised by how thick the air was with the warm emanations of plants and animals. Enna had never realized before just how much was growing around her, how much life filled up every inch. She entered her empty little house, sat on her cot, and stared at the wood grain of the floor. She refused to look at the door, fighting a ridiculous hope that any moment her brother could come through it. Her old restlessness was so profound now that it was almost audible, a discontented buzzing that could compete with the crickets.

Enna spent much of that night with open eyes, wondering how Leifer had slept so soundly. How could he not lie awake, constantly marveling at the ribbons of heat that seeped out of trees and animals and through the cracks in the walls? Her awareness of it felt like a last link to Leifer. As she paid closer attention, her sense of the heat became more distinct. She thought she could tell the difference between heat from an animal, a tree, a fern. Everywhere, things were alive, awake, and growing. The heat tickled her skin and felt as pleasant as baking bread smells.

The hearth was cold. She stubbornly refused to light a fire, even with flint.

In the morning she shut the house up tight and made Doda a present of half of her egg layers in exchange for looking after the hens and the goat indefinitely. By the next week's end, Enna was back in Ostekin. She greeted the west gate sentries and headed to the councilman's house where Geric had set up headquarters.

Up the main road a bit, she thought she saw Isi dressed plainly with her hair in a scarf as though out for a walk. Two young soldiers, clearly agitated about something, stopped her and began speaking with energy. Enna picked up her pace.

"I'm sorry, I don't think that's a very fair request," Enna heard Isi say. "You should speak to your captain. . . ."

"No, I'm telling you," one of the soldiers said. "My brother died out on that field, and I'm not going to just sit here and wait until my captain says I can fight again."

"That's right." The other soldier stepped in closer, pointing his finger at Isi. "And if you don't . . . "

"What do you mean, threatening the yellow lady?" Enna reached the group and stepped between Isi and the soldiers, shoving their chests until they backed up. "What, are you some Tiran pig dressed Bayern?"

The soldiers stiffened. "We're just saying what's true."

"Oh, you're just humming to hear the pretty noise. Get out of here, go on. If I hear you disrespecting our princess again, I'll whip your hide so you'd think I was your own ma."

The soldiers hesitated.

"Did you hear me, little boys?" said Enna. "Go on!"

They turned and walked swiftly away.

Isi sighed. "Those poor boys are grieving and don't know what to do about it."

"I do. Give the word and I'll flog them for you."

Isi laughed briefly and bowed her head. "I know you will, but I don't think it'll be necessary. This time." She met her eyes. "You make me feel safe, Enna. I'm so glad you're back."

Enna inhaled against an uncomfortable feeling, as though she had dreamed she had hurt Isi and was only now remembering. *The fire. I haven't told her.* She realized now that part of the reason she left Ostekin so soon after the battle was to avoid telling her friend that she had read the vellum. She did not want Isi to look at her as Enna had looked at Leifer, wondering how much of what he did was really Leifer, how much was fire, and always feeling on edge, waiting for him to break and flames to rise. *You make me feel safe*, Isi had said. How could Enna betray that?

"What's wrong?" asked Isi.

"I, nothing. I'm glad I'm back, too. How can I help you, Isi? I'd like to be useful, if I can."

"You're still my maiden."

"Yes, that's something," said Enna. "Well then, I'll be the most valiant queen's maiden in Bayern history."

Isi shook her head. "Queen. For my first sixteen years, my mother was the queen, and when I came to Bayern there had been no queen for a decade. Now suddenly I'm the queen. I'm still not used to it."

"I don't think most people are. Just now when I arrived, I said to the sentries, 'Where's the princess, or the queen, rather?' and they said, 'You mean the yellow lady?'"

"I'm not surprised." Isi patted the scarf that hid her hair. "I know I stand out too much with my hair so long and yellow as well, but I just can't bring myself to cut it."

"Cut it?" said Enna. "No, you can't. It's part of who you are."

Isi smiled and entered the councilman's house, but Enna

paused at the door. She turned to face southeast, the direction of the kingdom of Tira and the direction of Eylbold, the closest Bayern town Tira had taken. She felt the hairs on her arms rise. They were so close. So close that she imagined she could close her eyes and feel her way southeast just by the heat of their bodies. The feeling twisted her stomach.

Enna turned her back on the south and followed Isi inside to prepare for a war council, one of many that autumn. The leaves turned and pinecones fell, and there were councils and meetings and strategies, unexpected clashes with Tiran troops and dozens of Tiran prisoners. And then the weather turned decisively toward winter. The skirmishes between Bayern and Tira slowed and then stopped like tree sap in the cold. Tira had taken two more border towns but had launched no great battles, and now both sides seemed content to wait out the winter and strike again in the thaw of spring.

And Enna grew restless.

One evening she sat in the main room of the councilman's house, darning an apron to keep her hands busy. Isi was with Geric somewhere, and it had been a week since the queen's maiden was needed for anything more than being a friend. She found herself staring southeast again, toward Eylbold. A mild winter storm pushed on the shutters, thrumming the wood against the house, noises that made Enna feel as though she were inside a drum. She pricked her finger with the needle and angrily sucked away the drop of blood.

"Lovely girls you have here."

The careful, dry accent put ice in her stomach even before she knew who had spoken. Through the room three soldiers escorted a bound Tiran prisoner. He caught her eyes and sneered. "Glad to see there will be something lovely for Tira in this dismal country."

A soldier shoved him roughly, and they left through the back of the house.

Enna sat glaring at the still swinging door, wishing she had had something burning and clever to say back. Her anger at the prisoner and her lack of response and her own uselessness lately while all of Tira sat snuggly on Bayern land heated her face and sped up her breath. The heat pouring from the hearth fire wrapped around her ankles and rose to her neck. The heat those soldiers had left behind shoved against her skin. It swathed her like hot hands over her face. The room seemed to dim, and she rubbed her eyes and wondered if she was seeing clearly.

Inside her chest, that place she had filled with heat the day Leifer died began to pulse expectantly, and Enna felt a pleasant, slippery desire to comply. Get rid of all the clinging heat, draw it tight into that space, and make just one tiny fire. . . .

Enna bolted upright, grabbed her cloak from its peg, and walked out of the house and into a cold burst of wind. Immediately the heat left her, and she sighed. So strong an impulse to make another fire had never taunted her before.

She felt her limbs shiver, and she imagined it was not just the sudden cold.

The wind pushed against her back, so she walked with it, feeling its pressure move her toward the edge of camp. She felt better, but she did not want to go back into that house just yet to wait while loose scraps of heat from people and from fires stuck to her again.

Suddenly she remembered what Leifer had said when she had asked him if he could stop. *You don't understand if you ask me that question. I have to use it.*

Had he tried to resist and discovered that eventually the fire would have its way? Enna felt her muscles tighten at the prospect of a challenge. She had not anticipated that the fire could be so forceful, but now that she knew, she was even more determined to overcome.

The town was mildly busy with the activity of an early winter evening. Every building was occupied with captains and ministers and blacksmiths and tanners. On both sides of the town wall, brown tents pooled in groups under individual hundred-band banners. There was no place for her to be alone.

She stopped at the stables near the east gates and had a stable-hand saddle for her a sweet gray mare named Merry. Being a queen's maiden did have some advantages.

She had nowhere in particular to go, so she gave Merry free rein and let the wind whip at her skin. The sky kept to itself, cloudy and dim. The low hills were nearly colorless and clenched with a hard crust of snow. The absence of life was exhilarating, and Enna squeezed Merry's middle a little tighter and rode on.

The sun lowered faster than she had expected, and the land filled with that ghostly gray light that could slip into black without warning. She turned the mare back northwest, fairly sure that was where she had left Ostekin, and started a trot back.

Minutes later, the breeze was pushed aside by a wind from the north, and this one brought snow.

Gusts of wet wind pushed her around and washed the horizon in streaks of gray. Enna tied the ends of her head-scarf under her chin for warmth. The sun had left completely now, and the snow seemed endless. She could see no farther than a few paces in any direction. Enna shook her head at the bewildering, pale landscape and banged her fist on the saddle.

"Curse you, Enna," she said with chattering teeth. "I curse you up and down, stupid girl."

There was no point in trying to find her way in this weather. She walked Merry away from the wind, scanning for shelter. The night deepened.

Sometime later, she brushed snowflakes from her eye-lashes and squinted into the storm at a point of orange. Fire. She could not feel its heat from there, disrupted by snow and wind. Cautiously she moved closer, hoping to catch sight of any person before she was seen herself. If it were not for the wind, she was sure she could have already felt their heat. Closer, she spotted a tent and three horses in a curve of hill protected by a few scrub trees. A camp. But of whom? Closer. A figure hunched up against the wind moved around the perimeter of the camp. A guard. She waited until he walked to the far side of the little camp, then she moved in closer still.

The tent was white. None of the tents of Ostekin were white. But perhaps, she hoped, perhaps the Bayern scouts used such. Then a man opened the tent flap and moved into the light of the fire. Pale hair. Blue jacket.

"Tiran," she whispered.

She kept her eyes on the man by the fire and slowly backed Merry away.

"Spy!"

A shout from beside her. She jerked the reins and tried to gallop away, but the guard had come upon her unawares, and he stood now at the mare's head, gripping her bridle. He yelled to his companions. The man at the fire leaped forward, and another emerged from the tent gripping a spear.

Enna wrenched at Merry's reins. The mare whinnied and lifted onto her back legs, but the guard did not let go. He pulled her closer to the camp. The other two were almost upon her.

For a moment, the wind was breathless. It created a pocket of stillness inside the constant howling. Enna could at last feel a band of heat from the fire, and wisps from the mare and the Tiran guard, touching her face and hands. Frantically she grabbed at it, pulled it inside her chest, felt the burn, and sent it tearing into the tent. In the flash of yellow light, the two running guards faltered and looked behind them by the tent for another foe. The guard's grip on Merry's bridle loosened. Enna booted the man in the head, steered Merry away from the camp, and kicked her into a gallop.

now stung her eyes and cheeks. She could not hear anything but wind. Sometimes she looked behind her for pursuing horsemen, but soon the storm made it impossible to know which direction was behind.

She rode low, her face near Merry's neck, stunned as much by her heedless fire lighting as her near capture. Her hands were numb, her body ached. When at last the winds died and the sky cleared, Enna walked Merry until the distant fires of Ostekin directed her home. She entered its gates just after dawn.

Enna let a stable-hand help her dismount. When her feet touched earth, she gripped his shoulder and nearly crumpled to the ground.

"Long ride." He was looking over the mare's sweat-streaked neck with disapproval.

"I got lost," Enna said vaguely, and made for the town center. Walking on her own legs felt at once unbelievably refreshing and dreadfully painful.

She slowed her walk as she passed the councilman's house. Inside was her cot, and the idea of rest made her feel dreamy. Inside, too, was Isi. Enna imagined telling Isi at last about the vellum, and the uncomfortable heat last night when the prisoner made her angry, and her quickness in the snow-storm to use the fire to escape. Isi would probably under-stand, and she might even start working on how to erase what Enna had learned. Enna remembered now that Isi had not known of a way to erase such knowledge from Leifer but had wondered if those fire worshippers in Yasid might.

A door swung open to emit a messenger, and Enna caught sight of Isi sitting in the back room with Geric, deep in talk. No, it was not fair to burden Isi with this now. In compari-son with war and the death of the king, Enna's concerns seemed a mild matter.

Instead, Enna turned from the town center and wove through the brown tents and roped-off fighting rings to find Finn. The army was organized by hundred-bands, the smaller villages and three Forest areas offering only one each, the larger towns supplying several. The hundred-bands camped together, so she followed the painted shields until she started seeing those painted with twin pines—one green, one yellow. The yellow tree was meant to honor Isi, the yellow lady, for convincing the king to recognize the Forest boys as citizens and soldiers in the first place. But just then, Enna realized it looked like a tree aflame.

Finn sat at the mouth of a tent, attaching an iron head to

his javelin. She felt suddenly nervous to confess to him her secret, though she felt she should tell someone. He had always been a good listener, and she had missed their closeness these last weeks.

Before Finn, a couple of Forest lads sparred in a rope circle. The chief of their hundred-band called out, "Watch the left side! Lift up your shield!"

"Hello, Finn."

Finn glanced up, and at seeing her, a painful smile tightened his mouth.

"Hello, Enna. I'm just about to spar."

She sat beside him. "We haven't spoken in a while, and I thought we'd—"

"Mm-hm," he said as though he had not heard her, then put down his javelin and stood.

"Oh," said Enna.

Finn ducked under the rope of the fighting ring without a look back. "I'll relieve one," he said to the fight master.

A short boy about Finn's age nodded, too out of breath to speak, and exited the ring. He smiled when he saw Enna and sat beside her.

"How's it, Razo?" she said. Despite her exhaustion and the slight trembling that still shook her deep inside, she could not help but smile whenever she saw Razo. His unkempt hair stood nearly straight on his head, and his expressive face could never hide his current mood, which generally seemed to be either amused or confused.

She waited for him to get back his speaking breath and watched Finn in the rope ring. He fought with great energy, rushing his opponent and knocking him to the ground. Once he looked back to see if Enna watched, then turned away again just as quickly.

"He's getting better," said Enna.

"Who, Finn? No question." Razo tried to wipe the sweat from his brow on her shoulder, and she shoved him away.

"He practice much?"

Razo nodded, wiping his face on his already filthy tunic. It left a brown smear. "The most. It's scary to face him. He looks like he's going to pound you into the ground, and then afterwards you see he's not angry at all, just serious. Remember how he used to be?"

"Seems like the 'used to be' was only a few weeks ago," said Enna.

Finn was relentless and focused. Though his gestures seemed rough, his attacks were fierce, and Enna thought he looked natural swinging a sword.

"Why didn't you two ever . . . " Razo gestured back and forth from the fighting Finn to Enna at his side.

"What do you mean?"

"Don't be dumb, Enna-girl. I know there used to be something there."

"There was not, you dope. Finn and I've been good friends, but he never pursued me."

"Ah, get off," he said. "I pursued pretty, pretty Bettin

from Sprucegrove to Longpines, and that didn't keep her from marrying that impostor Offo."

"Razo, we're talking about me and Finn. A snake and a hare."

"Does that look like a hare to you?"

Enna watched as Finn attacked a fresh opponent, hammering the boy's shield until he cried halt.

"He's . . . changing, isn't he? I don't know what to think of him."

"It's the war," Razo said matter-of-factly. "It's getting all of us, including you. Your forehead's always knotted up and worried now, like I haven't seen since I had you completely and utterly convinced that your hen had a crazy chicken disease."

Enna laughed. At the sound, Finn turned and looked. His opponent used the opening to throw himself against his shield, and Finn tumbled to the ground. Angrily, he stood and rushed in return, pounding his sword against the other's until the training master shouted, "Match!"

"I'll admit, I've never seen him like this," Enna continued. "Do you think he's just trying to . . . impress someone?"

"Absolutely," said Razo. "You know, Finn's got a girl now."

"Finn's got a what? What do you mean?"

Razo jerked his head toward a slim girl leaning against a fence post. She was completely absorbed in the sparring, half a smile forgotten on her lips.

"Hesel?" Enna said with unconcealed wonder. "Finn and Hesel?"

"So it would seem," said Razo.

"But, but, she's not even a Forest girl, and she's too skinny."

"She's Captain Monulf's niece, and not bad to look at, and a pretty good cook besides."

"Ha." Enna smugly remembered seeing her once in the councilman's house overcook a loaf of bread. "Pretty and a captain's niece is scarcely a recipe for Finn's true love."

Razo gave her a toothy smile. "Are you jealous, then, Enna-girl?"

Enna glared back. "Don't be daft, Razo. I'm just thinking that a town girl's hardly what Finn needs."

"Match," said the fight master.

Finn knocked sword tips with his opponent in friendly dismissal and left the ring. Enna looked to where Hesel had been standing. She was gone, too.

A page tapped Enna's shoulder and told her the yellow lady wanted her for council in the public building, and she stood to go.

"Come see us again," said Razo. "When Finn's in a better mood."

"Wait," she said. Razo turned and waited for her to speak. And she wanted to. Yesterday she had nearly lost control, and that frightened her. She needed to tell someone what was happening inside her, someone who would not judge, who could help. She did not want to bother Isi, and it seemed Finn was past his listening stage. Could she tell Razo?

His face was young and boyish, but he had an arrowhead-shaped scar on one cheek and another peering out from the neck of his tunic. Those had been frightening injuries, but she remembered he had never been concerned about them. When he first received his javelin and shield from the king, he had wept openly. He was the least threatening, most ridiculous, and impossibly likable person she knew. So much like Leifer.

"I, uh, I'll see you around," was all she could say.

Razo snorted. "Sure." He started to leave, then turned back to her. "Enna, don't you breathe a word to Offo on what I said about Bettin. I know I'm hopeless, but I'll never love a soul besides Bettin and I'll die alone."

She sighed. "Your head's all full of silliness, saying things like 'I'll die alone.' You and Finn, you're still just little boys."

The public building was a single-story, one-room structure with the only glass windows in the town, and today it was surrounded by soldiers. The door ward let her pass. Inside, several small tables sat touching to form a larger, oddly rectangular one in the center of the room. Geric, Isi, Thiaddag the prime minister, and the two chief captains in the region, Talone and Monulf, sat at the table. Several other captains stood behind them. Isi and Talone were conversing quietly. Enna remembered that they were compatriots, Talone having accompanied Isi on her journey from her birth kingdom of Kildenree. He had stayed in Bayern as her personal protector and, later, as the captain of Bayern's Own, the king's personal hundred-band.

When Enna approached, Talone nodded to her and took his seat by Monulf.

"What's happening?" asked Enna.

"War council with Tira," said Isi. "A messenger came from their camp at Eylbold yesterday morning. We're all a bit nervous. I could use you beside me."

"Yes, of course. Have you . . . are you all right?" Enna just then noticed how calm Isi looked. "You seem different."

"You noticed?" Isi smiled. "I must normally be pretty agitated. A physician gave me a rather bitter tea. It makes me drowsy, but at least I slept last night. And it dulls me, I guess. I hear most of the news that comes to me on scraps of wind, but not so loudly. I didn't know you had entered the room until just before I saw you."

Hoofbeats and voices outside quieted the room. Everyone seemed to sit up a little straighter. Enna took her place standing behind Isi's chair. It was her usual position and a place of honor, but exhaustion made her legs feel loose, and she grabbed the back of Isi's chair for support. Moments later, the Tiran delegation entered. Most wore blue jackets and leather piecemeal vests and carried short spears. Enna stared at them openly, glaring whenever one caught her eye. The leader seemed to be a gray-haired captain named Tiedan. Enna had heard that the Tiran royalty did not enter battle, and their women stayed home.

After stiff formalities, Tiedan and Geric spoke almost exclusively, and Enna wondered why everyone else was needed there at all. She found herself not paying much attention to the talk, instead looking over the Tiran men and thinking about the battle of Ostekin Fields, of the soldiers who had been killed, of Leifer. A log in the hearth cracked, a noise as loud and distinct as a word. Enna felt herself begin to sweat.

Geric was speaking. "I think it wise to remember that this is not just an issue of land. It's people. The people you attacked in those villages and towns are Bayern."

"For now," said Tiedan. "Once they were Tiran. They can be again."

"You don't know that." Geric rubbed his eyes. "You say that, but you have no proof, nor does that fact live in the memories of my people."

Enna was not sure if the fierceness of Tiedan's speech meant he was angry or if it was just the effect of his rigid, pronounced accent. "The facts reside in more than memories. The facts embed themselves in our very natures. Look at your people, all with dark hair, most with dark eyes. Farther south in Bayern the people begin to have lighter hair—almost like us."

"But Captain Tiedan, that doesn't mean—"

Tiedan interrupted Geric. "And how is it that we speak the same language? I hear that lands farther south and east speak barbaric tongues. Clearly Bayern was born from Tira."

Bayern born from Tira. The thought made Enna scowl. She narrowed her eyes at the captain called Tiedan and hoped he would notice.

"You make no sense, sir." Geric was fighting anger. "And even if we agreed that, yes, once long ago, before memory, our people were one, that doesn't justify your butchery of this people! In truth, it makes your aggression even more senseless."

Tiedan chuckled and then spoke in a low, growling voice. "Then how, pray tell us, sir, do you justify the butcheries your grandfathers committed against Tira?"

Enna had a sudden and powerful conviction that she could set the room on fire. All the deadwood of the walls, tables, and floors would burn beautifully. All those living bodies and the hearth fire were just oozing heat into the room. She could with a thought bring the heat inside her, feel it change, and thrust it out again. The realization made her shiver.

She took a deep breath and focused on the cool sounds of a winter breeze whistling in the chimney. How could such a thought enter her mind?

"If this is just about revenge," said Geric, "then feel fulfilled and go home. You've killed the king, you've killed a goodly number of Bayern soldiers. Those who attacked you in the past are dead, and now so are many of their children. Let it end here."

Enna wiped her brow. All those people in one small space,

all generating heat. Isi shifted in her chair. Enna noticed that Isi had wrapped her yellow hair in a Forest woman's head-scarf, and her face was down. Many times Geric had begged Isi not to draw attention, afraid as he was that the Tiran would recognize her as the wind worker of the first battle and target her. Enna squeezed Isi's shoulder. Isi reached up and touched Enna's hand. Her cool fingers felt comforting and familiar.

"If your only solution for peace is keeping the towns you've taken," Geric was saying, "then I can't accept. We won't abandon our people. We're willing to discuss compromise, but ultimately it must include peace for all of Bayern."

"Sileph, first rank. Allow me a question, sir." A new Tiran captain spoke up. His hair was the lighter brown of lowland soil, his aspect confident but unassuming. He spoke properly, but with a casual arrogance, as though he knew he would not be denied. Tiedan acknowledged his request.

"King," said Sileph, stating the title with neither courtesy nor mockery, "you say you are here for peace, and yet on the eve of these talks you send your witchery to attack a camp of Tiran men."

There was a stir among the Bayern. Geric glanced at Talone and Monulf to see both offer slight shakes of their heads. Enna squinted at the soldier called Sileph. Had he been among the three last night in the storm? Even if he had, surely he could not know her face.

"We know nothing," Geric said, cutting through noise,

"we know nothing of attacks last night. If they happened, they were not of our people."

"Come now, King," said Sileph. "Those at the first battle of Ostekin Field reported fire workers. They set fire to the men's clothing. The ground around them flamed." He turned and looked directly at Enna. She blinked in surprise and resisted taking a step backward. "Perhaps the women, since you see fit to include them in war councils, would care to explain."

"No need," said Geric. "I can tell you. We'd a man with fire talents, but he was killed in that battle. Have you seen fire used in the skirmishes this autumn? He's dead, and no other works fire."

Sileph did not give up. "I have heard tale of fire-witches from the south, in the kingdom called Yasid. Is Bayern in league with the desert dwellers to crush Tira?"

Isi looked up, but Geric answered. "I know nothing of fire-witches in Yasid."

"Let the woman speak," said Sileph.

At first Enna thought Sileph meant for Isi to speak, but his gaze did not leave her own face. She let go of Isi's chair and stood straighter, temper flashing in her chest. Silence followed Sileph's words; then Geric said her name gently.

"The king speaks true," she said, relishing her Forest accent, slurring her words more than usual just to contrast with the Tiran's careful speech. "Your boys thought we women conjured the fire, but we just watched atop the hill.

Leifer, the fire worker, he stood in the midst of you. Then he burned himself up. I saw the body." She almost choked on emotion then, but she stayed cool and was proud of herself.

"And the others?" He seemed to take her in wholly, not acknowledging any other person in the room.

"I've never seen or heard of a Yasid fire-witch in Bayern. Leifer's dead, and he taught no one his art. Of that I'm certain." She smiled at how deftly she avoided an outright lie.

Sileph stared at her a moment longer, and she felt her face heat under his gaze. Then he nodded once and stepped back to his position behind Tiedan.

The men finished their talking, accomplishing little but an agreed standstill for the winter, and the council broke up. Enna sighed and stretched as the Tiran captains left the room. One looked at her disapprovingly. She returned his look with a saucy tip of her head. Sileph, the first rank captain, caught sight of her and looked down, smiling. He was a handsome man, more so than any she had ever known. Indeed, she had never given much thought to what made a man handsome, but looking at him, she was sure she understood.

When he glanced up again, she smiled back boldly.

As soon as the last Tiran left, the Bayern breathed out and began to talk. The council would continue, and Enna felt panicked at having to stay in that room any longer. The sounds of the departing Tiran horses felt like blows to her belly. There seemed to be no air to breathe in the heat.

Quickly she ducked out of the door and onto the street.

She could see the last Tiran horseman just leaving the town gates, and impulse bade her follow and do . . . something, hurt them, chase them out of Bayern. The place in her chest throbbed, and her skin felt feverish and raw. She took a breath and turned away, allowing the cool winter air to soak into her, a snaking breeze to push the heat away.

When she reentered the building, Prime Minister Thiaddag was pounding a javelin against the wood floor. "Captains, ministers, ladies, quiet for the king."

Enna sat beside Isi in a vacated chair and listened to the ensuing discussion. Geric brought up each point dealt with in the meeting and asked the Bayern captains if he had done right. Most of the men brandished their javelins, some thumping the ends on the wooden floor to mark passionate assent. Whenever some gave to inarticulate murmuring, the murmurers were asked to speak their mind, and their dissatisfaction was discussed and resolved.

The fire crackled louder, it seemed to Enna, than the men spoke. An hour crawled by, and the heat of the room clung to her skin. But though her vision tilted a little, and the heat began to scratch, she felt calm. She looked at the fields out the window masked in snow and listened to the wind humming in the chimney, and no urge to burn bothered her thoughts.

The council voted to wait out the winter and not attack the taken towns. The king and queen were to return to the capital to oversee recruiting, supplies, and civic peace. Last, they chose a captain to lead training, defending, and spying from Ostekin. For Talone, the javelins waved. Monulf inclined his head in agreement. Monulf was the senior captain, but he had led the assault at Ostekin Fields, so under his leadership the king had been killed. This post required one untainted by such a defeat.

At one point, Talone said, "Though the best scout we could have is leaving us for the capital."

"I can't," said Isi. "I'm unreliable of late. I can't focus on what I hear."

Talone nodded respectfully. Enna shook her head. It was a shame that in a war, with two nations dangling in the balance, Isi was not able to use her gift.

Before the council broke up, Geric turned to Enna. "Have you anything to add, queen's maiden?"

Enna blinked in surprise, but one thought did push forward. "Actually, I have heard the people in camp talking about an augury. Many are doing their own, but shouldn't we conduct a war augury?"

"Yes," said one of the captains in agreement. "We should council with fate to see if we fight in vain or can sacrifice our lives with the good assurance of victory."

The thumping of javelins sounded like the heavy footfalls of fate, though Enna did not know why she perceived it so.

"The council's in agreement," said Thiaddag. "Let the king pronounce the augury."

Geric turned to Monulf. "Sir, I've never led such an exercise. I allot this to you."

Monulf inclined his head. "A combat of countries, man versus man, is the traditional war augury. There are healthy Tiran prisoners in this camp. I'll ask one to volunteer for combat unknown. He'll sleep this night on a mattress and eat with me. Tomorrow I'll give him his own weapons and pitch him in a death match against one of our own—also a volunteer. The results will give us a glimpse of our future against Tira."

"Captains, ministers, women, speak not of this until the morrow," said Thiaddag, "as foreknowledge for the fighters will tamper with the outcome. We are released from council."

The men were quiet as they left the public house. Enna felt her mouth go dry. She had thought an augury might show an encouraging sign, something to get them all through this winter. She had not considered that a war augury would require someone to die.

Though the captains gave no details, it seemed the entire camp felt the new tension. Every night for the two months that she had slept under a south-facing window in the councilman's house, Enna had heard men's jocular voices intoning tavern songs or men's solemn voices singing lost love and death songs. That night, silence. In the stillness, the hungry, crackling sound of fires wafted from the camp through her window. To Enna, it seemed that the sound itself could ignite the wooden shutters.

Chapter 8

t dawn, men were already gathering around the town square. Everyone was fully armed. Monulf and another man drove stakes into the hard earth and made a rope ring. When the soldiers saw it, they murmured to one another.

Enna accompanied Isi and Geric to the rope through a mob of soldiers who occasionally patted Geric on the back or touched Isi's loose-hanging hair. They passed Hesel in the crowd, and Enna felt her face twist into a scowl. No, the girl was definitely not worthy of Finn. She had no substance—all face and hair and bright eyes.

At last they broke through the crowd to face the empty ring, and Enna took a breath, feeling suffocated by the heat of all those people.

"I'm nervous," Enna said to Isi, holding a hand on her stomach. "This all feels so big."

"Too big." Isi frowned. "I don't like it. We should do it in private. That way if our Bayern man dies, the army won't know, and it won't get them down with ideas that we're doomed to lose the war."

"What difference would that make?" said Enna. "The result'll be the same no matter how many people see. Don't you believe the augury foretells the truth?"

"Well, no."

"Oh," said Enna. She had never met anyone who doubted the signs all around them. Since she was a baby, her mother had taught her to predict the weather by the flight of wild geese or the harshness of coming winter by the movement of bumblebees. Perhaps such things had power only in Bayern, so Isi was never taught. But Enna looked at the rope ring, felt her stomach harden and freeze, and had no doubts. This augury was unlike anything her mother had shown her. It meant the life of at least one person today and the fate of their kingdom in the future.

Monulf entered the arena and held up his hands for silence. He turned around slowly, as though he meant to meet eyes with every observer. At last he spoke. "Who among us will enter this ring and represent us all?"

Perhaps thinking it no more than an exercise to rouse loyalty and energy, hundreds of soldiers raised their javelins and hollered, "I will! I will!" But others took him quite seriously and pushed their way toward the ring. One young man rolled under the rope before any other. He stood, straightened his shield bearing two trees, and lifted his javelin.

"No, no," said Enna.

"I will," said Finn.

Isi gripped Enna's arm. "Oh, Finn," she said quietly.

He looked as calm as he ever did coring apples or leading a wagon into market-square. The weapons did not fit him. Clearly his sword was not his own, the belt hanging low on his hips and sword point dangling near the ground. His expression was his same, soft expression that Enna knew. She almost expected him to duck his head and break out into one of his huge, bashful grins. But Razo was right—there was something more serious in him now. Tighter lips, perhaps, or a line across his brow. But she knew for all his seriousness that he was not the ideal champion of Bayern. Most likely the first time a sword hilt touched his hand was the day he joined Geric's camp for the battle of Ostekin Fields.

Monulf raised Finn's hand and said to the crowd, "This boy is Bayern. Now bring in Tira."

Guards led a blue-coated man into the ring. He wore a leather helmet, and the tips of hair escaping its hold were a lighter color than most Bayern. He carried a sword, an unpainted square shield, and a short spear. Enna was relieved to see that Finn was taller than the prisoner and a little broader, too. But the Tiran was older by perhaps ten years. He moved with a ruthless grace, and his expression was hard with calm desperation. She had no doubt he meant to kill Finn as quickly as he could.

At the sight of the Tiran, the crowd erupted into a deafening cheer, beginning to understand what this match meant.

Monulf held his fist in the air to command silence. The outer rings of the crowd took longer to quiet. Soldiers were climbing on one another's shoulders and on top of wagons, barrels, and nearby roofs to see the match. Four of the king's guard held large shields in a defensive position between the king's party and the rope, and Enna stood on her toes to get a better view. The opponents faced each other, circling slowly, each clutching his javelin or spear. In the quiet, Enna could hear their boots scrape against the earth. Monulf backed out of the ring, his fist still in the air.

"To predict the future of our war, combat to the death!"

He dropped his hand. The crowd reclaimed their cheers.

The Tiran was the first to move. He looked at Monulf as if expecting more instruction. Then with his eyes still averted he threw the spear. Finn deflected it with his shield. He moved forward quickly, stabbing at the Tiran with his javelin, making wide, swinging cuts. The Tiran held him off with his sword. Finn swiped upward, caught the Tiran's shield with his javelin tip, and tore it out of his hand. The crowd cheered. But in the next move, the Tiran dodged a javelin thrust, grabbed the haft, and pulled it out of Finn's hand. It clattered to the ground.

Now both were left to their swords.

Again the Tiran attacked first, and Finn met him in the center. In the uproar, Enna could not hear their swords meet. She could feel the crowd's emotion through the noise— anger, frustration, excitement, dread. Her own heart yelled back while her stomach cringed away.

Finn returned the attack, battering at his opponent's sword as though trying to break his arm. The Tiran jabbed from underneath, and Finn jumped back to keep from being skewered in the belly. Now Finn was on the defensive, backing away from the attack, defending with his shield. The Tiran's sword caught him on the leg, and Finn opened his mouth in a silent cry of pain. Quickly he dropped to one knee, rolled out of the way, and turned around to meet sword against sword.

Enna felt helpless. When had the world turned so grave? The Tiran struck Finn's shield with a force that knocked it from his arm, and Enna could not help but cry out. She felt as though she were tied up and being made to watch while her country fell. Enna saw Geric frown, but she knew he would let this go to the finish and accept the results. Isi bowed her head, her eyes closed. Apparently she heard enough from the wind that she did not want to see the action as well.

Please. Enna thought. *Please, Finn.*

The Tiran combated with the fierceness of a dying man, growling and spitting. Finn's face was nearly without expression. He bled a little from his knee and from his bare arm where his shield once sat. His chest heaved with the effort of dodging blows, yet he still attacked relentlessly.

He's persistent, Enna thought. She had a sudden memory of Finn visiting her home just after the death of her mother. A chicken had broken loose from the coop, and Enna had been too grieved to seek it out. Finn had scoured the Forest and returned hours later, carrying just a clump of feathers in both outstretched hands. He had cried for the chicken. No, Enna realized, he had cried for her, for having to bring her a corpse so soon after her mother's death, for failing her, for the sorrow he imagined she would feel.

Finn continued to fight, but the crowd's calls were becoming anxious. They pleaded now instead of cheered. Some put their faces in their hands. In a quick and desperate move, Finn dropped to his knees under his opponent's swing and pricked him in the side. The crowd roared anew, but instead of doubling at the pain and allowing Finn to gain his feet again, the Tiran continued in his swing, met Finn's sword, and twisted it from his hand.

The crowd gasped. Finn dodged the following blow, but he was now completely disarmed. "No," came the mutters and cries from all sides, "no, not to us." Finn tried to leap for the fallen spear, but the Tiran rushed him and cut off contact. Finn was now close to the rope with very little room to run. The Tiran approached. Finn stood on the balls of his feet, his arms held out in a ready posture, his face deathly still. Blood dripped off his forearm and hit the cold ground. Enna thought she could detect its heat. Despite the noise of hundreds of men around her, she could hear her own heart keeping time in her ears. The beat seemed to chant, *Do something, do it, burn it, burn and burn.*

The Tiran lunged. Finn dropped to his back and kicked up into his foe's belly. The Tiran was pushed back but swung around quickly, his sword in a steady arc reaching, diving, circling around, and plunging toward Finn's chest.

Enna saw this last movement slowly, the plunge of the enemy's sword as though it were many swords, the outcome plain before it happened. The enemy on his feet, and Finn, sweet, harmless Finn, on his back on the ground. That was wrong. And all she had to do was pull and push. So simple. So small an action. And so much heat ready, hanging around her in the winter air. And in this slowed moment, reasons raced in her mind. She could help. But she should not. She had sworn that she would not. But if she did not, then Finn would die, and not only Finn, but the war would be lost, the augury spoken.

So she did. The heat was waiting around her. She pulled it into her chest with a small sigh of pain, then she sent it boiling into the Tiran's sword, up into the iron hilt.

The Tiran faltered, and the arc of his sword swerved, just grazing Finn's shoulder. Finn grabbed the Tiran's tunic and slammed his forehead into the man's nose. The Tiran dropped the sword and stumbled backward, blood spilling down his face. Still on the ground, Finn grabbed the fallen spear and hurled it. The iron tip flew through the soldier's side and sent him to the earth. The crowd went utterly quiet. Enna could hear the Tiran's labored breath. Finn stood, went to his fallen shield, and strapped it on his bleeding arm. He picked his sword off the ground. Slowly, without glory or fear, Finn walked to the fallen man, hefted his sword in the air, and brought it down across the Tiran's neck.

The crowd exploded with noise. Men embraced one another and wept, tore down the rope, and mauled Finn with kisses and thumps. Guards immediately circled the king's company, shields facing out to protect them in the riot, but even they were cheering.

Monulf was at Geric's side. "We're assured, sire. We fight as valiantly as that Forest lad, and we'll be victorious."

Enna was holding a hand to her mouth. She did not remember putting it there. Had she been holding back a scream? Or was she trying to hide? She looked back on the image of that last struggle again and again—Finn kicks, the Tiran turns, plunges, then falters. To others, surely it would just seem that his balance failed, that his sword missed, and that Finn seized the opportunity to attack. And in all that commotion, she believed no one but her would notice that the leather-wrapped hilt of the Tiran's sword let off a thin gray string of smoke.

Enna could not sigh in relief. She felt Isi staring at her.

"Enna, what just happened?"

"We . . . What do you mean? We won, Isi. Finn's all right."

"Enna." Isi shook her head. "Is there something going on that—"

"No." Enna looked down, exhaling slowly. She needed to be alone, time to think about what she had done, what she

would do now. The moment she had interfered with the
augury, Enna knew she had made a promise, a silent com-
mitment to all of Bayern. It was not just Finn in that ring
representing Bayern's armies—Enna had added her fire.
Without her help, Finn would have been killed, Bayern's fate
sealed. She felt that if she refused to fight now, she was
giving her kingdom to Tira.

Enna slowly met Isi's eyes, tried not to blink, and prepared to lie to her best friend for the first time.

"There's nothing," she said. "Nothing's going on, except
Finn just won, so we should be happy. I should go and . . .
and let you be alone with Geric."

As soon as she broke free from the throng, Enna ran
down the central road to the east end of town.

"What happened?" the sentries called to her as she
passed.

"War augury—our boy beat the Tiran."

The men on watch howled gleefully as she left them and
ran out to the frozen fields where the ground sank away
from the town's view.

"You've done it now, Enna-girl." She sat on the ground
and leaned back to look at the sky, a winter blue spoiled with
patches of hostile winter clouds. The sun against the white
snow burned her eyes, and she blinked away stinging tears.
Again and again, she went over the augury in her mind,
Finn's fall, her intervention. The omen was clear—with her
help, Bayern's armies would be victorious, and without, there

was only defeat.

"Ahh," she wailed at nothing, and stood and paced and pulled at her hair. It was wrong; she had done wrong. She had promised never to use the fire, and now she had lied to Isi. But Finn would have been killed and the outcome of the augury sealed. There had been no other choice.

She faced southeast. Tira. The taken towns. Lately she always knew where southeast was, even at night, even with eyes closed. She fancied she could sense the enemy in her land, a great hulking presence. Just by facing that direction, her new decision to fight still raw but real inside her, she felt everything slide and click into place—Leifer's sacrifice, the vellum in her hands, the augury, all steps to bring her to this choice. She would save Bayern.

nna lay awake most the night staring at the cross-beams of the councilman's house and thinking of Leifer. If she was to succeed, then she had to avoid his mistakes. She went over what things he must have done wrong—telling others, using fire against his sister in a moment of rash anger, then using too much all at once on the battlefield.

"All right, then," she whispered so low that she could barely hear herself. "I will never tell a soul, I'll never burn a living person, and I'll keep it small, just bits at a time. I swear, Leifer, I swear."

Enna hoped such caution meant she would not end up charred on a battlefield, but it also meant she could not fight as Leifer had. Remembering the Tiran tent in the snowstorm, Enna decided that stealth attacks might do just as well as a grand fire show. She would be the mouse that could bring down an oak tree, chewing one woody fiber at a time.

A woman beside her snorted gratingly. Enna smiled,

imagining it was Hesel.

She spent all that day anxious, waiting for evening. Isi was busy with Geric, Razo and Finn with their hundred-band, and chores bored her when something so crucial was waiting. To pass the time, she battled with herself over what to do with the vellum. It was not safe hiding under her cot. She could not bury it—the ground was frozen, and besides, Leifer had found it under a fir tree. Perhaps long ago, someone like Enna had buried it to hide it, which meant that someone like Leifer could find it again. Enna did not want to commit the same error.

So Enna hid in a corner of the tanner's house, unstitched her hem, and sewed the vellum inside her skirt. She had read it so many times now that entire sentences entered her mind unbidden, but she did not know if she would need it again. She dared not destroy it or lose it, not until the war was over and her part in the augury fulfilled.

At sundown she made the ride to the nearest taken town—Eylbold.

The dark gray Merry was a ghost of the night landscape. A light snowfall from that morning had taken the icy edge from the air. It felt like a gentle winter, a sleepy winter.

"I won't be long," said Enna, tethering Merry to a tree. She wished she had a bond with this mare as Isi had with her horse. If only she could ask Merry to keep quiet, she could probably take her closer. It would be a real benefit to have an animal by her side and draw on all that life heat for her task.

Enna rubbed the mare's rabbit-soft nose regretfully and left her for the night.

The last scouting report said the Tiran camp sprawled from the edge of the northeast wood and into the taken Bayern town of Eylbold. The woods supplied good cover and a nice buffer between her escape route and the town, so she stayed in its moonshade, creeping from tree to tree. Intermittent patches of snow gave soft moans under her boot. She was grateful the night was not cold enough to freeze it, grateful to avoid crunching snow and that sound like a small beast eating, the noise of clumsy stealth.

She was aware of all the living around her. She could feel its heat—the trees, the sleeping animals in their arms or in holes in the ground. Even the frozen grass was still alive at its root, still emanating tiny strings of heat. Her sense of it was so much stronger than at first, and she knew she could draw on it at any moment. At first, the thought of at last giving rein to the fire was exciting.

Enna could feel the increase of heat before she saw the camp. Trees and plants let off so little in comparison, theirs a sleepy, measured life, a slow growth. But animals, and humans especially, gave off chunks of it, swirls and waves drifting off their bodies as though they had life to burn. And live fire was a powerful, steady source. So close to the men and fires of the camp, this edge of the wood throbbed with heat adrift.

She pulled her body against a fir and concentrated on drawing all that loose heat around her, readying herself to pull it inside. And hesitated. She closed her eyes, focused, and tried again. But her rapid breath seemed so loud, she could not focus on the push of the heat against her skin. Enna lowered her head and realized the excitement was gone, and her stomach moaned and twisted uncomfortably. She had resisted it for so long. That night in the snowstorm and at the augury, she had acted instinctively, to save herself or Finn. Now actually making the choice to pull the heat inside her felt as impossible as looking over a cliff edge and making her body lean forward.

Then a noise like a snapping twig.

Enna clutched the tree to keep still. It could be soldiers moving in on her, or it could be a branch settling in the cold. She listened, holding very still, breathing into the neck of her cloak to mask the sign of her icy breath. No other noise.

Her heart leaping in her chest reminded her why she had ridden so far and what she still must do. From nearby she could hear the shuddering, hollow sound of wind against a tent. She watched it a few moments to see if she could detect any inhabitants—no one entered or left, no lantern lit it from the inside. It seemed a safe target. This time she held her breath and closed her eyes. The heat was so close, so willing. She let go of her fears.

She inhaled and spoke to the heat touching her skin with a thought, a sensation, an invitation to enter. Her eyes opened wide, her voice nearly escaped in an indrawn scream from the unbearable burn. Focusing on the space before her where the tent stood, she felt a release and heard an outburst of fire whipping against cloth. Men began to shout.

Then a whisk she thought might be an arrow. Enna dropped to the ground, scurried a distance on her hands and feet, then drew up in panic for a full run.

"It's all right, it's all right," she chanted to the mare as she mounted and set her at a gallop. By the time she left the Eylbold woods, no pursuer was in sight.

The ride back to Ostekin took her until dawn. It was a strange and long journey with nothing to fear or look forward to, the heat left behind. Everything seemed frozen. The mare's hooves clipped against the icy earth, the mare's breath made a silver mist, the air around her seemed frozen hard in the dark as though she could crack it with a wood wedge.

She, too, felt iced over. That fire she mustered left her momentarily numb to the heat she had become used to sensing. Strangest, though, was the hollowness inside her chest, and for some time she could feel nothing stronger than a vacant ache deeper than she could touch. But still clinging to her was the memory that the rush of indrawn heat and release into fire had felt . . . astonishing. Unbearable. Lovely.

She neared Ostekin's town wall in the dull, cloudy dawn. One of the sentries watching the east gate was Razo.

"Enna-girl, where've you been riding?"

"Scouting," she said.

Two of the sentries squinted at each other. Razo looked up, slack jawed and unassuming.

"Talone put you on scouting duty?"

"Could be." She still felt the vibration of the arrow like a cold spot on her neck. The long, freezing ride back made her feel she had lost part of herself somewhere in the woods, somewhere on the dark fields. She leaned over to stroke her mount's neck and felt as though only the mare were real in all the cold, dim world.

"Come on, now, mistress chicken-girl, you know you've got to answer a sentry's questions when entering the camp."

"Talone said that . . . " Enna feigned looking embarrassed, as if she had let slip too much. "Oh, I'm not supposed to say."

A stable-hand took Merry to the stables. Enna wrapped her arms around herself and walked into town, avoiding looking back at Razo. It was better to lie than to break her promise of secrecy. But just then, numb and dazed and lonely, the wisdom felt like cold comfort.

Enna slept all day, flopping and kicking, dreaming that she was exhausted but could not sleep. She woke when the afternoon light had a sheen of winter gold, as though promising that what came next was even better than day. Isi was sitting by her cot, holding a mug. The sight of her felt like such a relief, Enna felt her throat tighten as if she were holding back tears.

"Good morning," said Isi with a smile. She held out the mug. "Mint tea. It was warm an hour ago, but you might still like it."

Enna drank it all without a breath, her eyes on Isi's, wondering what Isi suspected and, if she asked, what Enna could tell her. Would she have to lie? Could she tell Isi and make her understand? The ashes of one little tent seemed feeble to her now, and the weight of the augury pressed her chest like a stone.

"Thank you," said Enna.

"Are you sick?"

Enna nodded. She did feel ill and tired, cold from the inside out. A rush of memory brushed down through her chest—the intake of heat, the release of fire. She shivered.

Isi frowned. "The wind—it sees you a little differently. I thought you might be sick. You should rest. We're riding back to the capital in three days."

"I can't go," Enna said with conviction, before she had thought about it.

Isi pressed her hand to Enna's forehead. "Are you terribly ill, then?"

"No." Enna turned her head to look out the window. She could not leave Ostekin and the war front, not until she had done her part. Last night was not enough to win a war. "I can't leave here so soon—not so soon after Leifer has died."

"You need to stay because you are still mourning?"

Enna blinked only once before she said, "Yes."

Lying to Isi felt like the start of something irreversible, as significant as reading the vellum or lighting the first fire. To assuage her guilt, Enna barely left Isi's side for three days, aggressively protecting her from pushy ministers or soldiers, even when she knew it was not necessary.

It felt strange not to tell Isi everything. It seemed to Enna that her secret hung between them, always pushing them a little farther apart. Sometimes Enna was so conscious of the unspoken, she could not believe Isi did not know. She felt it keenly the morning she stood by Avlado and helped Isi mount, said good-bye, and watched Isi and Geric ride north. Then she turned around, back to the south. That very night she rode to Eylbold again, set another tent on fire, and fled into the morning.

Each afternoon the week after, Enna made a point to be in the main room of the councilman's house when Talone gathered his scouts for the report. She swept the floor, oiled shutters, mended tunics. A few days after her second attack, she stooped over the hearth for some time, stoking the coals, her eyes on the fire, impatient with the lack of word about her exploits. Nothing was changing. Still the Tiran armies sat on Bayern land, waiting through winter.

Talone dismissed the men, and Enna swung around.

"What about Eylbold?" she asked.

Talone seemed surprised at her question, though his face rarely showed emotion. Some of the departing scouts stopped to look at Enna. Razo was among them.

"Why do you ask, maiden?" said Talone.

Enna shrugged. "They're so close by. I just didn't hear you mention them, and it seems like there'd be more information."

"No word from Eylbold," said Talone. "I thank you for your interest."

Enna left the building with hot cheeks. No word. Was her burning accomplishing anything? That night she would return, and she must find a way inside.

This time she came upon Eylbold from the east and the open lands, thinking that the wood might now be well guarded. She left the mare in a copse of thorns and shrubs and crept across the frozen landscape. The moon was covered in cloud, and the only light in the world came from the campfires just over the next rolling field. She found herself looking forward to setting a fire in the night. The anticipation almost flooded out her fear.

She neared the edge of the encampment and saw the silhouettes of guards, spears in hand. At their backs the white tents seemed to glow like windows in the firelight. She stopped, lay down flat on the ground, and crawled closer. Her breath came from her throat in short gasps. Her hands tingled with cold and then grew numb against the frosty ground.

It was easy in the winter cold to pull the drifting camp heat out of the air, like stripping fibers from beaten flax. She also called on the roots of living things, asleep for the winter, and felt the curled-up body of some hibernating animal under the dirt. She would not pull heat directly from any creature, just gather what naturally left and wafted unused in the air.

Then, about a hundred paces from the nearest guard, Enna stopped. She looked carefully along the perimeter of tents. Guards every twenty paces. There was no way to enter the camp without being seen. She felt foolish for not having an alternate plan and, discouraged, started to crawl away.

Her limbs began to tremble and she collapsed, her face scraping the ground. Again she tried to pull herself along and again crumpled weakly. Her own breath was hot in her face, and she felt frustrated and helpless, the sensation of trying to run away in a dream but not moving at all.

What's the matter with me? she thought angrily. *Just get away, go.*

But she paused and looked back at the camp. The Tiran, warm in their tents, snug on Bayern land, safe from attack all winter long. Her power, the augury, all useless if she did not act. *To come all this way and not burn.* The desire assaulted her, sharp as hatchet strikes, and she winced. Avoiding the thought seemed impossible. The longer she crouched there, hesitating, the more the pain built and boiled, filling her body.

"All right," she whispered.

In that moment, she felt her insides bend as though leaning toward something, and her careful grip on the desire of the fire twisted like a snake in her fist.

Her eyes rested on a stack of barrels. She pulled in the heat, smooth and slick as butter, felt it change inside her, and sent it flying into her target. There was a satisfying explosion as the contents blew into the air.

A chill shook her as the heat left and shouts buffeted the night. She scrambled away, still keeping close to the ground. As soon as she dipped down over the first rise, she stood and ran. Immediately she heard bootfalls behind her and then a voice, clear and commanding.

"Stop or I will put this spear in you."

Enna stopped, her skin wincing in anticipation of the spear. She had expelled all her waiting heat at those barrels. She held no weapon. He came closer.

"You will surrender yourself," he said.

She was not quite numb yet, but she had no more gathered heat to attack. If only he were closer . . . *No, no,* she argued with herself, *I can't set fire to a person.*

"I said, surrender," he said.

But if I don't, I die. In that moment the maddening need to survive filled her, and she recognized in that need the same feeling the heat created when it pushed against her to be made into fire. *Just do it. Just burn him.* There seemed no other option. If only she were not alone.

Closer. She could feel him now. With a gasp she tugged at his body heat, what rose from his skin and circled around his head. Suddenly she knew she could get more, if she wished. She kept pulling and felt as though she tugged on a rope and someone on the other end tugged back, but she pulled harder and felt it give, freeing heat that was not loose, but what lived in his skin and beneath it. She heard him wheeze. She drew it in and sent it back at him again in its new and perfect form.

He screamed. Smoke rushed into her throat. Coughing, Enna turned and fled.

She did not look back, afraid to see him, afraid that if she looked, the image would burn itself in her eyes and she might never forget. Instead, what she did not see stayed with her, the orange flames thick in his tunic, licking his face, rising into his eyes. She shook her head and tried to focus on the moment—the darkness before her, the frozen grass crushed beneath her boot, the sensation that just behind her was something terrible and if she turned slightly, she would see.

At last she reached Merry and rode off to the northwest, holding close to the mare's warm neck. She was numb from the fire making and from crawling on the cold ground and from fear, and she wanted the very real heat she could feel when she pressed her fingers into the horse's fur.

As the mare galloped, Enna felt her insides rattle. She breathed in and out quickly, trying to clear her lungs, but the smell of smoke still clung like grease to her skin. She squinted into the cold wind and clutched the mare tighter. She had sworn never to set flame to a person, but she had failed. Her mind clung to Leifer and tried to avoid the pulsing thought of what she had just done. That sensation of something horrible just over her shoulder stayed with her on the long ride back.

She arrived in Ostekin well after dawn, dismounted west of the town, and walked the mare slowly to the stables.

"Come along, pudding," she said, stroking her mane. "Come along, honeysuckle."

The mare neighed sleepily, and Enna stopped to hold her neck and breathe into her mane. It felt so good to have a companion. And the horse was such a brave, patient creature to go out into the cold night world, risking the invisible drone of arrows and spears.

I'm brave, too, Enna thought gently, feeling like a little girl in need of comfort.

Enna waved off the stable-hand and took the mare in herself, taking off the saddle, hanging up the tack, brushing her down with great care. Work felt like the only comfort just then. Burning Eylbold perimeter tents was not chasing Tira off Bayern land, and she had broken a promise, had actually set fire to a person. Her mission was failing.

When she led the mare back to her stall, she found Razo curled up in the corner on a pile of clean straw.

"Razo." She rubbed her face in exhaustion.

He coughed in his sleep, then bolted upright and saw her. "Enna."

"Razo, this mare is falling asleep as I stand here. Can she have her stall back?"

Razo scuttled to his feet and out of the stall. His upright hair supported even taller bits of straw, and they wobbled dangerously when he moved.

"Enna, you're not a scout."

"No, not officially." She put the mare in the stall and rubbed her down again, not matching Razo's gaze.

"I know that. I mean, I thought you might be, but Talone made me a scout and I asked him and he said, no, of course not."

"No, of course not, you Forest yokel. They'd never make a Forest woman a spy for all of Bayern."

"He would've made Isi one. He asked her."

"Well, yes, of course." Enna would want Isi by her side. What a companionship they would make, wind and fire. But her connection to her best friend felt sliced, the weight of the augury unbending and, after last night, her mission brutal and pointless. She sat down heavily on the hay. "I'm not a very good friend, Razo."

"Enna." His voice, worried and hopeful, made her look up. "There's a scouting report from Eylbold. I heard last night. One of the villagers told our man that there're fires again. It's given them all a real fright."

"Has it now."

Razo looked at her meaningfully. "Talone, he thinks it's just rumor, or maybe coincidence. But if he knew it was someone under his command, the stone face might actually pop a vein. He'd get fired up about sabotage during peace agreement, you know he would. But I think someone from our camp is sneaking a mount and riding out to burn Tiran tents."

More than tents. Enna's stomach cramped as she thought of the sentry. "Yes, I know." She pressed her lips together and weighed her two options: break a promise and tell Razo, or continue on her own and risk another encounter like the sentry last night. If Razo could help her avoid burning another person, would that be a promise worth breaking?

"You're not really asking me, are you? You've already guessed."

"No," said Razo, feigning sincerity, "I've been waiting in every horse's stall to ask them if they've been out burning Tiran camps."

"Yes, yes, all right." She gathered clean straw over her lap like a blanket and told him her story, of reading the vellum, of swearing never to burn, and then the augury.

"Do you remember those last moments of Finn's fight?" she asked. "I do. I can still see that Tiran sword coming down toward Finn's chest. I know the outcome of this war if I don't play my part."

Razo nodded. He had not spoken since she began, just listened and picked at a knot in the wood grain. Now, slowly, he said, "And you need my help."

"I need another pair of eyes," she said. "The fire, it's strong, and I think I can fight it, I think I'm doing better than Leifer, but last night I had to . . . I almost lost control, or maybe I did, and then there was someone chasing me . . ." She took a breath. "I want someone not just to watch out for enemies, but to watch me, pull me back if I go too far."

Razo frowned thoughtfully.

"I'm asking you because you're nosy enough to've figured it out on your own," said Enna, "and you've got good eyes, and being a scout, you might have a way to get us inside a taken town, where I can have a bigger effect."

She bit her lip and waited for his reaction. At last he looked at her.

"What?" said Razo. "What's that look you're giving me? You're not making fun of me, are you?"

"Razo, come on, I'm waiting for your answer."

"You are? Well, you know that I will. We have to, of course. I was just thinking of how to explain to Talone, but since you're so set on secrecy I guess I won't. Anyway, I'm sure he'd agree it's of more use than just scouting." He smiled and crossed his heart with his fist. "We'll do it, Enna. For the Forest. For Bayern! Though I should admit to you that my first thought was that if I became a hero, wouldn't Bettin be sorry then that she picked Offo?"

"Ha."

Razo's eyes brightened at some thought, and he smiled excitedly. "And won't we be proud when those white tents go fleeing back to Tira and all Bayern shouts our names and says, Hooray for the Forest dwellers! Hooray for Razo!

And, uh, Enna, too!"

Enna shook her head. "And if they never chant our names?"

"No matter. We'll feel like we're living in a tale, like the ones Isi used to spin for us. It has to end well."

"Hmm," she said, "in my memory, not all her tales ended well."

"Ours will," he said confidently. "You'll see."

"In that case, Razo, if you become a hero, there'll be plenty of girls besides Bettin. If we succeed, I might even be willing to wink at you."

Razo made a gagging face, and Enna laughed and slugged him in the arm. A lightness in her chest felt like hope.

Chapter 10

olcmar." Razo pointed on the map to a town southeast of Eylbold. "Talone gave me the assignment this morning. I'm to report back in two days. Thought this might be our opportunity."

Enna nodded. She had stayed in Ostekin for a week, waiting for Razo. She felt an itch on the inside of her skin. Heat accompanied her everywhere, like a gaggle of children promised a treat out of grandmother's pocket. At last she could work again.

Enna met him that afternoon a league east of Ostekin. He waved when he saw her, then quickly returned his hands to the reins and eyed his moving mount suspiciously. She laughed at both of them, a couple of Forest cubs riding horses like nobles, sneaking around on hush-hush missions.

"You look like a rooster up there with your wobbling cock's comb and arms flapping for balance."

Razo glowered. "You've had more practice than I have."

128

"I thought you'd love it. On a horse, you triple in height."

"Yes, yes, let's just go."

Enna followed him east and then southeast. The low sun cast their shadows forward so that Enna felt she was running after herself, always a stride behind. It was a relief when the sun set and she felt herself in that familiar place again, hidden inside the night. At such times, the world seemed sad and depleted of light and heat, and aching to be set on fire.

It was a long ride to Folcmar, so Razo stopped in a ravine formed by a chain of low hills. They slept in a small gray tent meant to fit one man. Enna did not dare build a campfire in case Tiran scouts were near. That night, when her numb feet woke her, she sleepily gathered Razo's lost heat, careful not to take any from his living body. She found she could pull little bits inside her, not to make fire, just to push them into her toes and fingers. They stung, then throbbed, then warmed so that she could sleep again. She closed her eyes, and swirling images of orange and red pulsed behind her lids.

In the morning, Razo showed Enna a Tiran blue coat and leather jerkin.

"I've got two complete outfits from the supply taken from captives. We'll dance in there tomorrow and call the place home."

"So easily?" asked Enna, remembering her failed entry into Eylbold and the sentry she burned.

"It'll be a lot easier for us to get into their camp

pretending to be Tiran than it would for a Tiran in Ostekin, or so Talone figures. Bayern hundred-bands all come from the same villages, so everyone knows everybody else. But the Tiran group their armies differently. A fellow from the north might share a tent with a fellow from the seacoast, so they could have a stranger at their fire and not think two things of it."

They rode over the long, empty plains, then wove through woods until Enna could see the roofs of Folcmar beyond the clusters of white tents. If they were required to say more than a word or two, their Bayern accents—worse, their thick Forest accents—would break their disguise. And should anyone look at her too closely, even in leggings and leather helmet, Enna did not believe she would pass as a boy.

No one stopped them as they entered, their hands gripping the reins so hard that their fingers turned blue. Enna looked around the busy camp and caught sight of several captive town women. She noted that they all wore blue strips of cloth tied around their waists, tagged like cattle that belong to one herd.

Razo looked to be memorizing the layout of the camp and estimating the number of soldiers. His eyes darted frantically, his lips moved as though he counted under his breath. Enna swallowed against a shudder and felt her body tense, her blood run faster. She realized now that for days she had been holding off thoughts of fire, but now, so close to being able to burn, the heat whirled around her like pecking birds.

Just looking for a target eased her discomfort and gave her a little thrill.

Up ahead, a wood rack supported dozens of spears. Beside it, stacks of leather armor. That was much better than a perimeter tent. Now she would start to make a difference.

They were getting quite close. Enna tried to figure how far she could send the fire-forging heat, how much heat would be lost over the distance, and if it would be enough to produce a fire big and hot enough to grab the leather, too. Just a little closer, she decided. She urged Merry faster. The mare seemed as anxious as she.

"Where are you going?" A fatherly looking soldier with a guard's spear called to them. She and Razo exchanged looks, and Razo pointed up ahead.

The soldier squinted at them, and he frowned slightly. "What is your unit name?"

Caught, thought Enna. How to get out? She had only one weapon. She saw Razo open his mouth as if to speak, make up a name.

"Look," Enna said hurriedly, pointing straight ahead.

The Tiran soldier turned to see. It was easy for her to collect the heat around her body and find more with so many bodies, the sun shining, the cookfires sizzling. The burn as the fire entered her chest almost felt good now, a necessary pain like pulling a sore tooth. The release was better. Before the soldier turned completely, before his eyes rested on the rack of spears, it was blazing. The fire seized and blistered the leather armor. Men ran for water. Serving women stopped and watched.

Enna and Razo had to move away slowly so as not to draw attention. Enna knew this. But setting those weapons on fire sparked her desire to do more, and she was not numb yet to the heat. Here she was surrounded by enemy tents and supplies. Here she could make a difference now, speed the war to an end. But she had promised caution, and not to burn big as Leifer had. She became aware of pain in her hands from squeezing the reins so tightly. It took all her focus to ignore the fire, keep her eyes on the back of Razo's head, and let Merry walk to the edge of camp.

Once clear of the white tents, they trotted, and when their trembling muscles could not hold back anymore, they kicked their mounts into a run. Enna found her chest hiccuping oddly as they rode, and after a moment she realized she was sobbing. She breathed deeply and smeared the wet from her cheeks. She pounded a fist against her chest and rode on harder. The wind helped ease away clinging heat, and the exercise of the ride helped her forget the unused fire.

They camped that night in the same ravine. She expected Razo to be jubilant after their successful entry and escape, but he seemed more sober than usual as he prepared their meal and set up camp. After a meal around the fire, he finally spoke.

"You seemed pretty upset on the ride back."

Enna shrugged. "It was a little worse than normal, but

I did all right."

"You told me you were worried about it," said Razo. "But I was so busy counting stuff and trying not to look like a boy in a stolen helmet that I didn't even notice you, not until later."

"It's all right, I kept it under control."

Razo nodded. "Still, I think we need someone to be a third. I'm not the best swordsman, and I can't be guarding if I need to be scouting, so I'll grab someone trustworthy next time we ride."

Enna nearly argued, but she did not want Razo to think she was ignoring caution, so she just shrugged. "But he'd better be trustworthy."

Enna kept herself busy for a week and two days. She washed clothes like a woman starved for work. When the washing water was too cold and nobody was near enough to hear the hiss, she set off a quiet bubble of submerged fire. It warmed her hands and gave her a little burst of pleasure. But both passed quickly. Compared to the danger and significance of their burning raids, everything else was mundane.

Sometimes to stretch her back she walked through camp, always hoping for sight of Razo, who might give her a nod, finally some indication that they could move forward.

"Patience," she told herself, scratching her arms and refusing to acknowledge the pressing heat. But she could not ignore the knowledge of the Tiran camped just to the south. The awareness of their presence was constant now and felt like a splinter stinging her back, just out of reach.

She scanned one of the Forest band camps for Razo, then turned quickly, bumping into the chest of a soldier.

"Where'd you come from?" she said, then, "Oh," when she saw it was Finn. She had never realized before that he was so tall, and his chest felt as solid as a Forest pine.

He took a step back, pushing his dark hair off his brow. "Sorry. My fault. I was too close. I like your . . . your apron. The yellow is nice."

Enna ran a hand over her damp, stained apron and laughed a little. "Thanks, Finn. I dyed it myself."

"Mmm." He looked down. "I help my ma dye, in the summers."

"Yes, I know. I stayed with you once and helped out, about a year ago, right?"

"Yes, you did." He flashed a pleased smile, then looked back at his boots. He seemed to have nothing more to say.

"Well, I should get back to the house."

"I'll walk you back," he said.

"Don't bother, Finn," said Enna, "Hesel isn't there now."

Enna gave him a smug grin as she walked away, but Finn did not laugh. She kept walking and thought that Finn needed some backbone if he could not even be teased about his little love affair.

At last Razo came with the word: Adelmund the day after next. It would be a three-day trip. She filled the Tiran-style, long-necked water skins, packed her bedroll, stashed dried venison, hard bread, some oats in case there was little for the mare to forage, and an oiled skin. Razo would have the tent and Tiran uniforms.

When she neared the spot where they had agreed to meet, about a league west of Ostekin, she saw two riders instead of one.

"It's all right," said Razo, "it's just Finn."

"Finn?" Enna strained to see the figure in the distance. A boy sat patiently on horseback, his spine straight, looking away as though he wished to give them privacy.

"You must've known I'd ask Finn," Razo said with an acutely innocent expression. "You have to admit he's the most trustworthy person we know, besides being a good soldier and good company. Why do you look all surprised?"

Enna shrugged. "I just didn't expect him."

"I didn't tell him about you, if that's what you're worried about. So you can still send him home, if you like. But I think we need him, and I'll be honest"—he leaned across his horse as though he were telling a secret—"now that he knows we go on scouts together, I don't think he'll leave easily. He about spitted me when he found out we'd been sharing a tent. Called me some name I didn't know. He thought he had to defend your honor." Razo looked dead serious, then laughed as though it were a great joke.

Enna glared at him, and Razo rolled his eyes.

"Oh, just talk to him so we can get moving." Razo trotted

his horse past Finn and made southwest as though intending to go whether or not she followed.

"Hello, Finn," said Enna, and pulled up beside him. They began to walk their mounts toward Razo. "How'd you manage to get away from your commander? You're not assigned scout duty."

"They call me the champion," he said. "It's because of the augury match. No one seems to mind much where I go." He turned in his saddle to better see her face. "Were you there?"

"Yes, I was."

He inspected his reins. "I didn't know if you'd seen it. I was thinking about you."

"I was thinking about you, too. We all were," she added quickly. "So, what did Razo say to convince you to come?"

Finn swallowed. "He said—you might need some protection."

"Maybe I can defend myself." She reached down and loosed a piece of straw from her bootstraps. "I'm going to show you something, but you can't tell a soul, all right?" When he nodded, Enna sent heat at the tip of the straw. It blazed briefly, then smoked and glowed, before she dropped it.

"Just like Leifer." Finn was clutching the hilt of his sword, but he slowly let it go. His brow creased, and he looked at her shrewdly. "Are you being careful, Enna?"

"Yes," she said.

Finn tilted his head with an expression that was almost

accusatory.

"I *am*," said Enna. "You don't need to be so snappish about it."

"I saw him, you know, do that to you." He glanced down at her ankles, and from the look in his eyes Enna thought he was seeing her on fire again. "It didn't seem like Leifer to do that. I've wondered if it was him what did it, or if he couldn't control the fire, or . . . " He shrugged.

Enna looked at him straight on. "I can control it, Finn. And that's why Razo's here, and you, to help me make sure."

"Well, I'm glad you'll have a sword watching your back."

"Come on, you two," said Razo, slowing down to their pace. "If we want to reach a campsite before middle night, we need to give these animals some exercise."

They found the spot long after dark. It was protected from a south view by a swell in the land and a line of river trees. The river still ran, and they watered their horses. The day had warmed the land, and the wild grasses did not break under their feet. Because of Finn, Razo had managed to come by a larger tent, but when he and Enna pulled their bedrolls inside, Finn remained outside.

"Come on, Finn," said Razo, "it's warmer with people around you."

Finn refused, not meeting their looks. "It's warm enough out here."

During the night, whenever Razo's snarled breathing or her frozen feet woke her, Enna fed heat back into the fire.

She watched its initial blaze light up Finn's curled-up body.

In the morning, they donned their stolen uniforms. Finn insisted that he and Razo hold up the oiled skin and allow Enna to undress behind. The ride from their camp to Adelmund took them half the day. They rode right through the outer circles of the camp into the town and down the main road. Enna noticed Tiran citizens who were not soldiers—women with pale, cropped hair who did not wear the blue sash of Bayern prisoners, Tiran men in working clothes, Tiran men in robes of leadership. *They're planning to stay*, thought Enna. Their heat wrapped around her and scratched against her skin. *Burn, burn, burn.* Everything looked flammable.

"Razo," Enna said softly. She gripped her saddle and felt her chin start to quiver.

"Just a minute," said Razo, distracted by his counting.

Enna looked back at Finn. He was scanning the surroundings, but when he saw her, he nodded that all was well. They did not notice her agitation, and that encouraged her. Perhaps it was not as bad as she thought. She scratched her arms and watched the road before her tilt and twist. *Ignore it. It's just the heat*, she told herself. The buildings around her seemed to crackle in anticipation. A breeze whipped up the tent flaps like the dancing flames of a white fire. Smoky plumes of steam poured upward from a cook pot. All the world wanted to burn.

She felt the need twisting and writhing under her control.

If she was not careful . . . but was that not why she was here? To burn? Perhaps the desire was powerful right now simply because it was time to burn. But she had promised Razo to wait for his cue.

"Razo, say it's all right," she said.

Razo looked at her, bewildered. "What's all right?"

"Just tell me I can. Now."

Razo blinked a few times, then seemed to understand. "Go ahead, I guess."

Before he finished speaking, fire ruptured the roof of a large storage tent and licked the air as though grasping for more. The relief of letting go was so fierce, she wanted to either sob or laugh out loud. The tightness in her chest loosened, her hands stopped shaking, and she took a deep breath and felt cleaner.

"Over there," said Finn, pointing away from the three. He had practiced those two words for hours on the ride to their campsite, trying to imitate as best as they could guess how one from Tira might sound. It seemed to work. A general rush of soldiers ran toward the fire and the direction he pointed.

Enna found she could still burn. No one seemed to suspect them, and burning more than once made sense, so she gave herself permission. The freedom was exhilarating. She found another target farther from the road so it would appear that the fire-witch was running away. A pile of hay under an oiled cloth began to snap and smoke.

"Over there," said Finn, pointing to the right of the hay.

More rushing, more shouting. Razo fought a smile.

Farther ahead, Enna spotted stacked barrels of wine and felt giddy to discover that place in her chest expanded to receive yet more heat.

"Ov—" Finn started, then stopped. In the excitement, he was getting ahead of himself as Enna had not yet set the fire. She glanced back at him with a laughing smirk and then sent heat hurtling into barrels of wine. The explosion splattered the surrounding white tents with purple like the blood of a huge beast. At last the fire in her was sated, and the heat near her skin drifted away.

"Over there," said Finn, confidently this time.

"Where?" A frantic soldier came up to Finn and grabbed his ankle. "What do you see?"

"Over there," said Enna, pointing beyond the barrels. The soldier ran off with his sword drawn. Razo bit his lip.

The three rode around the camp as though aiming to head off any escaping criminals, then veered off to the north and galloped away. After a league or so, they slowed their horses and began to chuckle.

"Over there," said Razo in an extreme Tiran accent, pointing ahead.

Finn looked left, right, left, with the quick movements of a bird.

"Where?" Enna asked with mock panic. "Do you see something?"

"Over there," said Finn, relishing every syllable and pointing up in the air with a look of complete bewilderment.

They laughed, clutching their saddles to stay upright.

"I've missed you, Finn," Enna said unexpectedly.

"Yes, me too." Finn smiled one of his large, gracious smiles.

There was still some light when they returned to the campsite. In celebration, Enna tried to roast a squirrel out of a tree, but the meat tasted as it smelled—like singed fur.

"Well, that's enough of that," said Enna, dumping the uneaten meat into the fire. The flames snapped into it gleefully.

They feasted instead on the two squirrels Razo had downed with his sling. The taste of roasted meat, the success of the day, and the sound of Finn and Razo laughing felt like a bubble of contentment expanding in her chest. She thought, *Fire does good things*, and wondered why she had never thought of it before.

After eating, they stared at the fire, always a startling sight when the rest of the world was dark, and retold stories they had learned from Isi back in the animal worker days. Each told their favorite—Razo about the warrior whose mother bathed him in her own blood to make him invincible; Enna about the girl who could weave living animals on her loom that carried her to the land where music was first forged; Finn about the man who so loved an imprisoned woman that his heart broke and flew out of his chest and sang to her each day through her barred window.

Enna watched the fire as he spoke and imagined what he saw, the face of the woman as she listened to the song, gaining the courage to escape her prison, learning that the bird's wings sprouted from the two halves of the man's broken heart. And then the woman followed the bird back to its master to find him dead, so she bade the heart rejoin with the man and swore to love him as he loved her. Enna glanced up then. The ending she knew was not so tidy, but Finn seemed to relish his improved version.

With night fell a fresh winter cold. Light, airy flakes of snow like gray ashes fell on the fire and made sweet, soft hisses. Razo stood and stretched.

"Come on in the tent tonight, Finn," he said. "It's cramped but cozy, and I don't want to have to dig you out in the morning."

"You'd better," said Enna. "I shouldn't have to be the only one suffering through Razo's snoring. He sounds like an entire pen of angry piglets."

Razo shoved her shoulder and crawled into the tent. Finn hesitated, glanced at Enna, and nodded.

Late in the night, Enna woke. She was lying on her side facing Finn, though she could barely make him out in the blackness. She felt his breath touch her forehead in soft, rhythmic sighs. What woke her was his hand on her hair. He pulled back, and her head felt lighter for losing his touch. She had never imagined this before, what it might be like to lie beside him, to feel so warm and safe and content. Her heart hit against her ribs, and she tried to peer through the darkness and see if he was awake and, if so, how he looked at her.

Suddenly she realized she was holding her breath and quickly released it, long and slow, moaning slightly so that he might think she was still asleep.

In a hush-soft voice, Finn said, "All I've ever wanted was to be near you." Then he rolled onto his back and sighed into sleep.

Enna held very still. Her muscles tightened from her brow to her feet, afraid he would touch her, afraid he would not. The sound of her heart would not leave her ears. She gasped in pain and realized she had pulled heat inside her and held it. Frantically her mind sought a place to expel it. She found the dying warmth of their fire pit and she sent the heat through the break in the tent flap. In the brief burst of light, she saw Finn. One hand curled under his chin. His eyes were closed, his lashes touched the tops of his cheeks. He smiled slightly.

With nothing to feed on but ash, the fire quickly died. The darkness was more absolute for the sudden lack of light, and Enna could not see even the outline of his body.

"You're awake?" she whispered. No response.

She turned on her back, stared at the patterns that moved in the darkness, and wondered why she suddenly felt as vulnerable as a hare in a meadow, a trout in clear water. She put a hand over her smile to prevent a laugh. In the morning she woke that way, her fingers resting on her mouth as though holding back words so secret and insistent, they might slip out while she slept.

he next day, Enna noticed for the first time that Finn's brown eyes had specks of yellow around the edges. It gave the effect of deepness, and she found herself looking at him more than before. His hands were a man's hands, callused and strong. His face had lost its boyish roundness some time ago, and since the war began, his timid grins were rare gifts. He was pleasant to look at.

The first time she found herself alone with him after Adelmund, they were walking back from the stables. In the distance, they both spotted Hesel hanging laundry. Finn said, "Razo told me what he said about Hesel. And me. I just want you to know it's not true."

"Oh," she said, wanting to ask him why it mattered, to talk at last about what that might mean to her. But they passed near a cookfire, and the heat stretched out toward her, and the hollowness in her chest pulsed eagerly. Her throat itched, her stomach hurt, and she forgot what she was going to say. She thought she must be coming down with a cold.

Scout reports came from Eylbold, where Enna had first set her fires, that the Tiran were building a gallows. Speculation was rampant in Ostekin. Were they planning to execute Bayern townsfolk? Captured soldiers? Or something even worse? The talk bothered her, like being pinched over and over again in the same place. When she faced southwest and thought of the Tiran encampment, the gallows were on her mind.

"We should go to Eylbold," she said to Razo. "We should burn the gallows."

Razo shook his head. "Talone gave me the next assignment—Adelmund."

But the mission went badly. This time they were quizzed at the perimeter, and when Razo did not dare to answer for his accent and Finn said, "Over there," and no one looked, they fled. Enna set a couple of tents on fire as they left. She hoped it might serve as a distraction, turn a few eyes from them to the fires. They escaped all right after Finn fought off two soldiers, but still she ached for something else. She was irritated and anxious, and as she rode everything seemed slightly off angle, as though the earth were tipping slowly to one side.

They rode east all night, thinking to confuse any followers. After two hours or more, they saw a lone rider ahead, flying east as well. The three exchanged looks and understood—this was someone from Adelmund, most likely riding with word of Bayern dressed as Tiran entering towns to light fires. They spurred their mounts in a chase. As they neared, Razo loaded his sling with a stone and at full gallop shot it at the rider's back. He slumped forward and his mount slowed for a moment, long enough for Enna to get close.

She had not decided yet what to do with the fire when she brought the heat inside her. As soon as it spun in her chest, it began to pull out, seeking the closest target—the Tiran's body. Enna cried out, struggling briefly with the nascent fire. *Into him*, it prompted. *Send the fire inside.* She grappled, the heat searing her chest, and finally released the fire against the ground at the horse's feet. The animal spooked, rearing back from the flames, and sent the rider to the ground.

Razo helped Finn tie the spy's ankles and wrists and sling him over Finn's pommel.

"Well, that was good luck," said Razo. "He was on his way to Eylbold, no doubt, ready to go screaming about the fire-witch. Well done, Champion Finn, and that wasn't bad slinging on my part, if I can say so."

"You just did," said Finn. He smiled at Enna, but his smile quickly faded. "Are you all right?"

"Mm? Oh, yes, fine. Well done." She did not feel much up to talking.

It was a long ride back to Ostekin for Enna. She tried to flinch away from the memory of where she had almost sent the fire, but the long, chilled hours on Merry's back gave no escape. She shivered, wanting to rid herself of that feeling the way a horse shakes off flies.

She had wanted to set a person on fire.

But I didn't, she comforted herself. *I resisted. That's all that matters.* By the time they arrived back in Ostekin, she was nearly recovered. The numbness in her chest had eased, and she felt warm and comfortable.

After Razo and Finn delivered the scout to the prison guards, the three sat around a Forest band campfire. Razo's eyes were so tired, they looked bruised purple. Finn pushed his sword tip into the ground and rested his forehead on the hilt.

"What a night," said Razo. "I thought it'd never end. I thought we'd end up filleted and battered and buttered on bread."

"Good that we stopped that spy," said Finn.

"Suppose." Razo glanced at Enna to gauge her reaction. "Still, I don't think we should raid again for some time, maybe weeks."

"Ha," Enna said playfully. She hoped he was kidding. The thought of not burning for weeks gave her a sick, panicky feeling in her gut. "You've heard the rumors. We have to go to Eylbold."

Razo twisted small holes in the ground with a stick. He looked close to nodding off. "I think you burned there too many times in the beginning."

Enna handed Finn her empty cup, and he stood to fetch another round of heated milk and honey from the Forest band cookfire.

"They might not know to look for us," she said, "Bayern dressed as Tiran, since we stopped the scout. Not if we go soon. Tomorrow."

Razo tossed his stick into the fire. "Scouting reports also say that's their center now. It's dangerous. We might have a better chance if you hadn't set those tents aflame in Adelmund after they already suspected us."

"Someone should go," said Enna.

"Talone'll probably send someone. . . . "

"But he doesn't know about me, and I'm the best choice. Finn?"

Finn stood by, her mug warming his hands. He met Razo's eyes and looked down.

"Enna," he said gently.

Enna stood up, looking back and forth between the two. "What is it? What's going on? You two have something you want to tell me?"

Razo glanced at Finn again and sighed. "You're not going to say a word, are you, Finn? Well, I'm not afraid." He met Enna's eyes defiantly, then blinked and looked away. "You're spooking us, Enna-girl. You're, you're not right."

Enna felt her jaw tighten. "What do you mean I'm not right?"

"I'll tell you straight," said Razo. "Sometimes when

we're out there, the expression on your face gives me skin prickles to my scalp."

"I've been doing fine," she said. "Am I a charred corpse lying in Adelmund? Have I set the town on fire and every Tiran in sight? I'm doing well. I made promises and I'm keeping them. I mean, I let you two in on the secret about the fire, but I had to, and I promised I wouldn't burn people and I haven't, except that once, but it was a mistake and I haven't done it again. You don't know how hard it is sometimes, but I still hold back."

"But it's hard," said Finn. "I've been worried, Enna. If it's hard for you, then maybe, for a little bit, you could take a break."

"No, I can't take a break." *The augury*, she thought, but she did not want to tell Finn what she had done during his combat. "I don't need it. I'm fine."

"You looked funny after we caught that spy," said Razo. "I don't know what to say. It'd be a shame to stop. I mean, we've been doing so well, but you . . . " His voice got quiet as he stared at the fire. "You've changed. You've got that wild look in you, like Leifer had before the end. I think you're one loop short of a knot, Enna. A little tug, and you're undone."

Enna snorted a laugh. "I'm telling you I'm fine. I would know if I was close to losing control, and I'm not. Finn, don't you trust me?"

Finn paused. "Not just now," he said sadly.

They all went silent then. Enna turned her back to stare

at the fire and dry the shock from her face. Panting flames
the color of scarecrow straw twisted and writhed out of
blackened wood. Someone laid a hand on her shoulder,
probably Finn, but she ignored him. She played at sending
bits of heat into its orange core, the fire splashing in brief
higher bursts, like tossing stones in a pond. The exercise
made her twitch.

When she looked up again, the flames still burned in
memory in her eyes. It was a few moments before her sight
adjusted again to the night and she saw that Razo and Finn
were gone.

A cough shook her chest, and she coughed harder, trying
to dislodge something caught in her throat. Nothing
budged, so she tried to ignore the sensation. She sat down,
closed her eyes, and through her eyelids saw the campfire
tensing and turning. She imagined she was watching her own
insides. Her heart was stoked coals, pulsing heat. Making
ash. She felt like the loneliest person in the world.

Eylbold. The gallows. She would have to go alone. The
thought of the mission made her sad. She hugged her knees
against her chest. It was true that at moments her grip on the
fire felt like trying to squeeze soap underwater, but she knew
she had to fight through it anyway, and she knew she would
win. The augury had spoken. There had to be a way to make
an impact without breaking her promise not to burn people
and not to burn big, as Leifer had done.

This gallows felt like the first good target, and she would

hit it hard. She promised the desire inside her that she would see the gallows burn. She had to or all was lost. Beyond reason or thought, that certainty held her, soothed her, allowed her to breathe out and wait. At that decision, the heat loosened around her, and she cooled and calmed and felt secure again that though the fate of the war tugged at her like a rope around her neck, she would succeed.

She waited until full night. Her sense of the Tiran sitting in Eylbold just a few hours' ride to the south was so powerful now that it made her dizzy, like being shut indoors with a strong smell. She did not see Razo or Finn on her way to the stables. Everything she needed was in Merry's saddle-bag—water, food, a bundle of Tiran clothing. She led the mare to the edge of town, keeping her head down, not wanting to see the boys. She was afraid, and hopeless, and determined. A cool thought slid through her and gave her goose bumps—she could just not go. She could forget the gallows and Eylbold and the augury. She recoiled from the thought as she might from proffered poison. *I have to,* she reminded herself. *For Bayern. For everyone.*

Enna passed the east gate and heard a familiar voice call her name. She turned and felt relief briefly lighten her shoulders.

"Isi," she said, "you're back."

They stood just outside the town. The fires of Ostekin camp were behind Isi, but Enna did not need more light to know the long pale hair hanging loose, tall stature, and slight frame. Isi was dressed in her travel clothes, wide riding skirts, thick tunic, and cloak, all dyed dull colors. The Bayern liked things bright and colorful, but wartime seemed to stultify everything.

Isi's tone was frank. "Enna, the wind thinks you're on fire. You smell like smoke."

"I'm not. I'm just . . . Isi, so much has happened. If I could explain it all, you'd understand. I've been afraid to tell you. But really, I'm all right, and I'm doing good . . . good things."

Isi looked down. "Geric received reports of burning. We returned today and heard details from Talone. He doesn't suspect you, of course. He thinks you're my friend and would never sneak around like that. But there's a Tiran scout in the cells whom Razo and Finn captured, and he's babbling about how a fire-witch stopped him. Geric thinks he's just paranoid, but I, I think it was you."

Enna felt her breath get short. "I have to go, Isi."

"I can't let you, Enna."

Enna clenched her fists. Heat swirled around her like chaotic dancers, bumping into her, grazing against her skin. She felt herself sway. "Leifer tried to tell me what it was like, but I didn't understand then, and you don't now."

"Let me try," said Isi. "You read Leifer's vellum, and you meant well. You want to help Bayern with the fire. But things in you have begun to change. All this time in the city I've been thinking on this and reading what I could. The wind's changed me, so it makes sense that fire could change Leifer and you. Nothing it touches can remain unscathed."

Enna shook her head. "It's not an evil thing, Isi. I'm not. Please don't hate me. You don't believe in the augury, so you can't see what I'm seeing. Finn would've died, Isi. He was fighting for all Bayern, and he would've died. I'm so afraid." She felt her chin start to tremble, and she wanted to rush forward and cry on Isi's neck. "Please don't make it harder. I know what I have to do, but I'm so scared, and I just need to keep moving, keep going until it's done. If I stop to think, I might get too scared, and I can't stop now."

Isi took a step closer. "Enna, are you sure you have to? Really sure? Because you seem seized by all this. It's not your fault. It's just that the fire is bigger than any one person."

Enna felt her legs tremble. *Not bigger than me.*

"Fire must burn." Isi spoke more frantically, as though chasing down each thought before speaking. "That's its only need. It doesn't have a human mind. But I wonder, when it got inside of you, or Leifer, its need must be overpowering you, and the desire you feel to burn might just be your own human mind making up human reasons to see it through. Like Leifer, at first seeing Bayern as an enemy and then switching his need for an enemy to Tira. And now it's using you."

Chills shook Enna. She started to think about what Isi said, but it was getting hard to see. A yellow haze was thickening before her, and she rubbed her eyes and tried to breathe. *The gallows,* was her only clear thought. *The mission, the gallows. I promised to stop the war.*

Enna started to turn.

"Wait, Enna, don't. Just be still a moment and think."

"I can't," said Enna, pleading. The heat was pressing itself against her face, into her mouth when she spoke, into her eyes so they stung. "Please, just let me go. If you knew . . . if you could feel . . . you'd let me go, Isi."

Isi advanced. Her expression was grim and serious. "This isn't you, Enna. I will stop you if I can." She took Enna's wrist.

"No!" said Enna, tearing away. She could not bear it another moment. The heat was pressing, pressing; the enemy sat unchallenged, Finn would be dead, and so would all of Bayern. And Isi was in the way. Enna pulled all that built-up heat inside her, gasping at the burning pain. Isi was in the way. She had to get away. Now. The heat was blazing in her chest. She thrust it out.

The heat poured toward Isi, toward all that lovely, combustible cloth, that long, dead hair yearning to live again in heat and fire. But in that moment before the heat grabbed Isi and blazed into life, the wind came. Enna felt it swoop between them, a flash flood of cold. Enna struggled for breath and found none. The shooting heat was blown away, dissipating into the night before it could become fire. All gone. The air continued to roll over and around Enna, loosening any heat still clinging to her. She gasped and found air at last, her lungs aching with each breath. The wind left her cold, and she felt like a corpse standing.

She looked up. Isi was holding a hand over her mouth.

"Isi," Enna whispered. "I didn't, I . . . "

Enna felt as though all her words and feeling had been blown away with the fire. Isi, her best friend, she had sent the heat, she had tried to set her aflame. The whole world seemed to tilt crazily, and she just wanted to rush forward and fall at her feet and swear it was a mistake. Then the heat began to return to her, and she shuddered at its touch. The heat from Isi's body. The heat from her mare. And with it the persistent reminder of the gallows, begging to be burned. Her head throbbed with her pulse, and it seemed to say, *Burn, burn, burn.*

Isi dropped the hand from her mouth. Enna opened her mouth to speak but found no words. She turned around to look southeast. Eylbold. She could hear Isi start to run toward town.

"Help!" Isi shouted. "Guards, come quick!"

Enna clambered into the saddle and rode away.

The cold rush of night wind pushed against Enna's face, and she winced under its incessant swipe. She could not forget the exquisite release when she had sent fire at her friend. How easy it was. Enna did not believe she could ever live to forget that feeling, could ever look at Isi again without remembering what she had tried to do. And now, Bayern guards might be riding at her heels, and ahead the invaders waited. All the world was wrong, and the only way she could see to make it right was by burning.

The wind current loosened her headscarf and whipped away the heat. She felt naked and raw. But even the wind and cold could not reach that bit of deep heat inside that was always ready, always waiting to burn again. Her body trembled in the saddle. She fought to hold on.

At last she knew Leifer's mind that night in the Forest. At last she could see herself from his eyes, looking at his sister as an obstacle to what everything inside him insisted he must do. He had been unable to resist the heat, unbelieving that it was that simple to set someone you love on fire. Unbelievably simple. There seemed no way to ever return, to ever be just Enna again. Razo and Finn had looked at her as at a stranger, and Isi . . . No, nothing could be the same. Why had the augury not even hinted that to fulfill her mission, she would have to give up everything?

Leifer's fate seemed unavoidable to her now. She had broken two of her rules. She had told Razo and Finn of the fire, and she had burned the living, setting fire to that Tiran soldier and trying to burn Isi. So far, she had honored the third rule by keeping her fires small, but perhaps only because she did not know how to burn big.

She pulled the mare short near the woods outside Eylbold and dismounted. The woods seemed unfriendly to her—the living trees unburnable and selfish with their slow heat locked inside bark, closed and dark, relishing the sunless hours. She wrapped her arms around the mare's neck and tried to soak in her warmth. Gently. Without drawing it. Just feeling it. The mare held still and received the affection. She felt an impulse to do something recklessly noble.

"I won't let you get hurt," she said, removed Merry's bridle, stuffed it in the emptied saddlebag, and slapped the mare's rump. It felt like a good, clean sacrifice to let the horse go, make sure the mare was out of danger and not think about herself. She slapped Merry again, and the mare hesitated, then began a halting trot north. Enna watched her horse go and felt small and alone. She would have to walk back to Ostekin, or perhaps to the Forest, when this was done. But she could not think clearly just then, and she turned her back to the north to face Eylbold.

Enna tied her blue headscarf around her waist. It was nearly the color of the sashes she had seen the taken Bayern women wear in the Tiran camps, and she thought it would serve. She clutched an armload of Tiran clothing as though it were laundry and set off toward town. Her hair brushed the tops of her shoulders as she walked and kept the cold off her neck, though the top of her head felt too exposed. She thought of pulling heat in to warm herself and resisted.

She slipped between two tents and was in the camp. The paths were deserted, only an occasional sentry at his post. The sentries ignored her, a Bayern girl wearing the blue sash of a taken woman, carrying a bundle of Tiran laundry. She drew on their escaping heat and carried it around her. Her muscles had stopped shaking, and the calm of her resolve felt heavier than wearing wet clothes, heavier than mud. She imagined Leifer had felt this way burning the battlefield. Perhaps he knew that he must be near the end, but conviction of his purpose propelled him on.

Enna made her way to the center of the town. There, indeed, stood a gallows. In the moonlight the pale wood looked blue, as though it were underwater. From its massive lintel swung three bodies, their necks roped. No, as she got closer she could see they were not bodies, but scarecrows. One wore a Bayern skirt and tunic, long, blackened straws for hair, and a clumsy crown. Isi. Enna realized that Isi had worn a Forest head wrap at the initial battle and the war councils, and the Tiran likely did not know that she was a foreigner with yellow hair. The other two wore Bayern uniforms. One was crowned—Geric. The other had strips of orange cloth hanging from his mouth. A breeze stirred the cloth, and Enna understood. Fire. The third was the fire-witch.

She could feel the camp's heat—sleeping bodies of men, sleeping horses, sleeping prisoners. She did not need to call to it. Heat seemed to know her now, and it wrapped around her, ready for use. In a bound, the heat pulled inside her, formed into flame, and tore out again. The scarecrows popped and fried.

"Ah," she sighed aloud. The burden was gone, and she felt joy.

She gathered more heat and sent it again. The lintel blazed. She repeated it again and again, gulping bits of heat, sending the fire in rapid succession like an archer going through a quiver of arrows. Soon the entire structure was a brilliant bonfire. Under the flames, the wood cracked and moaned and coughed. The scarecrows fell from their blackened ropes and sizzled on the ground. The place felt radiant with life.

She tried to pull in heat one more time, one more blow, but choked on the effort. She could feel the scorching fire in front of her, but the pocket in her chest was cold and tight. The attempt made her gag and shiver, and she took two steps back.

She was conscious of herself standing alone in that square, dark, quiet, cold, and started to back away from the fire into the shadow of a tent. No one appeared. Surely others saw the fire, and those near would even smell and feel it. But there was no one. Silence.

Then, across the square, someone stepped forward into the light of the blaze. Sileph, the captain from the war council who had spoken to her. He was staring right at her.

"What?" she said with a breath, dropping her bundle of clothes and stumbling backward. Inside her burned-out, cold chest she could feel the prickling of fear.

On either side of the square, two archers arranged themselves, their bows cocked, one eye closed, arrows aiming at her heart. She fumbled to muster heat and send it flying quicker than their arrows. Then a new source of heat emerged right behind her. She tugged at it and gasped. It was a person. She started to turn when pain struck the back of her head, and then blackness.

Part Three

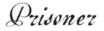

Prisoner

nna began to ache. She did not know where it came from. Everywhere. The entire world was ache and thirst and darkness. She heard herself moan. It scraped against her throat, a grounding sensation that roused her. Her eyelids felt sticky and hard, as though glued down with pine sap.

There was the sound of someone approaching, and then a cup was held to her lips. She gulped down the water and had time to notice that it had a sour, dry taste like green cherries before she again succumbed to the dreams.

And more dreams. Villages burned as she walked through them. Cornstalks sprouted ears of fire, and the fields caught it and burned green. A flock of white geese flew out of the ashes toward a silver sky. Their hard wings beat against the sky and it broke like a mirror, raining glass shards onto Enna's head. She ducked, then woke groggily. Someone nearby shoved a cup against her mouth. She pinched her lips together and tried to push it away, but her hands would not move. Water dripped down her chin. The cup withdrew.

"Who?" she said, trying to look around. It was either very dark or she still could not force open her lids. Hands held her face and pinched her nose. She struggled, then gasped, and the sour water poured down her throat.

She slept fitfully, and even inside the dreams she could feel herself shaking. Sometime later, she felt a blanket wrapped over her body. The warmth was so welcome that she struggled to say, "Thank you," but only managed a groan. Her tongue felt bigger than her mouth. She thought if she could just clear her head, she could will her tongue to shrink.

A hand stroked her cheek. Or was she already inside another dream?

When she began to discern the waking world again, she was force-fed another cup of water. The flavor was lighter than the others, and she slowly, painfully, awoke. At once she noticed a terrible pain in her stomach. As she focused on it, the pain shrank to a tight, sore realization of hunger. How long had she been dreaming?

She stilled her mind and tried to reason out where she was. She was lying on her side. Beneath her was rough cloth over cold ground. It must still be winter. No wind or sun— she was in some kind of enclosure. She could barely move with her ankles bound and her hands tied behind her back. She tried to move her head and winced. The gallows, the square, the person who came up from behind. So, she had been hit on the head. She gagged and tasted again the unripe-fruit tang of the unnatural water. First hit and then drugged.

Something else was very wrong. With a start she realized what it was—she could not feel heat. It was as though she had set the world on fire and there was nothing left living. Or just, she realized with alarm, that the drugs brought an artificial numbness. A world without heat felt cruel and empty, and she found she wanted to weep as though some-one had died. Carefully she probed about her, trying to sense any traces of heat. Through the ground, around her body, farther away. Something was there. She felt it faintly, and her abused and woozy body assured her she could not drag any of the heat into her.

Her powerlessness angered her, and she focused all her strength on opening her eyes. She saw white. She was inside a tent. Daylight seeped through the cloth walls. A gray wool blanket was tucked around her body. She blinked, worked those tiny muscles, and tried to send her gaze farther than a few feet.

A person. A face. The lines became sharper. Sileph sat on the ground and watched her calmly. She was not surprised.

"Hello," she said with a dry croak.

He nodded. "Do you see me, then? The watcher is watched at last." He lifted a gourd cup from a pail. "Would you like some water?"

"I don't want to sleep." Her voice sounded as though it came from far away.

"This is just water. See?" He drank fully from the cup and wiped his chin. When she did not protest again, Sileph dipped the gourd and brought it to her side. He placed a hand under her neck and helped raise her to drink. She gulped the cold water and felt her body take it like parched earth takes in rain.

He lowered her head to the ground and left the tent. Her eyes open now and her consciousness sullenly returning, Enna felt every strand of her body throb and complain. She tried to heave herself onto her back, but the effort sent ribbons of pain into her bound wrists and ankles, and her head spun. She lay still and concentrated on the crossing threads of the ground cloth before her, wishing the dizziness to abate. A tear spilled from the corner of her eye and wobbled on the surface of the oiled cloth.

She heard someone enter and looked up. Sileph held a wooden bowl and spoon.

"There is food," he said. "Will you eat?"

"Untie me."

He frowned, as though the suggestion wounded him. "I think I will assist you first. You can stretch after."

She realized then that even if she had free hands, she probably could not hold a spoon. She could not even hold herself up. Perhaps he had thought of that and wanted her to keep some dignity. She felt very little dignity just then with her face pressed to the ground. She was certain she had soiled herself while in the drugged sleep.

"Let me see," said Sileph, looking around. There was no hard wall to prop Enna up against. He sat on the ground beside her and pulled her upright, leaning her back against his chest. She had to rest her head on his neck to keep it upright.

"Now, my lady, if you do not mind, I will bring the food to your lips. I assure you there is nothing in here but barley, potatoes, venison, water, and salt. I brought it from my own fire. All right?"

She nodded, ashamed that she would have eaten the stew no matter what was in it. Just to smell food was agonizing. Her stomach twisted smaller, and she was afraid it would growl embarrassingly. Why should she be embarrassed? she suddenly wondered. She was a captive warrior, ruthlessly tied and drugged. But Sileph's manners made her feel in his debt. Her head buzzed and her stomach snapped. She would try to think on this later.

Sileph lifted a steaming spoonful, blew on it, and held it to her lips. She nearly swallowed the spoon with the stew.

"It has been some time since you ate. I should think you would want to take it slowly."

In truth, Enna wanted the entire bowl upended in her mouth. But as she swallowed the third spoonful, her stomach lurched. She bolted forward, constricting her throat, shaking with little convulsions. He pulled her back against him and put a hand on her forehead.

"Easy. Relax. It will be better if you can relax. Breathe."

She took slow, deep breaths, trying to keep the food down. He slipped his hand from her forehead to her stomach and rubbed her softly. She twisted under his hold.

"Don't," she said.

He took away his hand and was quiet for several moments. She began to wonder if she had offended him. She could smell him—beef soap, leather, greenwood smoke. And another smell, maybe sweat, that she associated with men.

After a time, he began to talk. His voice was calm and confident, and it soothed her. She liked the sound of the deep tones she heard vibrating through his neck. She nodded at the spoon, and he began to feed her again. His voice and the food made her feel sleepy and safe. *You're not safe*, she reminded herself, but her body eased.

"I wonder if you remember, but we have met before. My name is Sileph. I saw you in that Bayern prince's council in Ostekin. Enna, isn't it? I remember you well. How you stared at me! As though you wished to light me on fire with your gaze. How could I forget that expression? Your mistress the queen just looked down and didn't say moo. There is not much to her, is there? But not so with her maiden. I will admit I was struck with you. And I wondered what hair you hid up under that scarf."

She felt him finger a strand of her hair.

"Black as night. I've seen you three times at night. I don't think you know that, do you? First was in a snowstorm, and you burned our tent. It was dark, and I did not see your face well." He laughed lightly, and she could feel the rumble through her back. "We were mighty cold that night.

"Another time, I watched you in the woods outside this town. You crept up alone, hiding from tree to tree. You were fascinating. I found I would much rather watch you than stop you. I don't know how you do what you do, but I could see in your face that you enjoyed it. Would you like to set a fire right now?"

Even the suggestion of it filled Enna with hope, and she nodded breathlessly.

"Not on me, I hope. Why don't you set just a little one? Just this spoon?"

He held out the wooden spoon an arm's length in front of her face. She knew it yearned to be given life again, all those tiny, empty spaces inside it void of living juices, perfect to give root to flame. But she could not even feel that— not heat, not the lack of heat. Nothing. *He's trying to find out how much I can do*, she thought. But his voice and the food loosened her resolve to keep him ignorant.

"I can't," she said.

"Ah. The drugs. They are powerful. What they are giving you is a mixture of several herbs, but it is the king's-tongue that is the key. So named, says the tale, for its insidious use on King Husilef, four kings before the present. His daughter fed it to him subtly for months. His mind slowed, his body weakened, and the damage after all that time was permanent. His daughter had him declared incompetent and became ruler in his stead. It could be rumor, I suppose, but there have not been any queens since, just in case."

The word *permanent* rang in her head like a ball in a bell. Sileph put down the empty bowl and continued to hold her. His head moved a little closer to hers, his jaw pressing lightly against her brow. It rubbed against her as he talked, and she felt herself drowsing.

"Have you always had this gift with fire?"

"No," she said.

"Of course. I've thought of something you said in the war council with your king, that the fire worker had taught no one his arts. It seems to me, then, that this is a gift that one can be taught, no? Enna, I want you to teach me."

Enna opened her eyes, and fear returned with a jolt.

"It would help your position here if you could be a teacher," he said. "Just to me. Show me how you do it and I can protect you."

An arrow of thought whipped through her drugged mind. *War.* She was forgetting the war. She had entered an enemy camp in an attempt to cripple them, and instead they were wrestling her weapon away for their own use.

And it would be even easier than they knew. Her eyes darted to the right side of her skirt. There, sewn inside the wide hem, was the vellum. She had wanted it to be safe, and instead she had walked right into the enemy's home, bringing the means to destroy Bayern. She had no idea how many Tiran would have the ability she and Leifer shared. Maybe hundreds, maybe none. But as Leifer had proved, even one could be devastating on the battlefield. Enna realized grimly that she had thought she could end the war herself, but she had not considered that she could do it from either side.

Her thoughts looped around one another, and she blinked hard to try to still them. He was waiting for her to speak, so she said, "I can't," again because it was the easiest thing to say.

"Do you mean you won't?"

"I don't think it's possible."

Sileph took a breath. "Was that you out there burning on the battlefield?"

"No, my brother."

"And he taught you?"

"No," Enna said firmly. "He didn't teach me. It just happened."

In frustration, she had been trying to sit up and convince him with her effort that it was impossible. But the tent and ground tilted queasily, and she found herself back in his arms, her cheek pressed against his chest.

"I can't," she said into his shirt. "I can't think."

"Yes. With a clear mind you might find a way."

"The drug." Perhaps with that incentive, they would find a reason not to feed her the king's-tongue anymore. Then she could have her mind back and think a way out of there.

Sileph patted her hand. "Soon, I hope. Now I think you would like to stretch and wash. Tiedan wants a look at you tomorrow, and we should have you in some clean clothes."

Enna stiffened. They would take away her skirt. They could find the vellum.

"Don't worry, I will send in a woman to take your things," he said, mistaking the reason of her reaction.

"I'd rather not," she said, but he ignored her. He lowered her to the ground, pulled a knife from his boot, and sliced through her wrist and ankle binds. With the sudden release, slivers of pain drove into her arms and legs and ran in sharp shivers all over her body. She cried out. Sileph stopped and looked at her.

"You . . . you should not suffer." His voice trembled a little at the end. Enna stared up at him, mouth agape. She believed that he honestly felt for her. But a moment later when he called out to a sentry, his voice was low and commanding again.

Before she could test her strength enough to try to dispose of the vellum, Sileph returned with two guards and a Bayern woman wearing a blue sash. Sileph gave orders so quickly that Enna's slowed mind did not catch them completely, and then he left. The two guards stayed in the tent with their backs turned to Enna, ostensibly to make sure no illicit communication passed between the two prisoners.

The woman clucked and *tsk*ed as she undressed Enna, but her eyes were tender. Though perhaps only ten years Enna's senior, her face was lined and sun scarred. Eylbold was a farming town, and Enna imagined the years working fields were rough. She stared at the woman, caught up by her eyes, blue as the high, lonely sky. It was good to see someone's eyes. Enna wanted to tell her with her own eyes to ignore what she might feel inside the skirt hem, to just return it without a word. She shook her head in a silent plea. The woman surely did not understand the warning, but she returned a comforting nod.

Once Enna was stripped down, the woman washed her with a rag and warm water in quick strokes. Enna wanted to protest and say she could do it herself, then realized that she could not. So she just kept the woman's blue eyes, felt like a kitten washed by its mother's rough tongue, and thought of what she would do later, when she was free.

The woman wrapped Enna in a large wool blanket that vaguely itched against her bare skin and left the tent with the dirty clothes. The two guards followed her out. Enna could see they kept post just outside the tent door.

It was quiet. The tent got darker. Outside, she could hear campfires pop and hiss. She wanted that sound to feel comforting, like the voice of an old friend, but it seemed so far away. She did not want to be alone to feel how cold and untouchable the world was now, to feel the absence of the heat like heavy grief. Alone, her thoughts would catch and fling her back to the moment with Isi, the unforgivable moment. She winced again and again at the memory, and dark regret rode with her into sleep.

She heard a voice and woke slowly. The air and darkness felt like deeper night. The voice that had awakened her still vibrated inside her head. She listened to it again. A voice she did not know. A man's. She opened her eyes.

"There you are." It was one of the guards. He had removed his helmet, and his yellowish hair stuck up in a way that reminded her of Razo. He was in the tent, alone, looking at her.

"All nice and comfortable, are you? For a moment I thought you might be dead. Were you dead?" He smiled.

"No," said Enna, since he seemed to be waiting for an answer.

"Good, because I'm curious." He took slow steps toward her. "I wondered what a girl looks like who cooks people alive. A friend of mine, Duris, he was sleeping in a tent just like this one when it caught fire somehow. Do you know how?"

She did not answer this time. In the near darkness, his face was disturbingly shadowed. That empty place inside her that she used to fill with heat was now sick with dread.

"You must be too good to answer to me, yes? Our precious little prisoner. Our resident fire-witch. Deserves death, but instead is washed and fed and guarded like a prized puppy. You took something away from me that night. Do I not get something in return?"

Ah, she thought, *ah, that.* He came toward her, and she

fought rolling pains of disgust and the nauseating realization of her own powerlessness. Her limbs felt like stripped corpses. Her mind swayed like a motion-sick child rolling around in the back of a wagon. She concentrated on the pit of dread inside her and how to change it to anger, and how that anger could free her, wake her skin to awareness of heat again, loose the sleeping fire. He knelt over her, and his hands touched her blanket where she gripped it closed.

His voice was soft and mocking. "I just want to see what a fire-witch looks like."

She could feel the heat of his wet breath on her face. *Good. Heat. Go ahead,* she thought, *go ahead and touch me and let's see what happens.* But she held the blanket even tighter, a maddening grip that reminded her just how weak she was. She sobbed once and felt a little heat bubble inside her. His face leered over her, and she could see pale glints of his teeth. With his bony finger he stabbed her a few times in her side as though he were prodding meat or teasing a sibling. Then he grabbed the corners of her blanket and said, "Hush."

She heard the sound of the tent flap whipping aside.

The guard sprang to his feet. "Captain," he said with an effort at normalcy.

Sileph looked around wildly, at him, at Enna, back at him. Enna pulled a loosed corner of the blanket tight over her chest. Her hand shook like a baby's gourd-rattle.

Sileph's face tightened in rage. He rushed forward and released his fist into the guard's face. The punch sent the guard spinning to the ground. Sileph swore, looked down, and hit him again. And then again, and again, cursing him and his family and his stench and his greasy heart. The guard covered his head with his arms and whined like a beaten dog. Sileph seemed unwilling to stop, and his fists shook with unspent fury, but he grabbed the man by his neck and the back of his tunic, ran him through the tent, and flung him out the door.

Sileph put a hand over his face and breathed hard through his nose, his entire body clenched up in a reluctant effort to calm. His forehead shone with perspiration.

Enna pushed herself up a little on her elbow. "You should've let him try." Her voice shook more than she thought it would. "He would've . . . I would've found a way . . . to burn . . . " She stopped, angry and humiliated, aware that even in anger the fire was a stranger to her drugged mind.

Sileph tightened his fists and looked around as though wishing for something new to hit. He pointed at her, and his voice trembled with rage.

"Nobody touches you." He paced a moment, put a fist to his mouth, discovered a trickle of blood from where he had bitten his own lip, and wiped it away angrily. "Nobody."

After a moment, when his breathing slowed, he sat beside her. Enna watched his face, amazed that this was the same man from the war council in Ostekin. She thought unexpectedly, *He's nothing like Finn.*

He sat for a few moments just looking at her, then said, "I am sorry, Enna," and stood to go.

"Wait," she said.

He turned back to her, his expression almost hopeful. She realized that she was going to ask him to stay and that was ridiculous, so she curled back up on the ground and said no more. Sileph waited a moment and then left.

Enna tried to keep her eyes open for as long as possible. Under her blanket, she rubbed her bare arms and tried to still her shivering muscles. She had never felt so empty.

arly, when the tent walls began to brighten with shaded light, the tent flap moved again. Enna jumped, but it was only the blue-eyed woman with her clothes. The skinny man with his hard finger and hot breath and sneer was not among the guards who accompanied her. The woman dressed Enna tenderly. Her clothes smelled of beef soap and wood smoke. Enna ran her weak hand along the hem—the vellum was still there.

Sileph waited outside the tent until the woman departed, then entered quietly, a small water skin in his hand. Enna nearly sobbed.

"Please," she said, pride combating the pleading tone in her voice. "I want to be able to think and move again."

"I wish I did not have to. Tiedan spoke with me this morning. His orders are that you remain drugged." He uncapped a flask and held it to her lips. With his other hand he smoothed her brow. "Just a little. Just enough to hold the fire back. It won't be forever, not if they can find another way to protect themselves from you."

He began to pour and she gagged on the bitter water, her hands gripping his wrist. She coughed, gulped one, two, three swallows; then he allowed her to push his hand away. He wiped the dribbled water from her cheek with a corner of his shirt.

"You are very brave, Enna."

That one word was too much. Brave. She choked on it, clutched his wrist tighter, and started to cry. The fear and powerlessness were so overwhelming, Enna could scarcely remember who she had been. Sileph held her against his chest, smoothing her hair and rocking her slightly. His voice changed again, softer, lighter.

"You are, Enna. You are amazing. This is temporary. You will shine again, I promise. I will see you burn again."

"Why?" she asked.

He did not speak, just held her while the king's-tongue spread through her body, pressed down her hands and feet, and cooled her skin so that it felt dead. The pit inside her was empty and cold, and it weighed down her chest. Soon she was aware of Sileph but could not feel him. Only her sense of smell remained completely keen. She pondered the smell of his leather vest—dust, smoke, oil, animal.

She looked at the dark hairs on the back of his hand and thought of him last night in his rage. What had he done to the hard-fingered guard? Was that guard now dead? Finn would not have killed him, but Sileph might. She wanted to ask him these questions, as well as others that would start with "Why?" But she was comfortable against him in her nearly numb body. And she liked his smell.

Smell was her only strong sense for days, as Sileph and the king's-tongue became her only companions. When the drug began to wear itself out, Sileph was there. She leaned against him and told him of home, of the Forest and being a worker in the city, of Leifer's death and how the queen tried to stop Enna from burning. She told him because she wanted his trust, sure that he was the best hope she had of someday escaping. And she told him because she wanted to. Those moments with Sileph, the grip of the king's-tongue loosening, were the times she felt a little like Enna.

She left the tent only to go to the privy. Sileph picked her up, one arm under her knees, one supporting her back, and carried her into the winter sun. She closed her eyes, leaned back her head, and let the light touch her entire face. The warmth and light made her feel pretty. Her skin tingled and her heart swelled, and she breathed deeply of the cool air that brought the tang of pine trees and warming earth. She had spent most of her life out of doors, and just leaving the confines of the tent felt like going home.

It also made her ache. Inside the plain, windowless white tent, her numb state seemed almost natural. Outside, with the sun and wind and colors and people and fires, she remembered dimly how much she used to feel.

Sileph always arranged to have a woman help Enna at the privy and then returned to take her back to her tent. Once he let her try to walk, holding her arm over his shoulders and steadying her with his other arm around her waist. It was almost fun for the first few steps to feel the rough ground under her thin boots and feel her ankles and knees move. But soon her legs crumpled, the drugged and unused muscles cramped and useless. In that moment Sileph swept an arm under her legs, held her again in his arms, and kept walking as though that had been their intention. Enna wrapped her arms around his neck and held his head close to hers.

Returning to the tent, the washed-out light and smell of close quarters, caused Enna a physical pain. Sileph said nothing as he settled her onto her blanket. She did not let go of his neck, so he knelt beside her.

"I walked," she said.

"Yes, you did." He contemplated her face. "Someday, when this is over, we will walk together in Ingridan. It is a beautiful city. Not as harsh and cold as Bayern. It lies by the sea on a river delta. Seven small rivers weave through the city, and there are white stone bridges and white houses and palaces and squares, and when the fruit trees are in bloom all the air is sweet."

She gasped with a sudden sob. The image was beautiful, and she felt so ugly. "King's-tongue. I feel sorry for that king. I know how he felt. It's cruel what his daughter did to get power."

Sileph's brow was lined. "People do cruel things when they are afraid. They need leverage against you, Enna. They need a way to be sure you won't burn the tents around them. That's why, I thought, if you could teach me how . . . "

"If you'll let me go, I'll take an oath never to . . . to never . . . "

Sileph's grip on her arms was tighter, and there was a touch of desperation in his voice. "I can't let you go, Enna. You have to try. If you can teach me the fire, I can protect you. Once I can wield the power as well, Tiedan will feel safer around you and revoke the order to keep you on king's-tongue."

"But there's the war . . . " Enna rubbed her eyes irritably, unsure what she should say. When she looked up again, Sileph was watching her shrewdly.

"The war." He shook his head. "Do you really think I'm your enemy?"

Enna studied his face. *Sileph. Enemy.* No, she could not reconcile the two.

He straightened, and his manner spoke of the soldier he was. "You deserve to know something, Enna. This war will not last long. We have been allowing the Bayern spies to count our numbers this winter because they cannot see the armies yet to march from Tira. Soon, very soon, Tira will overwhelm Bayern. Don't resist teaching me the fire because you believe you are saving Bayern. Bayern is already lost. Save yourself."

He drew closer and smoothed her hair away from her brow. "You are not a traitor, Enna. You are a survivor. All I am asking is for you to show me what you do."

A way out, she thought.

"Just you," she said.

"Yes, just me."

Sileph stayed with her during those hours when the king's-tongue began to loosen its grip on her mind and before her next dose was due. For Enna, they became the most delicious and grueling hours she had known. The first time she could gather heat to her, she nearly cried out. And then resisting, not lighting the fire for fear of revealing too much, made her sweat and shake. Never had the gift brought her so much joy or forced such a struggle for control.

"Tell me how it works," he said.

"There's a place in here"—she put a hand on her chest—"that I fill with heat. Just bringing it inside changes it, then I direct it into some fuel, and it becomes fire."

"Where do you get the heat?"

"I don't know. It's all around. I can't remember anymore."

She did remember. Living things give off heat. But she would not reveal all willingly. She tried not to think about that place in her skirt that felt a little heavier against her ankle.

Just as Enna had wished, because Sileph became more hopeful of learning, he put off the drug until later and later.

They would sit together in the dark. Through a rift in the tent roof, a little moonlight slipped in and pooled on the surface of the king's-tongue water. It trembled in its cup like a threat.

Sileph would hold up a stick or piece of straw and say, "Concentrate."

She did. The later it was, the more she could feel him. Sileph. His heat leaving his skin, brushing by hers, rising against the shaft of moonlight and dispersing into the night sky. The nearness of the heat was intoxicating, and she would close her eyes and just feel it, play at drawing it near, imagine pulling it inside that dead space in her chest and feel the transformation to flame. Resistance sometimes took the little strength she had. Something about Sileph made her believe he was one who could be taught, and he might just be cunning enough to figure it out without reading the vellum.

"I'm sorry," she would say, and with a sigh he would nod and hand her the cup of drugged water. He always watched her drink it and stayed with her until the king's-tongue took effect. *So that I can't retch it up*, she thought. *Or perhaps he just wants to stay.* He would hold her until she slept, and his smell and the faraway feel of his hands on her hair made losing herself to the king's-tongue just a little more bearable.

In those last moments before her hands and feet began to feel like leaded fishnets, Enna thought of escape. One night perhaps something would happen to take Sileph away, an emergency, a call from Tiedan. When that happened, she would be prepared to act.

The chance came several days later. Enna was feeling alert enough to sit up cross-legged. Sileph was unaware that this also meant she was able to feel not only his heat, but also the quiet hibernating heat of the grass roots beneath her legs and snakes of heat that came from the guards outside, slithering through the tent flap and up against her skin.

Enna wiped her brow as if she were exhausted from trying to light a fire, though she was in fact tired out from trying not to. It was as though the ghosts of all that had lived pressed against her body and begged for life. She found the sensation a thousand times more pleasant than the numbness of the king's-tongue.

"You long to do it," he said. "I know you do. I remember your face when you used to run in this wood sending tents and wagons into flames. Remember that feeling. It could help you. What does it feel like to burn?"

"Relief."

Sileph nodded as if he understood. "And what about burning as your brother did on the battlefield, a great deal all at once. Is that different?"

"I can't do more than little fires, a little at a time. Maybe his talent was different."

Sileph considered, then shook his head once. "No. If he could, then I have no doubt you could as well. You seem to grasp at the fire, trying to control it and still protect yourself. I wonder what may happen if you surrender instead."

Surrender. The word frightened her.

"He died, you know," she said. "He died from burning, perhaps from surrendering."

"If there is a way of mastering it, you will find it." He smiled briefly.

"Why do you take such an interest, Sileph?" she asked.

"The sooner we can show Tiedan progress, the sooner you won't have to take the king's-tongue."

"And that's the only reason? For me?"

He leaned back, resting his arm on the ground, and looked at her unblinking, as though anticipating in advance what her reaction might be. "My father was a soldier in the king's army. As was his father. I was born a soldier, and if I have sons, they will be born soldiers, unless I can change that."

He cleared his throat and looked at his hands. Enna enjoyed the rare times when he seemed uncomfortable. One of the things she hated most about her king's-tongue state was that he could not see her as she was, that he might not know that in will and strength she surely was his match.

"These times," he said, "they allow for opportunities. I lead a fifty company; that is good for one my age. But I need to win more. You are so powerful, Enna. What you are, what you know, is an opportunity for me. But I also believe it is an opportunity for you, if you are willing to grab it."

"So, what'll you get if you become a burning man, Sileph? They'll give you a spot of land? Or maybe more—a title, a statue in some square, or just the satisfaction that people in the streets will nod to you and give your wife the fatter cut at the butcher's?"

"I expect military promotion and only that. The Tiran citizens would not know what to make of me, I imagine. We have no fire-witches in Tira, except in tales. And besides, I have no wife."

Enna raised her eyebrows. "No? And you must be past twenty." She sighed. "Well, I guess it's no surprise you couldn't catch a wife, a boy like yourself who goes around kidnapping poor girls and suffers such a sad lack of charm and good looks."

"And you, my lady? A husband awaits you at home, or at least a betrothed?"

She gave him a glare that had won her many arguments in the past.

He leaned back a little as if in surprise. "No? But you must be near seventeen. Well, I guess that cannot be helped. It is a shame your mother couldn't bear a girl with a witty tongue, or at the very least a pretty face."

"You're a rogue," she said with some pleasure.

"Am I now?" He sat up on his knees, his hands full of straw.

She slugged him once on the shoulder and started to scoot away. "Easy," she said, "what're you doing? It's not fair to attack a girl in a weakened state."

"Oh, I think you are plenty awake, my lady, and I am under orders to test out your weaknesses, for future reasons of torture, of course."

He began to pelt her with pieces of straw as though they were spears, and she batted them away. His look was one of deep concentration, though she noted the right corner of his mouth was twitching, as though his face fought his resolve not to smile.

"Ooh, that was a good throw," he said.

She took in a sharp, mocking intake of breath. "You almost got my eye."

She gathered up the fallen straw and began to hurl it back at him. As she dodged and threw, she found herself laughing.

"Captain!" The call came from outside the tent. Sileph stood, pulling straw from his hair, his demeanor losing all signs of playfulness.

A guard entered the tent. "Sir, you are needed immediately."

"Yes, Pol." He looked down at Enna with a frown, then said, "Drink the tea."

Enna felt as though she had been slapped. *Who are you? Which you is you?*

"Drink your tea," he said again. "I don't know when I will be back."

Enna snatched the cup angrily, spilling a little on her hand, and gulped down the liquid. It stung her throat to drink it that fast. She could feel her tongue begin to swell.

He watched her throat to make sure she swallowed and then stood there, giving it time to digest.

"You should come now, sir," said Pol.

Sileph nodded and started to follow him out. He looked back. "I will return as soon as I can, Enna."

She knew what he meant. He was always there when she took the drug, comforting her as it numbed her body and took away the world. Again she wondered, *Does he hold me to make sure I'm properly drugged or because he wants to?*

The instant he left, Enna scuttled to the corner of the tent and scratched up a flap of ground cloth. She jabbed at the back of her throat, vomited the clear liquid onto the ground, covered it up, and lay down before anyone came in to see her.

Some of the drug was already in her body. The dry, green taste of the king's-tongue seemed to coat her completely— the taste was a film on her eyes, the chapped skin on her fingertips. Her hands felt heavy, and a mild dizziness made it difficult to keep her eyes open. But she could still think, and dreams did not entangle her into fiery darkness. The mild effects would wear off soon, and then she would disable Sileph somehow (that thought still made her uncomfortable) and flee, burning her way out if necessary.

Enna curled up, trying to ease a sudden stomachache. *Get out.* That had been her thought all along, but now that the possibility neared, anxiety plucked at her. Where could she go? She had left nothing behind—she had tried to set fire to the queen, her closest friend, and she had nearly gotten Razo and Finn killed on their last raid. Leifer was dead. She knew she could not bear to return to the Forest again, the uneasy fire pulsing inside her, making her feel useless and small unless she burned. And if what Sileph said was true, if Bayern had no chance against Tira? Then there was no more home.

Enna cursed and slammed her fist against the hard ground. Her drug-numbed hand vibrated peculiarly. She looked at it as at a strange object and wished that she had somewhere to run.

There were more shouts outside. She was often too drugged to be curious, but now the noises tugged at her attention and her mind played at figuring them out. Not battle preparation. Not a celebration. *An intruder*, she thought.

Just then Sileph entered the tent. She sat up quickly as though she were caught doing something wrong and then remembered she was supposed to be drugged to unconsciousness. Weak dizziness took her, and she exaggerated its effects.

"Enna." There was eagerness in Sileph's voice, but also caution. "Enna, I have found our leverage. I have found a way to make them feel safe around you without the king's-tongue."

Her eyes widened, but she did not speak. She reminded herself, *You're drugged. You're nearly asleep.*

"It is good for us," he said. "Before you see what's waiting, you must remember that."

He picked her up like a baby and carried her out of the tent.

The first thing she noticed was a fire. It was night. She had not been around live fire since the night she razed the gallows. It was so beautiful in the dark, like gold cascades falling up into the air, dripping with heat and light. And she felt it, too, and recognized the desire that seeped from its center, the desire to stretch and grow and consume and be freed. It was her desire. She was the smoldering embers in the pit.

The night was very cold, and Sileph's arms gripped her as though he wished to warm her as much as to hold her up. He walked a short distance, stopping before a gathered group of soldiers.

"Here is our answer," he said.

Her eyes still burned from staring at campfires, and here it was dark. She focused on what stood before her until her eyes grew accustomed to the night. Slowly, the people's faces resolved into clarity.

Standing between the soldiers, their hands tied behind their backs, their faces swollen and bloodied, were Razo and Finn.

heir swords were gone. They breathed hard as if they had been fighting until moments ago. Razo had a scrap of cloth tied around his mouth— Enna did not doubt he had been cursing and shouting. And his hair, of course, stood straight up. A soldier beside him held a dagger at the point of his jaw as if prepared to slice his throat clean open.

Finn's mouth was uncovered, and his labored breath came rasping from his throat. In addition to his hands, his ankles were tied with rope, probably to stop him from kicking. Two men held his shoulders. Both Razo and Finn watched Enna, and their eyes were sad. They had come here, she knew, for her.

"No," Enna said softly.

"It is all right," said Sileph. "This is our chance, Enna."

"How dare you?" Finn spoke out with a rage that surprised Enna. "If you address her, you call her 'maiden'; she's not Enna to you!"

A soldier punched Finn in the belly. While he was doubled over, they gagged him with a filthy cloth someone pulled from his tunic.

"Let them go." Enna pushed her way out of Sileph's arms and landed on her feet. She wobbled, and Finn lurched forward as though he would catch her. Sileph grabbed her shoulders to steady her. She struggled out of his grip and fell to the ground.

"Listen to me," he said quietly, crouching beside her, "their presence gives you power now. You won't have to take the king's-tongue."

"But they can't be punished for me," she said. "They didn't do anything."

"They tried to sneak into a Tiran camp armed and outfitted for sabotage. They knew full well that—"

"No, they don't know anything. They're just stupid boys."

Enna saw Finn flinch at her words, and she rose unsteadily to her feet. "No, I didn't mean that. I just meant it's not your fault, it's mine, and I need to fix it."

She started to walk to Finn, unsure what she could do, just wanting to free them. Sileph grabbed her arms and held them behind her back.

"I will not let you hurt yourself for these boys," he said quietly in her ear.

"Let me go," she said. She felt dizzy, intoxicated, out of control.

"Take the prisoners to a holding room, double guard," said Sileph.

"No!" Enna in a rage grabbed at any loose heat that would heed her and pulled it into her chest. The cold hollowness filled with heat and nearly burst, sending shivers through her body. Enna gasped at the pain.

Sileph shook her once and shouted quickly and urgently, "Enna, if you set fire to one bootlace, those boys will be killed."

She shook her head, shuddering.

"They will, Enna. I swear they will."

She had already pulled the heat inside her, and she had to expel it into flame or be burned by it. She kept her eyes on the guards who held Razo and Finn, despairing that freeing her friends meant endangering their lives. Her throat burned, her stomach burned. The pain of held heat shook her body, and it burned hotter and hotter. She screamed and sent the heat barreling into the nearest campfire. It exploded into flames the height of a man, blasting wood and embers into the night air.

Enna gasped for air again and again and felt her insides cool. The hollowness in her chest now was small and hard like a curled-up potato bug. She was weary and angry and sick, and she felt Razo's and Finn's stares like the disappointed heat that still pressed against her skin.

Sileph grabbed her shoulders and faced her to him. "Listen, Enna, those guards have orders. The moment you set a fire in this camp, they kill the shorter one there. You do it again, the second one goes. And they will be happy to do it. Those Bayern boys injured three of my men before they were contained. Do you understand? Are you sober enough to comprehend all this?"

"Yes," she whispered, "yes, I understand. I burn, and you kill them."

"Not just if you attack, Enna. If they see a fire spreading from its pit, a tent aflame, any fire loose anywhere in the camp, their orders are that the first one goes. Tiedan will take no chances with you."

"It's not fair," she said through her scorched throat.

"It is the price. Any loose fire sighted and one dies."

Besides the guards who held Razo and Finn, others stood by, two with nocked arrows, two with naked daggers. She felt defeat as real as if she had been beaten and bruised with it.

"I understand," she said. The sting from holding heat too long, the night chill, and the effect of the drug all pressed and pained her, and she began to shake so badly that her teeth chattered.

"Come on," said Sileph, wrapping his arms around her shoulders.

Finn's forehead furrowed in anger or confusion, and Enna shrugged Sileph's arms away. Sileph glanced once at Finn and frowned.

"Back to the tent, girl," he said sternly.

She waited for the soldiers to march Razo and Finn away before she followed Sileph into her tent.

"It is for the best," he said.

"Whose best?"

He watched her as she sat and rested her head on her knees.

"Don't you want to know why I saved their lives?"

"What?" She glared up at him, daring him to make himself a hero now.

He shrugged and looked a little like a young boy hopeful and unsure of himself. "I told the guards that they broke into camp to try to rescue you. Tiedan would have them killed if he knew that they were assassins."

"Oh, stop with your Tiran rhetoric," said Enna. "Those soldiers aren't assassins."

Sileph seemed surprised. "I meant . . . you know they came to kill you."

Enna opened her mouth to protest, but the words dried in her throat.

"They came as assassins, Enna, so that Tira could not have you in its power. There was a third boy who threatened as much before my men killed him."

"No," she said, her voice a little higher, "they came to save me. I don't know who the other one was, but Razo and Finn would try to rescue me."

"Three people? Bayern sent three boys to pull you out of Tira's war camp and expected success? Didn't you notice how they looked?"

"Bruised, gagged," she said defiantly. He waited for more. "And sad. They were trying to tell me they were sorry."

"Sorry that they failed you? Or sorry that they had betrayed you?"

Enna started to answer, but her throat constricted, and she felt her lip tremble. It was ridiculous what he claimed, but she saw in memory their sad eyes, their worried brows. And who had been the third boy?

Sileph sat beside her. "I don't want to talk at you and convince you that they meant ill. I thought you would have known the truth. But if Tiedan and the rest believe that they came to rescue you, then we can use the boys as hostages. What I'm saying is, it would be wise if you pretended to care about those boys."

Enna met his eyes. "I do care. I . . . "

Sileph shook his head, and his jaw set in anger. "Those bastards. Sending *friends* to kill you, or worse, sending your friends to be captured and killed before you, and leave you knowing that no other rescue will come." He rubbed his jaw whiskers hard, keeping his gaze on her. "They must not value you at all, or you would not have come alone in the first place and would not now be subject to such a pathetic rescue."

Enna stared at him. Her wet eyes began to blur his image, and she could no longer make out his face. *Pathetic. Assassins.*

"Get out," she said.

"Enna . . . "

Enna stood and punched him in the jaw as hard as she could.

"Get out," she said. He did not move, so she swung again. He caught her arms by the wrists, his eyes flashing anger.

"Don't hit me," he said slowly, his jaw clenched. Enna's eyes widened, and she felt afraid of him for the first time. His grip on her wrists tightened, as if testing her strength; then he tossed her to the ground and left the tent.

Enna was alone for two days. The last of the king's-tongue seeped out of her body, leaving her muscles feeling thin and raw but workable. Her mind gradually became her own again. And as she felt heat once more and stuffed tiny bits into her extremities, she found that she was not cold for the first time in many days.

Alone, she paced in circles in her tent, waved her arms around, and tried to awaken and strengthen her ill-used body. When an opportunity came, she did not want weakness to prevent her from fighting or fleeing. But for two days the guards brought only water, and soon she huddled on the ground, wrestling down the pains of hunger, the renewed desire to set fire, and the fear that Razo and Finn had sworn her death.

Inside, deeper than the hollow spot in her chest, she did not believe they could be assassins. But Sileph's words still buzzed in her head, and she could not be sure. Regardless, she could not let her friends be killed. She would not burn.

On the third day, when the yellow shade of the tent walls told her it was midafternoon, Sileph returned. He put a hot loaf of bread and a slab of cheese before her without a word and turned to go. He stopped, one hand on the tent flap as if reconsidering, then turned and sat cross-legged before her.

"Eat," he said.

She met his eyes with a glare that would speak for two days without food and the capture and beating of her friends. The lines of his face relaxed.

"We were both angry," he said. "I'm sorry."

He looked at her, and though she was prepared to refuse his apology, instead she found herself momentarily breathless. She had not really seen him, not in all those king's-tongue hazy days. His pale brown hair was tied back, exposing the angular shape of his face, the sharp line of his jaw, his dark brown eyes. Just now, there were tired lines around his eyes that made him look heartbroken.

"Go on," he said, and she gratefully looked away from him to her meal. The food was welcome, though not quite enough to keep her from wanting more. She brushed the crumbs from her fingers, readied herself, then raised her eyes to Sileph's again.

"You're a fool," she said.

Sileph nodded. "Don't say it took you two days to realize this."

Enna nearly smiled. Sileph was thoughtful for a few

moments; then he closed his eyes as though shutting something out.

"Enna, from all you have told me, I assumed that Bayern had or would abandon you, and that those boys' clumsy assassination attempt"—Enna started to protest, and Sileph held up his hand and continued—"or rescue was just the final proof. But I understand now that you still had hopes of returning to Bayern. I was thoughtless. I know how I would feel were I betrayed by Tira, and I am sorry."

Sileph stood, pacing in the small space. "It makes me angry. How can they be so blind? If you were mine, I would not let you go so easily."

"Wouldn't you?" she said with some contempt.

He answered simply, "They are fools. They don't deserve you. To not only cast you off, but also to make so little attempt to bring you back? Huh. I'm not surprised, I suppose, when I think of that mousy little queen."

Enna winced. When Sileph spoke disparagingly of Isi, it was a temptation to agree and allow the persistent, pinching guilt to ease. But her heart would not allow it.

"Don't," said Enna. "Just don't. You don't know her."

Sileph nodded once. He knelt beside her and took her hands.

"Nevertheless, if they do not want you, we do. Tiedan has given me orders. You and I are riding out today—on a mission. If it goes well, things will change for you here."

"What do you expect me to do, forsake Bayern?"

"Haven't they already forsaken you?"

"Captain," came a voice from outside the tent.

Sileph let her hands go and stood. His face was smooth, and his voice regained its public hardness. "Come in, Pol."

Pol entered. She had seen him several times in her weeks there, but he never looked at her. None of the soldiers did, save Sileph.

"Horses are ready, sir."

Pol handed him a bag and departed, and Sileph dropped it at Enna's knees. Inside was a lady's riding dress, deep brown and cut in the Tiran style with fitted wrists and waist. Also leggings, a wool hat and mitts, a jacket, new boots, and a filled water bottle with a long neck like the one Razo had filched for their costumed expeditions.

"Get dressed. We go when you are ready," he said, leaving her alone.

Enna dressed quickly, feeling not only cold in those brief moments after she had flung off her worn Bayern clothes, but also vulnerable, vivid memories of the hard-fingered soldier leering before her, her only defense a thin wool blanket. She kept her old skirt on under the dress—they might think she wore layers for warmth.

When she emerged from the tent, she felt strange, the hat wonderfully warm but unfamiliar, the dress touching her in different places from her Bayern skirt and tunic. She felt as though she were no longer a prisoner but had shed herself and become Tiran. A thought scratched briefly against her good feelings: *that's how he wants you to feel.*

It was a relief to be dressed so. As she walked through the camp with Sileph and several other Tiran soldiers, she felt like one of them instead of trapped by them. She knew it was an illusion, but at least it lessened her feelings of vulnerability. Then they arrived at the horses. Ten soldiers were already mounted. One on a large horse held another on the saddle before him. It was Razo, gagged, his hands bound.

"Why?" she said.

"For our protection," said Sileph. "Whenever we go out, we will take one of your Bayern friends along." He helped her mount a horse, then hopped into the saddle behind her. He rested his head beside hers and whispered, "I trust you, but Tiedan does not."

Enna looked at Razo. The soldier had angled his horse so that she and Razo could not meet eyes, but she could see a bruise and an unbandaged cut on the side of his face. She thought, *I'll see Tiedan burn.*

"I can ride my own horse," she said, thinking fondly of Merry and hoping she got home safely. *Home.* Was Ostekin the mare's home? Was it hers?

One of the soldiers laughed at her request. "And let you gallop off to the Bayern? No luck."

Sileph laughed, too. She could feel his laugh muscles against her back. "Not yet, my lady. You will earn that right in time."

"And how'll I do that?"

He wrapped his arm around her waist, pulled her tighter against him, and kicked his horse into a canter.

They rode for a couple of hours, and as the winter sun descended and the horizon burned red, Enna felt more and more uneasy. Being kept in ignorance was as bad as being bound in ropes. She watched the gray ground slipping beneath them and caught a glint of metal in Sileph's boot. A knife.

"Slow down," said Sileph at last. The party came to a stop, and Enna looked around madly in the low, fiery light to see where they had come. Over the next rise was a farmhouse. Panic seized Enna as though by the throat. Why were they taking her to this remote place? Did they plan to torture her until she revealed how she controlled fire? Or would they make her watch as they tortured Razo? No, no, she would not let them.

She barely thought about her actions. Sileph dismounted and helped her down. She feigned weakness, wobbled over, and pulled the knife from his boot. In a swipe she brought it to his bare neck, her left hand holding the back of his head, clinging tight to let him know that if it came to a wrestle for the knife she would not let go until she had broken skin. His body stiffened, but he did not raise his hands to her knife hand.

"Let Razo go free," she said.

The soldiers drew their swords, and three strung and

armed their bows. Enna moved slightly so Sileph was part-way between her and the archers.

"Untie him, give him a horse, and let him go or I kill Sileph and burn the rest."

"Enna," said Sileph.

She gripped his neck tighter and let the blade press slightly. She stood on the balls of her feet to reach him, and her hands were already shaking. She wondered why he did not try to disarm her, but maybe it was the fire and not the knife that he feared.

"Why aren't you moving?" said Enna. "I said let him go."

"They won't move without my command, and I won't give it."

"Tell them," said Enna. She did not look at Sileph's face. Looking at him was like being on king's-tongue, and she needed to think clearly. Maybe they would obey her if she lit one of them on fire. Then again, maybe they would kill Razo.

Sileph swallowed against the pressure of the knife and spoke softly. "Enna, I said I won't. If you want to do this, you will have to try to kill us right now. You might get us all before the arrows hit you or Razo. But whether you live through this and escape or die trying, as soon as word reaches Eylbold, Finn will be executed."

She strained to make eye contact with Razo, but his rider still held him away so that she could not see his face.

"You don't have to do that. Just let Razo go. I'll stay with you, I promise, and you'll still have Finn to use over me."

"No." She was close enough to him to feel that word rumble in his chest. "My orders do not allow it. You must choose now if Finn lives or dies. And if you are going to kill me, Enna, you will have to slit my throat. I am too close to burn."

He put his arm around her waist and she jumped, pressing the knife a little harder.

"Easy, easy," he whispered. "I am just showing you that I won't let go until you kill me or put down the knife."

Enna looked at the faces of the soldiers in the dying orange light. They would kill Razo if they could, and they would kill Finn. She believed they would have killed her already if not for Sileph. She could see the blood thirst in their eyes, like her own fire thirst now, the heat from their bodies and the horses tickling the exposed skin of her face and neck.

It was hopeless, but she was reluctant to lose her momentary advantage, and she leaned away from their arrows and closer to Sileph. Her head touched his neck, and she looked at the dark intimation of his shaven beard, the hollow of his throat, a small white scar on his chin. He smelled as familiar as Forest pines, as her mother's soap, and she realized with a cold, achy thrill that she might be falling in love with him. And despite being a prisoner, despite Razo and Finn and king's-tongue and war and all, being there at that moment was in every way the fulfillment of all she had dreamed and longed for when feeling bored and unimportant on quiet Forest nights. She had a knife in her hand, fire aching in her chest, and a war captain by her side. Had she not wished to do things, to be involved in something bigger than herself, bigger than the Forest? *Oh, mercy, Enna,* she thought, *you would be this absurd.*

She grunted in defeat and threw the knife to the ground. Immediately the soldiers arranged themselves in formation, Razo in their center, all arrows pointing at her. Sileph waved them down and then laughed.

"Well, I am glad to get that taken care of." He wiped his neck and looked with delight at the smear of blood on his finger. "I was expecting something eventually, though I will admit that was a bit intense. What brought that on?"

Enna was not amused. Her anger was built, and there had been no release. And she was irritated at Sileph for tricking her into love.

"Why're we here, *Captain?*" she asked.

Sileph blinked once at hearing his title instead of his name. "I brought you here to burn."

Sileph signaled his soldiers, and most followed him on foot as he walked Enna toward the house. "There is something I can't get out of my mind, and that is the expression on your face when you were lighting fires outside Eylbold. It was pleasure. And relief. I know you must need to do it again, Enna."

She did not argue, not trusting herself to lie. Even the

thought of it gnawed at her belly with excitement. "But why this house?"

"Tiedan's orders. It's an empty house, just to get you practicing again."

Enna's fingers tingled and her instinct shouted warning. But already the hollow place in her chest was expanding and heat gathered around her, expectant.

"No, I shouldn't," she said.

Sileph removed her mitts and hat and loosened the neck of her jacket. The heat now had more skin to touch, and the temptation was rich and inviting. Why was she resisting, anyhow? She was not a prisoner out here. Finn and Razo would come to no harm from this fire. Isi was miles away. She pulled the ready heat inside her, converted it to the idea of fire, and sent it exploding into the roof.

Enna gasped as though she had been held underwater too long and just now could breathe. Flames clawed at the now dark sky. She could feel the heat of the soldiers behind her and used it to scorch the walls. She was tempted then to try the surrender Sileph had suggested and see just how far she could go, but she resisted, still cautious of Leifer's fate, still clinging to that last unbroken promise. And so, after a few rounds, her sense of the heat diminished, leaving her chest aching, tightened, and cold.

Then the door opened. Two figures fled the burning building, one of them beating at the flames licking his tunic. He fell to the ground, rolling away the fire. The other pulled out his sword in a defensive posture but quickly dropped it when he saw the number of soldiers gathered behind Enna. He fled behind the blazing house and emerged mounted. Before his horse took more than three strides toward Ostekin, a Tiran arrow thumped into his chest. He slumped over and tipped out of the saddle.

"No," said Enna. She swung around and faced Sileph. "You made me do this." She slapped his chest. "You made me attack my own people. How dare you?" She kept hitting him and cursing herself until he grabbed her arms and held her still.

"Stop it. Contain yourself, my lady." His grip tightened, and she stopped struggling. He met her gaze with his hard brown eyes. "This is Tiedan's work, not mine. How was I to know there were Bayern spies hiding inside. Did you?"

Enna froze, openmouthed. No, she had not known. Why not? Why had she not felt their heat emanating from the building? Perhaps, she admitted to herself, she had wanted so badly to burn again that she had not stopped and tried to sense them.

"Captain," said Pol. He pointed to where the first Bayern man had recovered from the fire and now ran to his companion's horse.

"Let him go," said Sileph. He whispered to Enna, "For you."

Arrows lowered, and the man mounted and galloped safely away.

he company rode back in silence in the quickly dying light. Enna tried vainly to meet eyes with Razo, to see if he understood or if he condemned her. Her thoughts were blazoned with the harrowing image of the Bayern man with an arrow in his chest, but that eased when her sense of heat returned. That empty place in Enna's chest relaxed, and she was conscious again of the stallion's heat, the riders all around, and, most of all, of Sileph's arm around her waist.

On arriving back at the Eylbold camp, Sileph grabbed Enna's arm and walked her quickly to her tent. His eyes looked over everything they passed without seeming to see anything, and his lips tightened and twitched. He ordered the tent guards to remove themselves a few paces and followed her into the tent.

He held her before him by her shoulders to look at her face, then ran his hands along her arms to take her hands. "That was marvelous. Did it feel good?"

Enna blinked twice and frowned. "Yes," she said like a question.

Sileph smiled. The result was shocking. His eyes brightened, the creases around his mouth expanded, his jaw widened. Enna felt her insides chill nervously.

He laughed, lifted her by her waist, and turned her around. "Of course it did. You are amazing."

Enna stumbled as he set her down, and she tried to pry his hands off her waist. Her stomach still made her feel as though she were spinning.

"For weeks, weeks that seem like years, I have been longing to watch you burn, Enna. It is what you were made to do."

"Well, I don't know why you have. I'm not forgetting that a Bayern man died today. . . . " Her argument sounded lame to her own ears.

"Never mind that." He looked into her eyes with such focus that Enna felt herself flush. "Ever since I saw you walking through the woods of Eylbold, I have thought of you relentlessly."

"Oh, please." Her voice cracked a little. She encouraged her indignation to flare up, angry at herself that this was exactly what she wanted to hear.

"I have wanted you to be with me," he said. "I knew how we would be together, didn't you? You must feel something."

He grabbed both her hands between his, and she pulled them loose.

"Still you resist," he said.

Outside she could hear a call from a sentry, and an answering cry, and the crackling of a near fire. She felt shut out from that world, as though in that tent only she and Sileph existed. She looked down at her hands and saw that they were still, which surprised her, as she felt both excited and afraid.

"You're trying to trick me somehow," she said. "I shouldn't've talked so much. I should've remembered what I am here. We're enemies."

"Why? Why are we enemies?" He paced in his familiar way, and in his earnestness some of the stoic Captain Sileph pushed into his voice. "You have told me yourself, there is nothing for you in Bayern. Your family is dead, your queen does not trust you, your friends are assassins, and that Bayern spy might ride home and report you burn for Tira."

Enna let her head bow and saw again that fleeing scout, the blazing house, and herself before it, no knife to her back, no arrow aimed at her chest while she burned.

"Oh," she said, and felt a funereal weight sink her chest. "I burn for Tira."

"We are not enemies," he said. "You need not be a prisoner here, not now. Tiedan wanted you to teach me the fire, and he would have counted that a proof of loyalty. No matter that you couldn't. What you did today, that is our answer. Burn for Tira. Help me end this war quickly. And then . . . "

His voice softened, losing its tones of exultations, melting down to woo her with the sounds. He held her hand in his, rubbing his thumb against her palm. "And then you and I return to Tira, honored warriors. I will buy you a large house in Ingridan. You will command a circle of servants, and at need we will serve the king in securing the country against foe and calamity."

He took her other hand. She did not pull it away.

"This house," she said, "it'd have plenty of hearths?"

He laughed and smoothed the hair from her brow. She remembered his doing that before, during the drugged days, but she had never felt much about it then. His eyes moved over her hair, her cheeks, her eyes, her lips. One hand shifted to the small of her back, the other held the back of her head, his thumb caressing her cheek.

"Hearths and wood," he said, still smiling. He leaned in closer to her, his voice softening to a whisper. "We'll keep a hay field just for you to burn. And sticks, and straw, and tents, all the tents you want . . . "

He kissed her lips. Her eyes closed for a moment, and she thought of nothing but the volume of her heartbeats banging around inside her head. Her hands trembled now in earnest. She hesitated, then wrapped her arms around his neck and kissed him back. Part of her was still hesitating. She thought of Sileph's advice on how to burn as Leifer had—*surrender*. She took that advice now, but not to make fires. She let go of fears and just let herself feel.

*   *   *

Enna was in love with Sileph all week. It was a relief to give up the struggle against him. They dined by his fire and walked together through the camp, smirking at how everyone else still saw them as master and prisoner. He was often gone, serving Tiedan and seeing to war matters, and Enna sat alone in her tent and missed him.

"There was no need for the king's-tongue after all," said Sileph when he returned.

"Without it, I'd've burned you all out of your boots."

Sileph laughed and kissed her hand.

"And Razo and Finn—they can go free?" said Enna.

"Soon," he said.

And they continued to ride out. The first time with a bound-and-gagged Finn, but on subsequent missions with no hostage at all. She burned another house north of Eylbold, and this time Enna had Sileph make certain no one was inside. The next day she burned two wagons full of supplies hidden in the cleavage of two hills. Then another house. When it proved to be a Bayern outpost and a spy ran out, she screamed, "Surrender! Surrender!" before he could try to flee and be downed by an arrow.

She was growing used to the pattern, the long, breathtaking rides, the open sky, the thrill of the fire, Sileph behind her on the horse, Sileph beside her as she burned. And when she questioned if what she did was right, he was there to assure her and comfort her and allow her to keep burning.

Then Sileph was gone for two days. Enna paced in the

tent, lighting bits of straw and blowing them out again. She could hear a lot of activity in the camp. More soldiers arrived from the south. Weapons were sharpened, wagons loaded with supplies. Around the fires at night, the noise was boisterous and excited. Enna lay on her side, watched the firelight spark through the tent cracks, and fell asleep wishing to join the camp.

It was dark when she awoke, the tent walls a night silver from the watch fires' glow, the camp quieted to a drowsy murmur. Someone was in the tent. She started, thinking of the hard-fingered soldier, then realizing that this time she could scorch him where he stood. Then, again, she remembered that if she burned, Razo and Finn died.

"Who's there?"

"Sileph." He knelt beside her. "Did I wake you? Oh, your skin is cold." He smoothed her blanket over her, tucking it around her sides.

"What is it?" asked Enna.

Sileph sighed. "It is time to march. My company joins a small army going east at dawn to see to another Bayern town. You are coming with me."

"To burn?"

"Yes. It is time to burn as you were meant to, Enna, end the war and be done with it. You are our hope."

Enna curled up on her side. "All right," she said sleepily.

She closed her eyes and breathed slowly. Sileph stayed beside her, touching her hair, and she did not respond, acting as though she slept. She wanted him to leave so she could decide what to do. It was too hard to think clearly with him so close. *End the war swiftly.* Yes, that sounded good, but she could not burn people. She wanted to cling to this rule and hoped it would somehow save her. Sileph stroked her hair, and Enna exhaled softly.

She found herself thinking of another time in a tent when she pretended to sleep, Finn beside her, his hands curled on his chest. *All I ever wanted was to be close to you.* They were so different, those two boys. Of her, Sileph wanted so much more than just to be close.

After a time, Sileph carefully lifted his hand from her head and whispered, "Are you sleeping?"

Enna did not answer. She heard Sileph stand and slip out of the tent. Immediately she opened her eyes, folded her arms, and smirked at the tent flap. He did not know her so well after all if he thought she could sleep on this night. Before her thoughts could begin to untangle the decision before her, a quiet conversation in the distance stirred her curiosity. She sat up to listen.

"There he is, our sharpest arrow."

"Captain Tiedan," Sileph said with respect.

"And the . . . ?" said Tiedan.

"Sleeping," said Sileph.

They're talking about me, Enna thought. She crawled across the tent and peered through the flap.

"Your Pol came to me a month ago with some doubts,"

said Tiedan, "thought you were attached to the girl, thought you would not make her burn for us. I told him I would give you some space and wait, and my instincts were correct."

"Yes, sir."

"Your troops are ready for the morning march?"

"Yes, sir, we leave at dawn."

"Good. Make as much of a ruckus as you can. Burn farms along the way. If your plan works, my own troops will be marching in two days." Enna could see Tiedan press his lips together and look at Sileph carefully. "The war is not yet won, but I believe some congratulations are due. I doubted your idea at first, but I see now that your every design, from building the gallows as bait, to the king's-tongue, to using her little friends, has been a decisive success. I think you will not long remain a fifty captain."

Sileph nodded once. "I thank you, sir."

Then Tiedan stepped in closer and whispered earnest words. Enna did not catch them, but she had already heard enough.

It was a relief when dawn came. Enna was tired of hating and cursing herself and pounding the cold ground. A shard of sunlight jabbed through the tent crack. Enna stood, waiting. Sileph entered, handsome, excited, ignorant.

"You are up? Good. It is time. . . . "

Enna crossed the tent and punched him in the jaw.

Sileph grabbed her wrists. "What are you . . . Are you

crazy?"

"You lying son of a goat. I should burn you." Enna bared her teeth at him. It had felt good to hit him. Very good.

"What are you talking about?" he said, shaking her.

"All the time about Tiedan: Tiedan insists on the king's-tongue; Tiedan holds your friends as hostages; Tiedan wants you to burn. Perhaps you should tell Tiedan what he's doing, then, because he certainly seemed to think it was all you last night."

Sileph stared at her a moment, his lips parted. He blinked and tried to resume his air of confidence. "I don't know what you mean."

"Oh, stop it, Sileph," she said, pulling her arms loose and pushing him a step back. "You've been lying to me since I was unconscious. I'm a prisoner because of you and only you. You said you let that Bayern scout go free for me. Ha! You probably let him go so he'd tell Bayern I'm burning and I couldn't return."

"I—"

"Hurry, quick, think of another lie."

Sileph rubbed his brow roughly. He shook his head, staring at the ground.

"I'm sorry," he said lamely.

"Mmm-hmm," she said, unimpressed, sounding to herself like her mother when the children had been naughty.

"Have you never lied, Enna?" She started to argue back, and he raised a silencing hand. "Just listen to me for a moment, all right?"

Enna shut her mouth emphatically and glared.

"Thank you," he said. "I have lied. I have lied and tricked and done everything I could think of to get you into this camp and keep you here. This is the part that you can believe—I want you here. With me. Now that you know that, nothing else should matter. You are still coming with me, Enna. Today. Now. We are burning together and we are ending this war, and then when we are in our big house in Ingridan you can harangue me in front of all the servants about my lying days."

He smiled at her, his sweetest, handsomest smile, and reached out to take her hand. "Come on, Enna," he said gently.

She slapped his hand away and laughed. "You are goat kin if you think that's all it would take. I'm not going, not now, and if you tie me and take me I *will* burn, I swear it, but wherever I please."

Sileph stared at her with such surprise, Enna wondered if anyone had ever said no to him before.

"Captain Sileph," came a call from outside, "the troops are ready to march."

"In a moment," he yelled back angrily.

Enna glowered. "Go on, Captain, your army's waiting."

Sileph tightened his jaw. His face was red. "You will change your mind. When battle after battle the war does not end, and your precious Bayern stubbornly resists, willing to be wiped out entirely rather than surrender, then you will know you could stop it, decisively, beautifully. You will want the war over then, and you will come to me."

He hesitated at the door, as if still expecting her to change her mind and go with him right then. She folded her arms.

"I am not letting you go, Enna. I will be back for you, and you will come."

He swept the tent flap out of his way and was gone.

Enna slumped down on the ground and cursed herself richly. She had acted boldly, but she felt torn up, split like a log. Her heart was hammering out a rhythm in her skull, and her stomach felt iced over. She was the greatest fool of all.

nna was uprooted. She could not stay, but she had nowhere to go. She would not burn for Sileph, and she could not burn against him in Eylbold for fear of hurting Razo and Finn. Never had she felt so imprisoned.

Leifer was dead. She had no more family, and the impatient nature of the fire that was a part of her now would never allow her to return to the slow, quiet life of the Forest. One night she had dreamed of the Forest reduced to steaming black stumps.

And what of Isi? She had tried to kill the queen. Enna had not thought that word before—*kill.* And now she had set fire to Bayern outposts and witnessed the death of at least one of their scouts. If she returned, she might be jailed or even executed for treason. How could she explain? No, she could never go back.

Razo and Finn. Perhaps when the war was over, she could agree to go to Tira with Sileph on condition of Razo's and Finn's release. The desire to burn rose blazing in her chest like a cough, and she choked it down. It worsened after Sileph's departure, and Enna wondered if without an enemy to burn, without targets like the gallows or Bayern outposts, if the fire would slowly consume *her* instead. Maybe, she thought bleakly, when Sileph came back from his current mission, she might agree help him end the war. She shook her head at how quickly she had changed from being tormented by desires to burn Tira to a willingness to burn Bayern. Just like Leifer. Perhaps Isi's warning had been right after all.

Two days after Sileph had ridden east with a small army, Enna heard a second army depart Eylbold. The camp was quieter after that and her evening stew a little thinner. As night softened the camp, several soldiers built a fire near the tent, and through her tent crack Enna watched the flames and their hot, twisting colors. She found herself daydreaming of Ingridan, Sileph's city of white arches and houses and bridges spanning blue rivers, and of being a Tiran warrior, a fearsome and famous woman.

From just beyond the fire, the tones of a Tiran woman caught her attention. All the Eylbold women she had seen were Bayern, and, curious, Enna eavesdropped on her conversation with some soldiers about her ride up from Folcmar and passing news of the war. In addition to some message from Folcmar, the woman brought several skins of wine that she passed around. Enna could hear the sounds of drinking, and the laughter and conversation took on a slightly higher pitch.

"They sent you carrying messages alone from Folcmar?" said a soldier.

"Now, sir, why should I be afraid to ride through my own country?" There was a pause. "Is this not Tiran land?"

Several soldiers laughed. "Indeed, lady, it is, and will remain so."

Enna felt irritated by their talk, and she was tired of waiting. She burst out of the tent and was immediately stopped by her two guards' crossed spears.

"Back inside," said the larger one.

"Sileph said I could join the camp," Enna lied.

"The captain said to keep you hidden away until he returned, witch. Back in."

"Ooh, is that the fire-witch?"

Enna met eyes with the Tiran woman and could not stop her mouth from widening into a silent gasp. It was Isi.

Enna almost did not recognize her in the Tiran clothing and speaking with a Tiran accent. But she knew her. And she clutched at her stomach to keep herself from crying out. Isi's yellow hair was uncovered and cut to her shoulders in the fashion of a laborer.

"Yes, that is the fire-witch, our own little Bayern demon," said a soldier with some disdain. He prodded Enna back inside by a spear tip. She sat down by the flap and watched through the gap.

"I have never seen a fire-witch before," said Isi in her perfect accent. That had always been her talent, Enna remembered. When Isi had first come to Bayern, she had imitated the Forest accent to hide her identity, and she could distinguish different bird sounds and repeat their words so perfectly, a crow thought she was another crow—or, apparently, a Tiran another Tiran. "May I go in and talk to her?"

"No, not a chance. This is no ordinary prisoner. This is our captain's special pet."

Enna winced at the word, and she saw Isi raise her eyebrows.

"Is that so? Would this be Captain Sileph, then? A great leader. He has his way with words, does he not?"

Some of the soldiers snickered.

"I heard a tale once," said Isi, "of the gifts of languages. Do you know it? How in faraway places, there are people who can speak with birds or horses or rain, and some when they speak to other people have the unnatural power to persuade, their every word a kind of magic? Once in Ingridan I heard Sileph speak and wondered if he had not just walked out of that old tale."

"Indeed," said a guard.

Enna's skin tingled with an icy chill. Isi was trying to tell her something—Sileph had the gift of people-speaking. *A dangerous gift*, Isi had said once. *When one with this gift speaks, it's not easy to resist the power of their persuasion. It's difficult not to adore them.*

Alone in her tent, Enna scowled. *Honey-tongued goat bastard.*

"Do you know some tales, then?" said a soldier out of Enna's sight. "Go on. It has been a long night since we have had entertainment."

There was a rumble of agreement.

"All right, but just one, as I am to ride back to Folcmar tonight."

"Slave drivers," someone said sympathetically.

Isi closed her eyes as though visualizing the story. "In a mountain kingdom, a landslide awoke a long-defeated dragon. She stretched her neck, sharpened her claws, and tore her way out of the cave. In the rush to freedom, the dragon burned the nearest village, gorged herself on cattle, and returned to her cave to sleep on her bulging belly."

"Oo-hoo, I would like to try my hand at one of those beasts," said a young soldier.

"They are not real, you fool," said the guard.

"Oh," he said, and hiccuped from the wine.

Isi cleared her throat. "So. A brave prince rode to the cave on his fastest horse. He entered, quietly stepped over burnt cattle bones and charred bits of armor, and got close enough to spear the beast through the eye. But it had been long since one of his kingdom had faced such an enemy, and he did not know that the great old wyrms slept with eyes half-closed and nostrils wide open. When he neared, the dragon woke and raked her mighty tail against the cave wall. The prince stumbled away from the falling rock and was trapped against the cave wall by a barrier of unmovable rubble."

Occasionally Isi batted the air around her face or paused a moment, gazing at nothing, but for the most part she seemed as much in control as she could be. Enna thought of that tea Isi took to help deaden the wind's touch, and she guessed that Isi had taken some recently. It might keep her mind focused, but Enna also knew it lessened her skill with wind and made her more vulnerable. The thought made her proud and sad, like watching a bird battle a cat to save her chicks.

Isi looked right through the crack in the flap as though she could see Enna watching, could meet her eyes. "The prince's many friends wanted to rescue him, but it was useless to try to get past the sleeping dragon. So they waited near the cave for an opportunity. For a great while, none came." She looked back at the soldiers. "When at last the dragon stirred, she took flight directly toward another village. The prince's companions knew they had a choice—free the prince or protect the land. With heavy hearts, they turned their mounts to the flying dragon and sped toward battle."

Isi stopped. There was a silence in which all Enna could hear was the fervent crackling of the fire as it feasted on a green pine bough.

"So, then what happened?" said a soldier.

"That is all I know of the story," said Isi. "What do you think happened?"

"I guess the companions caught up to the dragon and slew it, and then went back to rescue the trapped prince."

Isi smiled. "That would be a very good ending."

"Or," said another, grumbling that the tale had no ending, "they all got toasted, no one knew the prince was trapped, and he died, too."

"Yes," Isi said softly, "that could be an ending, too. Or perhaps while the dragon was gone, the prince found a way to free himself, though digging himself out of a collapsed cave could not be easy."

"Hmph," said one of the guards, his voice slurring slightly. "If you do not mind my saying, lady, you are fine at telling tales but lousy at ending them."

"But you bring good wine," said another cheerfully.

Isi wished them well and stood to leave, glancing once again at the tent flap, her eyes sad. Enna watched her depart and felt as though Isi had tied a string to her heart and pulled it as she walked away. Enna remembered Isi once bemoaning the fact that she did not have the gift of people-speaking. To Enna's mind, Isi did not need it.

Isi had come all that way just to tell Enna in a story that they could not rescue her. The thought made her chest burn. She thought of Sileph's assessment of the queen—a mousy woman with covered hair and lowered face. He never could have foreseen Isi entering the camp disguised as a Tiran woman, risking her life just to comfort her friend.

There were two details that kept returning to Enna's mind

and twisting her heart with a painful wonder. First was that in Isi's story, Enna had been the royalty and Isi the friend. And second, the possibility that just to disguise herself as a Tiran, just to tell her a story, Isi had cut off her hip-length hair.

Enna sat by the slit in the tent, hugging her knees and thinking about her quickly shifting future. An hour before, she had been ready to give up on Bayern and run off to the enemy country with a smooth-speaking captain. She had thought her friendship lost, but Isi would not let her go. The rumor of the campfire's heat threaded through the tent flap and battered at her skin, but her chest filled with a different kind of warmth. She yearned to do something, right then, to show her loyalty to Isi and Bayern.

Enna grimaced as she ripped open her Bayern skirt and pulled out the vellum. The leather was supple from sitting so close to her body heat. She ran a finger over the black writing, letting random phrases catch her eye: *Heat remembers that it was once a part of something living, and it seeks to be so again. That small, hollow place. Burns best in what once lived.*

She could destroy it right now. Isi had not believed the power for creating fire was contained in the vellum, just the knowledge of how to do so. But what could happen to Enna's gift with fire if the vellum was not just hidden but reduced to ashes? It felt like a worthy risk. But she hesitated, read over it one last time, rubbed the vellum between her fingers. She sighed a surrendering sigh, pulled in the loose heat

from the fire, and lit the vellum. A corner burst gold as flames crawled up its side. She held the far corner until the bite of the heat was blistering, then threw it on the ground, stomping out the ashes before the ground cloth lit.

And then she closed her eyes and just felt. Cold air swirled around her; then a stab of heat came in from the fire through the flap. Wrapped around that heat thread was the paler heat from the guards and bare wisps from the nearest trees. The hollow place in her chest throbbed, ready to take it in at her will. The vellum was gone, and nothing had changed.

She rubbed her forehead and thought of being angry or upset, or even relieved, but she could not pretend surprise. She had wanted to show herself that she was willing to give it up, just as Isi had been willing to cut her hair and risk her life. But she admitted to herself that she had not really believed burning the vellum could take away the knowledge that seemed to be branded into her mind and mingled with her skin, until she could not remember what life had been before fire.

From what Enna could hear through the tent walls, there was no end to the wine Isi brought, or it was particularly strong, for the soldiers seemed to get drunker by the moment. Even Enna's tent guards were sitting on the ground now, laughing and hooting at some slurred joke. She heard someone say "Bayern" and leaned forward to listen better.

"They won't know to run . . . to run or what."

"Bayern don't know terror till they have met Captain S-SSileph."

"It is Tiedan leading the army to the capital. Sileph's just going to Fedorthal."

"I know, I know." The speaker began to giggle. "But isn't the plan mav . . . marvl . . . fine? To attack some out-of-the-way place like Fedorthal and draw their army there, only to send our biggest force to the capital when no one's looking."

"Who would suspect us to march right on their capital? I wish I were going."

"You would be, you cowherd, if you had not been on watch duty twice when her highness the fire-witch there had come a-burning."

Enna stood, pacing again in the small space. Sileph harassing Fedorthal, Bayern responding and leaving the capital exposed, Tiedan on the march to the capital. She had to act. Sileph had seduced her with his people-speaking lies, but maybe Bayern was not lost after all. Besides, what of the augury? It said that Bayern would win, but with Enna's help. For a time, she had forgotten.

This was Enna's chance to set things right. Perhaps she could still catch Isi, warn her, and be back before they noticed and harmed Razo and Finn.

The soldiers outside had grown quiet. She peered out the flap. The guard and three soldiers she could see were asleep, the others gone. Scarcely believing it could be so easy, Enna slipped out into the chilly night.

The camp was quiet. Most of the soldiers stationed there must have marched with Sileph or Tiedan. If only she could catch up with Isi. There was little chance of finding Razo and Finn, freeing them, and getting to Isi in time, so she would have to get back to her tent before anyone noticed she had left. Trying to look casual and still not make noise, Enna picked her way through the sleeping bodies and toward the edge of camp.

"Stop there, fire-witch." Two soldiers returned carrying a pot of stew. Their cheeks were a rough red. "Just where are you so set on going?"

"To the privy," she said, nearly spitting at them with the words.

The heat from the soldiers and their fire was crashing against her skin as though it sensed her anxiety and wanted to aid her. Suddenly, everything looked like fodder. For a time, Sileph had tricked her into forgetting that Tira was her enemy. But the fire needed fuel, and she needed an enemy, and the two had converged once again. The urge had not been so powerful since the night she burned the gallows.

"Not without us, you don't. We will be glad to help you."

One of the soldiers grabbed her arm with a sickly smile. She pushed him off. He stepped closer, gripping the neck of her dress and pulling her face close to his. His breath was thick with the sweet, rotten-fruit smell of drunkenness. His hands were hot.

"Don't provoke me, my lady fire. All I need is one reason to kill you right now and call it an accident."

"Get your hands off me, pig-boy," she said through her teeth.

"That is a pretty good reason." He shoved her back and took up his sword.

As he raised his sword for a neck swipe and the other drew his sword, Enna pulled in heat and sent it into both their hilts. With a painful gasp they dropped their swords. Enna sucked the heat out of the metal to cool them, sent it into the still blazing fire, and picked up both swords. She held one aloft, the blade pointed at the neck of the nearest guard, and said in a low voice, "Call out or dash away and I'll either run you through or burn you up, whichever's easier."

Enna did not know how to use a sword and did not dare start a fire lest it spread and warn Razo and Finn's guards, but the drunken men believed her threat, nodding with frightened wide eyes. One took a step backward, slipped onto his rear, then looked at her as though she had made him do it. With a sword, Enna cut a length of rope off the nearest tent and told one to tie up the other. Then she cut more rope, letting the tent slump down, and tied up the second man. She hacked two pieces of fabric from the tent for gags and, smiling, turned to leave the camp.

And smelled burning cloth. The tent had fallen into the fire pit and was blazing.

Razo and Finn. Their guards had orders to kill them at the first sign of unusual fire. In panic, she sucked the heat out of the burning tent, enough to extinguish the flames, and with the heat raging in her chest looked around wildly for a place to send it. Nothing. She let it go on the bare ground, and the fire burst in a brief, bright explosion.

"What's all this?" The inebriated soldiers around her tent stirred at the sudden pop of her blaze. She was tugging the fallen tent away from the campfire, but it had lit again. One of her guards stood and began to shout, "Fire, fire!"

"Hush up. There's nothing. It's fine."

But he continued to shout. Across the camp, Enna heard the answering calls from sentries: *"Fire!"* She cursed, abandoned the tent to its flames, and ran toward the center of camp. Two of the soldiers roused and called after her, "Stop there! Fire-witch escaped!" She heard swords ringing free of sheaths. She could not stop to deal with them now. With a backward glance she sent fire into their swords.

The screams that followed stopped her cold. She looked back to see a soldier beating at the flames that clawed up his tunic. She rushed back, sucking the heat from that fire and setting the ground before him ablaze.

"I didn't mean . . . " Her stomach turned to see she had broken that rule again, as she had with the sentry, as she had tried with Isi. Keeping her promise felt like her only safeguard against losing herself completely to the fire. She looked around—soldiers yelled across camp to one another, one tent was crushed to black remains fuming smoke, one beside it split with fresh flames. The soldier lay before her, his tunic still smoking, and he watched her with angry, fearful eyes.

"I'm sorry," she said to him. "But Razo and Finn, and Bayern, they're more important." She fought a wave of nausea at her resolve as she turned and ran, but she knew now that to save them and stop the war, she would have to break all her rules, even the one that killed Leifer. Eventually she would have to surrender to the fire.

She raced through the tented camp to the town. To add to the confusion, she scorched the tents in passing. Wherever sentries or soldiers tried to stop her, she sent fire, hopefully into their blades and bows, but she did not look back.

The first building she reached appeared to be an old barn. Only one young guard stood before its bolted door, staring at her with wide eyes, holding up his sword in defense. She heated his sword and he dropped it, his expression barely changing, as though he had been expecting that. She held up her two swords to his throat, but they were too heavy, so she dropped one and held the other with both hands.

"Where're the two Bayern boys kept?"

The soldier shook his head. *Burn him*, prompted the fire. The excitement of burning was simmering in her, heating her up for more action. She felt invincible and dangerous and at the edge of surrender, the means to burn more than she ever had before. But she resisted, for now.

"I think you should run now," she said, and he did not delay.

Inside, several taken Bayern women and some townsmen stood in the center of the barn, fear in their faces. Enna recognized the blue-eyed woman.

"Where're my two friends?"

"In the old merchant's house," said the woman.

"Show me." Enna took her arm and hurried her out of the barn. Behind them, the Bayern prisoners fled, two picking up the swords Enna and the guard had dropped.

Enna let the woman lead her through town while she scanned for soldiers. She continued to send flames into tents, wagons, anything that was Tiran made. She was not conscious of having to pull the heat from anywhere—it seemed to follow her now, hover around her like a swarm of wasps. The woman struggled to loose her arm from Enna's.

"What're you doing?" Enna asked. "I need your help."

"Yes, I'll help, girl," said the woman, rubbing one arm with the other, "but you're so hot."

Enna glanced down at herself. Her clothes appeared to be steaming faintly in the cold air. She nodded. "Lead the way."

They ran to the house and found it guarded by four soldiers. One held his sword to the throat of a bound, blindfolded Finn. Enna did not hesitate. While still advancing, she set fire to three soldiers' leggings. They screamed and dropped to the ground, trying at once to put out the fire and move farther away. The soldier holding Finn blinked.

"Kill him and you're dead," said Enna. "Drop your sword and I'll let you run."

He blinked again, let his sword fall, and scurried down the dark street.

Enna ripped off the blindfold and sawed through the ropes around Finn's wrists and ankles. They fell, revealing raw, red welts. Enna hissed at the sight, and that place in her chest yawned, aching for heat. She met Finn's eyes. He would have a scar down his cheek when a cut there healed, and his eye was green with an old bruise, but he smiled.

"Hello, Enna," he said, his voice creaking from disuse.

"Hello, Finn," she said softly. The heat around her dissolved for a moment. She felt her heart beat in that emptiness, and for the first time in weeks she felt something like good, clean hope. Shouts from down the street were getting closer.

"Razo?"

"Inside," he said.

"More guards?"

Finn shook his head. Enna pushed them both in the door and out of view of any archers, gave Finn her sword to loose Razo, and turned to the blue-eyed woman.

"Have you heard anything?" she asked.

"Sileph's army marched three days ago, Tiedan's yesterday. Don't know where Sileph went, but I heard Tiedan is headed for the capital. They're marching west of Ostekin."

Enna smiled. "You've heard quite a bit. Thanks. Now we could use horses."

The woman pointed to the near end of camp.

"You should get out of here, and let others out if you can," said Enna.

"All right," she said, but stopped to put her fingers on Enna's forehead. She frowned. "Be careful," she said, and ran out of the barn.

Enna turned to see Razo and Finn, both armed with swords, both looking skinny, sickly, and anxious, but also a little pleased.

"Oh," she said, "they've been so cruel."

Razo shrugged, then winced in pain. "We're all right. You look pretty good, pretty well fed and all. That's a nice dress."

"It's new," she said, despising herself. "I'm sorry, Razo, Finn. I'm just so sorry."

Razo shrugged, then winced again. Something in his manner reminded her fiercely of Leifer. She nearly sighed in contentment just to be speaking with Finn and Razo again. She had thought she was alone, but she knew now that she had been wrong. Razo, Isi, and Finn felt like her last family, and one that she was determined to keep.

"You've got to stop shrugging," she said, almost laughing. "What happened to your shoulder?"

"It was that captain, uh, Silver or something. He came in one day, mad as a chased hornet, and just took to beating us."

Enna blinked slowly. "Sileph did."

Razo nodded. "Oh, I'm all right. Alive. Just pulled my arm out of joint or something. He hit Finn harder, huh?"

Finn just gave a half smile and looked at his boots.

"Who was the third boy who came with you, the one killed?" she asked.

Razo and Finn glanced at each other.

"Don't know what you mean," said Razo. "We two came alone. Talone didn't even know."

"But wasn't there . . . Sileph said . . ." Enna stopped. It had been another lie, of course, told to make her a little more unsure, work on her to believe that Razo and Finn had been assassins. Enna squinted, seeing Finn turn a sickly yellow, then noticed that the yellowish shade was everywhere. The heat was suddenly awful, and she realized that she was enraged. She spoke slowly with forced calm, almost afraid that if she spoke with her real anger, her very words could scorch them.

"We're getting horses and riding north. I've got to finish this."

From outside, they could hear soldiers shouting. The fire blazed inside her; she resisted and immediately felt her body cringe and loosen. Her knees gave and she slumped. Finn was beside her, his arm supporting her.

"Easy, Enna, you all right?"

She nodded and the room wobbled. "It's worse, Finn. I started to let go out there, burning people and all. The fire wants to keep going; it wants all of me." She swallowed and felt her dry throat scrape against itself. "I've got to stop for a minute, so I can last until we find the army."

Finn set her carefully against the wall. "Sit easy. We'll take care of them."

"No worries, Enna-girl," said Razo, raising his sword with an eagerness that belied his tired, bruised body.

The door thrust open and five soldiers entered. Enna managed to burn a few swords out of hands before she concentrated on letting go of the heat, on breathing clear air. Behind the swirls of yellow and orange, she heard Finn and Razo fighting. She had no doubt they would win. They had to win now that she knew what she must do.

After a time, Finn's mild voice said, "We're ready, Enna."

She opened her eyes and nodded. "Let's go."

Hours later, they rode in the wake of the army. The frozen grass and wheat stubble was well trampled, the area scarred with the black pockmarks of fire pits. Sometimes, from far ahead, Enna could feel a tremendous heat. The cold night and the wind of riding fast had cooled her off. Now the rim of the sun was blazing over the horizon, and the promise of battle and the heat of hundreds of bodies began to taunt her. The hollowness in her chest throbbed like a wound.

"Let's skirt them if we can," she said.

Razo and Finn nodded. They had managed to scavenge some armor and two shields in Eylbold. Finn's helm made him look much older. Razo's was ill-fitting and tended to slip forward over his brow, and he reminded Enna of a small boy playing at dress-up. She cringed at the thought of his getting killed.

"On second thought, I'll go alone," she said. "You two go straight to the capital or Ostekin—whichever you think best—and warn."

Finn and Razo glanced at each other.

"Enna," Razo said gently, as though talking to an ill person or a child. She noticed he did not call her Enna-girl, and the abbreviation seemed to warn of something ending. "I think it's a bit late for caution. Scouts must've seen them by now, and the king's reinforcements'll come as soon as they can."

"Still, I think, just in case—"

"You aim to stop 'em," said Finn. "We're your guards, Enna. We're staying with you till the end."

"All right." Her voice squeaked as she spoke. Tired, cold, thirsty, she did not think she was capable of much emotion, but Finn's words pulled some out of her as easily as a showman tugs a scarf from his sleeve. The entire world seemed to be rushing down an icy slope, but she felt resolved. It was the price of victory, and the price of her crimes. But the unsinged part of her wished differently for Razo and Finn.

"It's not over, Enna," said Finn. His expression was concerned, and something more, afraid maybe, though she knew he was not fearing the fight.

"I don't want it to be," said Enna. "I wish . . ."

She left her wish hanging and urged her mount forward.

They rode east of the trampled earth, close enough to Ostekin that they could have ridden there in an hour's time, but they did not spare it. Enna could feel the constant pressure of heat to her left, where the army marched just out of sight. She ached with it. Her chest arched and trembled, anxious for the fire. She found she could resist for now, though it cost her some pain.

Once they passed two scouts heading east. Razo tore after them when they began to flee, hollering that despite the Tiran garb it was he, Razo.

"Unbelievable," said one of the young scouts. "Razo, you are alive. Talone said no chance the Tiran could kill you."

Razo puffed up visibly. "Indeed. What's happening, Temo?"

"We haven't known much these weeks. They razed a lot of our scout network."

Enna swallowed, remembering the houses and wagons she had burned and the Bayern scout with an arrow in his chest.

"A couple of days ago," Temo continued, "the king sent a force to stop an invasion of Fedorthal. Then the queen came back from somewhere saying she'd heard on the wind of a greater army marching north."

"To the capital," said Finn.

"That's right. The king had time to pull his army back. They'll meet before the city by tomorrow, I shouldn't wonder. We're off with messages for reinforcements."

The other scout grimaced. "Looks bloody. Lots of Tiran."

They saluted and gave rein to their restless mounts, hurrying off to the east.

Enna, Razo, and Finn had to stop past midday to rest the horses by a partly frozen stream. The three lay down on the banks close together for warmth, Enna snug in the middle, and slept for a few hours. Near sundown they rode again and through the night, stopping once again for an hour's huddled rest. Finn lay against her back, his arm over hers. She tried to feel hope at his touch, but instead of warming her, his heat reminded her that there was burning to do.

They rose and rode again. Only a couple of hours later, in the murky light of winter dawn, they heard battle.

Enna led them a little farther north and up a gentle slope. The noise became deafening. In the valley just a few hours' ride from the capital, two armies collided. This battle was two or three times the size of the battle of Ostekin where Leifer had died, and it seemed to Enna that the blue-clothed Tiran soldiers outnumbered the Bayern by at least three to one. She felt her mount shiver.

"What do we do?" said Razo.

Enna rode farther until they were a hundred paces to the side of the Tiran central force. Finn pulled out his sword and readied his shield. Razo followed. The sun crested the horizon behind them and touched their backs like a push from a warm hand. Despite the heat that hung about her like a poisonous vapor, Enna felt clammy and chilled. She knew she could not turn back now, but she trembled to begin.

"I miss you, Leifer," she said softly. Without further hesitation, she looked at the nearest grouping of Tiran soldiers, pulled in heat, and set them on fire.

At first she tried to go slowly, wait for the heat to gather again, not give up control too quickly, but the deeper she swam, the more desire she felt to just be pulled by the current. The fire begged, the lake of soldiers moved and shimmered, seemingly restless for their deaths. *Surrender.* So before the hollowness in her chest could turn cold and hard, before her skin numbed to the heat, she let go. It felt like dropping the reins on a wild mount, like pushing away from shore. She had been prepared for the horror, but she had not anticipated the joy.

Her horse began to prance and whine. She slipped from his back and onto her knees and continued to burn. It seemed a great while before men broke from their ranks to come after her. Perhaps Enna's Tiran dress and the boys' Tiran armor had fooled them for a time. Enna was conscious of the closer sounds of swordplay, but she did not move her eyes from the battlefield.

Then something new. Enna sent fire not into a man's hair or clothes, the dead parts of him, but right inside him, into his bones. She stopped for the first time, stumbled away, and emptied her stomach. She had not realized before that the living could also be fuel, and she felt betrayed by the fire, its whispers justifying its existence because it burned only dead things. Lies. But to quit would be like stopping the water after swallowing. She turned back to the battle.

The burning field was mesmerizing. The heat from the sun, from the fires, the horses and living men, from Razo and Finn, it all met in her and became power. It was strange and beautiful how destruction and life were bound together in fire, and she marveled that she had never thought of it before. Her eyes stung, tears for the beauty of it scalded away before they could drop. Was that why she cried? For the beauty? And something else. Pain. She remembered that people cry for beauty and pain, and seeing both together was almost unbearable. She found she was on her stomach now, propped up by her shaking arms, straining her eyes at the field. She ripped apart her sleeves so that her bared arms could better feel the touch of heat.

Nearly a tenth of the field was on fire now, and the untouched pools of blue-coated Tiran seemed to be moving wrong, like a dammed stream. They were gushing out of the way of the fires. They were fleeing. *Burn them,* she thought, *before they're gone.* Again and again she filled up her chest with heat.

Then a noise like a twig underfoot. Something inside her cracked, and she felt the heat bleed into her, inside her chest, through her blood.

Now it's over, she thought, and she saw in her mind the hard, blackened body of Leifer crumpled on the battlefield. At last, here was burning pain without beauty, and it felt just. The world dimmed, the sounds of battle were muffled and far away. She felt herself fall forward, heard as from a distance her own cry. Everything seemed to be slipping away.

But before she was completely gone, a new sensation—wind. Cool, late-winter wind rolled over her skin, on her face, over her arms, into her lungs, touching her like a fall of water to wash away the grime. It was cool like a tree shade and carried with it the scents of snow, fox, pine, and hay. Wind reminded her of Isi, and Enna wondered if she were near. She thought she heard Finn say, "Hold on, Enna."

She breathed in as deep as her own roots, and when she breathed out again there was no pain, just sleep.

Part Four

Friend

he sleep now was different from that of the king's-tongue days. Then the drug had smothered her in numbness and loss of will. Now, even unconscious, Enna found herself fighting. The struggle with the fire became a struggle to survive.

She idly thought that she was still lying on the rise over the battlefield because the sun was so very hot, burning her right through her clothing. It seemed to always be high noon. Sometimes she thought that she awoke, opened her eyes, and saw her body was a charred clump of hard ash. *Nightmare.* She recoiled into deeper, imageless sleep.

After a time, the struggle included a fight not just to live, but not to wake. In that faraway place where she could think, she feared that if she woke, she would die. She did not want to open her eyes and see the valley and the remnants of her burning. But awareness came closer and closer. She was cognizant of people touching her, speaking around her, placing a cup to her lips.

King's-tongue, she thought intuitively, and spat out the water. She creaked open an eye and saw that she lay in her old room in the palace. A physician stood over her, said something soothing, and brought the water back to her mouth. She drank.

She was conscious at first for only a scattering of moments. Sometimes she opened her eyes and saw that the room was dark and the windows full of night, and she admitted to herself that the heat came from inside her and not the sun after all. Often Isi was there, asleep on a sofa or reading by candlelight.

Slowly, painfully, Enna at last allowed herself to fully wake. The room was quiet. Only Isi was present, sitting in her chair with a book, twirling one short lock around a finger. Enna took a deep, shuddering breath.

Isi looked up.

"I'm still alive," said Enna, her voice raspy and without melody.

"Barely," said Isi. Her smile was friendly, but there were dark patches under her eyes.

Enna thought of the animal worker days in the city when Isi wore a hat all the time to hide her hair and identity and only Enna in all of Bayern knew that Isi was the foreign princess. She remembered Isi by Eylbold firelight, her hair chopped short, telling the Tiran guards the story of the prince and the dragon. She remembered Isi standing outside Ostekin, her hair long and loose, and her expression of horror—no, of sadness—when Enna unleashed a torrent of flaming heat.

Enna took another deep breath, wanting to say something, to explain. Her breath caught in her lungs, tightened, and turned into a sob. She covered her face and let the tears come, then cried out in pain when the sob shook a cracked place inside her chest. She remembered that injury on the battlefield, taking in more heat, feeling the hollow place get so hot, too hot, and snap. A flood of heat followed and even now continued to leak into her blood. She was changed. The fire was not gone—it would never leave. Neither would the images of that last battle, seemingly burned into the underside of her eyelids, always there when she closed her eyes.

Isi moved her chair closer and turned the wet cloth on Enna's forehead over to the cooler side. Enna held her breath until she could control the desire to cry, then spoke with a stunned, sleepy calm.

"I killed. Hundreds of people. I burned them alive."

"It was war," said Isi.

"It was me," Enna said bitterly. "You were right about the fire, about its power being too much for one person. But you should know, nothing forced me to do it. I chose to . . . to . . ." She lifted up her hands and saw the smooth, natural skin. "Why aren't I burnt up?"

"You nearly were. I heard rumor of you on the wind, and then I cooled you. The wind had to keep at you, like putting out a hay fire that keeps relighting."

"Ah," said Enna, remembering.

They were quiet a moment. Enna studied the way strips of light from behind the curtains painted the wall.

"It's over?" she asked at last.

"It's over," said Isi.

"And?"

"We won, more or less. Our land is ours again. It will be. There's still some . . . reconstruction needed."

Enna nodded. "Razo and Finn?"

"Razo's going to live, but he took a sword in the ribs, on the hill beside you. He's still in bed. I believe Finn's fine. To tell the truth, I've been here with you for days and haven't let anyone else in. I can go find him. He's probably hovering somewhere nearby."

"Don't," said Enna.

"All right."

Enna thought of Finn sneaking into a Tiran camp ready to kill an army to get her free; of Finn bound, gagged, beaten by a jealous Sileph because of a look that passed between them; of Finn asleep beside her, his arm over hers. She had loved Sileph while he and Razo rotted, she had attacked Bayern, and she had slaughtered hundreds of people, and still Finn would forgive her. That knowledge felt like a needle pressed into her heart.

She watched Isi's hand straighten a creased page of her book.

"I know now why Leifer died," said Enna. "Part of it was

just what happens when you use that much fire, but part of it was choice. He surrendered to it and burned big, but then knew he couldn't live to see what he'd done, so he let himself burn out. It hurts, but not as much as seeing what you've made. I would've done the same as Leifer." Her chin trembled and her face tightened to stop the tears.

Isi sighed and took Enna's hand. "I want you to understand something, Enna, so listen to me. Are you listening? It's what I was trying to tell you that night . . . before you left Ostekin the last time. I've talked with Razo about you and I've read a bit, and I think no one could've come out of this as well as you. Between Sileph's power with words and the fire inside you aching for a reason to blaze, how could you resist? And yet you did for so long. Only Enna, stubborn, unyielding Enna. I know you've only done what you thought best."

Enna nodded. She would love a reason to give up the guilt. But she remembered the nascent flame leaving her body and shooting into a soldier, and before it fully became fire and left her awareness, she felt it enter his flesh, enter the soft center of his bones, the speed of his blood, and there burst into fire. She shivered from deep inside.

When Enna did not speak for a time, Isi said, "You didn't expect to live until now, did you?"

Enna shook her head.

"You still might not." Isi leaned forward, meeting Enna's eyes. "You're on fire, En. You've been living inside a fever now for over two weeks. The physicians don't know what to do. Is it just that you want to . . . burn out? Can you decide not to?"

Enna breathed in and winced at the tearing pain it made in her chest. "I don't know, Isi. I don't know how. It used to be that I had to find bits of heat and pull them to me, but near the end, the heat began to find me. It was like it recognized me, sought me out. It took all my concentration to keep it at bay. But on the battlefield, something in me . . . broke. I can't hold it back anymore. It's leaking inside me, all into me."

"Yes," Isi said thoughtfully.

"Is that how it is with you? Did the wind start to find you, stick to you, and you couldn't push it back?"

Isi looked about to respond, but they were interrupted by a physician bringing Enna food and a fresh cool cloth for her head. While he ministered to Enna, Isi stared at her book, though her eyes did not move across the lines. Enna slumbered, and when she woke again, she opened her eyes to a man standing over her. Instinctively she hunched deeper into the pillows.

Isi stood up. "Enna, it's Geric."

Enna's bleary eyes resolved the images before her, and she saw Geric standing by her bed, his brow furrowed.

"Should I go?" he asked.

"No, no," said Enna, trying to sit up. Isi put a hand on her shoulder that told her to relax. "You're fine, Geric."

"I think you must've had a rough time," he said, frowning. She smiled weakly. "So've you, I guess."

"Geric," said Isi, "I was just coming to tell you. I think I know what Enna needs to heal. I'm taking her back to her house in the Forest. There's nothing more the physicians can do. I've asked a packhorse be prepared with food supplies for us, and Avlado and Enna's Merry are saddled and waiting."

Isi waited, smiling a little as though fearing his reaction.

"I'll go, too," he said.

Isi shook her head. "There's too much for you to do right now. The king can't leave. I'll be back as soon as she's better."

Geric pressed his lips together. "You're right, but I'm sending an escort at least."

Isi hesitated, then said, "Fine." She kissed his cheek, his lips, and then they embraced. At their affection, Enna felt her heart reach and long for something. *Sileph*, came the unbidden thought.

"Oh," said Geric, squeezing her tighter, "I'll miss you, my yellow lady. Don't be long."

Isi pulled away and nodded. Her eyes were wet. It made Enna wonder how long Isi intended to be gone.

"Don't worry about me." Isi smiled and kissed him again.

Enna thought she was well enough to ride upright, and they left the city in the brightness of an early-spring morning, so unlike the last times she had ridden Merry over frozen midnight fields. She was happy to see the mare again and relieved she had made it home safely, but Enna could not enjoy the ride. A sensation like an empty walnut shell bounced in her chest. Heat clawed like rough fingernails on her skin.

Entering the Forest again was a skin-shuddering relief. The green buds and needles and creaking sounds were as familiar as the smell of her own bed, yet she felt like a stranger. She wiped her brow with the back of her hand. Everything seemed flammable, even her.

A day later, when they reached Enna's little house, Isi released the escort from their duty. "We're safe here. Tell the king we'll send word when we're ready to return, but not to bother checking for at least three weeks. I'm certain it will take longer than that."

"Three weeks is long, my queen," said the head guard.

"Two, then," said Isi. "Go on."

Enna frowned. The guards might be oblivious, but Enna could always tell when Isi was lying. Whatever Isi intended, it most likely would take much longer than two weeks.

Isi put Enna in her bed. The familiar smells of pinewood and chicken feathers reminded her so suddenly and profoundly of Leifer, she sat up coughing at the tightness in her chest. She breathed deeply and waved off Isi's concerned look.

Isi set up some split wood in the hearth. When she turned away to look for flint, Enna set it blazing.

Isi looked at her with creases around her eyes. "Should you . . . ?"

Enna shrugged. "The heat is constantly on me and inside me now. It can't hurt to expel a little."

"But not too much," said Isi.

Enna watched the tame little fire in the hearth, the pleasant ripples of orange and gold. The sound of heat-snapping wood was homey, like the click of knitting needles. She felt like that fire—it seemed lively enough, but eventually the fire would burn through the logs and go out completely. She already felt worn down to embers.

"I brought you here with an idea," said Isi. "I've done more reading while you were sick. Yasid."

"That kingdom to the south," said Enna.

Isi nodded. "More than one book mentions a people there called the *tata-rook*, the fire worshippers. Some claim that the *tata-rook* have a relationship with fire. If it's common in Yasid, they must have a secret for using it and not letting it destroy them."

Enna watched the flames rise suddenly higher, and she thought how the hotter and brighter a fire burns, the faster it burns out. "We're going there."

"Yes," said Isi. "Soon. Tomorrow. Before Geric . . . before anyone knows we've gone. We can't go riding down there with an escort of fifty soldiers. There are roving bands of Tiran still, and with numbers we'd attract attention. If we want to avoid notice and have speed, our best chance is just the two of us alone. And if trouble finds us, I believe we can handle ourselves."

Enna pulled her gaze away from the fire. "That could take three months. Or four."

Isi nodded. "Or more."

"So, you'll sneak away, leave Geric, travel for months, just on the chance that the fire worshippers might have a cure?"

Isi blinked and said simply, "Yes."

"No," said Enna. She did not believe that getting rid of the heat, the fever, the desire, could be so simple. Even the thought of trying caused her legs to shake. "You don't even know if it will work, and I could die on the way, and you'd be alone and months away from home and you could get hurt—"

"Look at me, queen's maiden," said Isi. Enna stopped and looked. Isi was intent, even a little angry. "There's no debate here. You owe me. This is what I want—I want you to live. I order you to live. Do you understand?"

Enna nodded. Isi had never ordered her in anything. Her instinct was to fight back, but she found she did not want to this time.

They departed in the dewy morning. Isi had risen early to saddle the mounts and prepare the packhorse. She had managed to bring many bulging bags of food from the palace and a small tent like the one Enna had slept in with Razo and Finn.

Enna's neighbor Doda stood in the yard to see them off. Isi had given her pleading instructions to put off the soldiers as best she could, and when the king came—for Isi was certain he would come—to tell him what she was doing and that they would be back before harvest.

The first few days they rode under the Forest canopy. The wet, green smells, the growing things, the ceaseless chatter of birds and squirrels, all seemed fresh and new. She had spent far too long in a small winter tent, and even longer subject to the impatient, ravenous desires of fire. She thought how it was the opposite of the slow life of the forest, lichen growing, moss, mushroom, one thing living off another. A tree did not have to die to support a nest.

Enna was battling constantly to restrain the heat and slow the fever's rise, and she had little energy for conversation. She soon realized that Isi was nearly as troubled as she. Enna watched her, imagining all Isi heard from the Forest breezes, and wondered if the voices of birds or the warm tones of her horse in her mind comforted her or added to the confusion.

At night they camped off the trails. Isi thought it best to avoid people in case they were recognized and word was sent back to the capital before they were out of Bayern. The winds helped direct her on paths where no people lived, and once they crossed the southern border of Bayern, she had a map sketch from the trader's book they could follow.

After one such day of long travel and silence, they set up camp inside a hollow made by the twining roots of two ancient firs. It was early spring, and the night air was a chill on their skin.

Isi was drinking a tea that smelled like steeped hay. She offered Enna a cup.

"It might help to resist the burning," said Isi.

"No," said Enna, "I'm done drinking teas and numbing control."

Isi nodded. "It helps me—a little. I don't dare take it during the day. I need to hear the wind to find our way. It's not so bad out here where we're alone. People are so much more complicated than trees and birds. But with it I sleep a little easier."

Enna shivered, despite the fire and the constant burn of her skin. She threw pieces of dead grass at the fire and got angry that they did not fly straight.

"Isi, I can't pretend that we're just great friends as always and go on. I tried to set you on fire, and I started burning against Bayern, and you'd be right to hate me."

Isi looked at the flames a long while, and Enna found she was holding her breath. After a time, Isi looked up.

"It did hurt," she said.

Enna shut her eyes against the ache.

"I didn't hate you, Enna, but you know, it took me so long to trust people again after being betrayed before. Then I remembered that it was you who got me to trust again a couple of years back, and that was for a reason. And I remembered that Leifer had burned you, and you forgave him."

"But why, Isi? Why do so much?"

Isi seemed stunned by the question. "You're the best friend I've ever had. When I was completely alone, you were there. I know you must feel so alone right now, and the thought wounds me. But I care mostly because I'm selfish. I don't want to lose you."

"I don't deserve you," said Enna.

"You've had a bad time of it, Enna. Be easier on yourself. I think about all you've been through . . . I had no idea what it must be like to have the world of fire nipping at you. I knew you were in deep with the fire, but I had no idea until I went into Eylbold that night that you were also in the clutches of a very dangerous man. I have a feeling it's extraordinary that you did resist him as much as you did. After a month alone with a man like that, so skilled in people-speaking, I imagine nearly any other person would've licked his boots at command."

Thinking of Sileph still made Enna feel odd, put together wrong, like a loosely stitched doll. She shifted uncomfortably.

"That was a brave thing you did, coming to Eylbold," said Enna. "I was . . . You made me better with your words."

"I would've been a poor friend not to attempt it. As I recall, a few years ago you stormed through a raging battle just to get by my side so I wouldn't feel alone."

"Did I?" Enna raised her eyebrows and smiled. "Yes, well, that wasn't half-bad, was it?"

"No, not half. That next day after the fighting was the best day of my life."

Enna grinned. "I remember you about smacked me when I suggested we call the newly formed Forest band the yellow band after you."

Isi rolled her eyes. "Oh, yes." She started to giggle. "And you remember when Razo got his javelin from the king, how his hands shook so hard he could hardly hold it?"

Enna laughed, too. "He had fish eyes; he didn't dare blink in case it'd all go away."

They laughed much harder than the memory was funny because it felt good to laugh. At first the shaking hurt Enna, and she felt that place in her chest shift uneasily like shards of broken bone scraping one another. But then something found its right place, the pain eased, and the laughter felt more natural.

That night for the first time since the battle, Enna did not worry when she went to sleep that she would not wake up again. The next day the travel was a little easier to bear. On rainy evenings, they set up the tent early and huddled together under its thin eave. Enna found her voice to tell the story she could not before. What Leifer's death was like, how she felt as though someone had grabbed her insides and ripped her like paper. And why she had read the vellum, how the knowledge had felt more important and beautiful than anything in all the warring world.

She told Isi about Finn and his whispered confession in

the tent at night. And she whispered Sileph's name at last, though it hurt her to admit that she had fallen for his words and lies and looks. She could barely confess that her heart still felt twisted and pained even at the thought of him.

And Isi always listened, never told Enna she had been foolish, never said hollow things like "You'll be all right." Enna knew that Isi had seen her own father killed, had lost her family, her homeland, her beloved horse Falada, and still, even in her joy with Geric, she carried an edge of that sadness. Isi saw Enna's struggle and her sadness, and she understood.

Then one evening the talk stilled, and drowsily, they found themselves playing with wind and fire. Enna set a pile of dead pine needles crackling, and Isi flung a suffocating wind to blow out the fire. Enna pushed out more heat and anticipated Isi's lighter wind that blazed the fire higher. Enna added heat, Isi added breath, and the fire grew. Each seemed to sense what the other would do in advance, and they worked together like an old couple long accustomed to shared chores. Then, when Isi pulled in a stronger wind, the kind that would take the air away from the fire and kill it, Enna stopped her short. She sent a rush of heat against the swoop of air, and the heat changed the air, split the wind into pieces, hot, erratic gusts that blew themselves away.

"A neat trick," said Isi.

Enna smiled. "It makes me wonder what else we could do."

✳   ✳   ✳

The next day they crossed Bayern's border. In Bayern, they had often passed within sight of farmhouses and close enough to Bayern hundred-bands on border patrol that Isi could sense them on the wind. But now they passed through unclaimed land. The grass was coarser, the ground stony, and there were few settlements. Even so, the risk of running into roaming bands of their recently defeated enemies was a dangerous possibility. Whenever Enna found herself wondering of Sileph, she quickly pushed his voice and face out of her mind. Isi looked back over her shoulder more and more. Twice Isi said she thought a man on horseback followed, someone familiar to her she could not name.

Some days past the border, Enna and Isi were filling their bottles at a stream. Isi stood up suddenly and turned, looking like a woodpecker listening at a trunk.

"What is it?" said Enna.

"Men." Isi opened her hands, listening to the wind curl through her fingers. "Not the single horseman—two different men. They're near. The wind was going north, so I didn't realize until now—"

A man's voice interrupted her. "There, now, look at that."

Enna saw two men ride up, both with at least a month of beard growth and sporting somewhat tattered Tiran uniforms. One seemed familiar, perhaps a guard she had seen on one of her raids or even in the Eylbold camp.

"Well, they are not rabbits, but they will do just fine. Three horses, some supplies, and two little girls to add to the treasure." He smiled at Enna and winked. "Hello there, pretty girl."

"Go away." Enna meant to sound commanding, but it came out sounding a bit bored. The tall man laughed. Isi took Merry and the packhorse and hooked their reins onto the strong arms of a shrub. It was then that Enna realized they would not avoid this without a fight.

"Well, well, Pilad, looks like we found ourselves a Bayern girl. One of them is, anyway," said the tall, more talkative soldier.

The one called Pilad did not seem capable of smiling. He leered at Enna, and his hands fumbled at his sword hilt anxiously. "Yes, that is fine. You there, girls, come on with us, now. It's up to you if we catch you easy or hard."

Isi stepped up beside Enna. They looked at each other and smiled a little.

"We're not running, pig-boys, as you can see," said Enna, the tiredness in her voice edged with laughter, "but I think you'd best run yourselves if you want your skulls to keep a good hold on your hair."

The tall man looked at her, stunned, then turned to his companion and guffawed. The other laughed, too, but without smiling. Enna and Isi exchanged glances again. Isi smirked.

"I don't understand," said Pilad. "Why do they look all giggly? Do they have warriors hidden in the brush somewhere?"

The other drew his sword. "Let's take them before their companions return."

He started to ride forward. Isi took Enna's hand, and Enna knew exactly what to do. She sent a spark into the brambling ground before the advancing rider. Even before it flamed, Isi seemed to know where Enna would send the spark, and she fanned it with the wind. The rider's steed reared, neighing in fear. Prodded by the wind, the fire rushed and crackled until it completely encircled both riders. Enna replenished the circle with more fire where she felt the wind leave gaps. She did not worry about Merry. With the same certainty that she knew where Isi would send her wind, she knew Isi, through Avlado, would calm their horses.

The flames of the circle leaped over one another, clawing the air higher and higher. The men dropped their swords and tried to soothe their anxious mounts. Enna smiled at them. The fire wanted the men, their clothes, their hair, their bones and blood. It wanted to push past the wind that maintained it like a flock of sheep. But it was easier to keep control with Isi beside her in silent communion. An understanding flowed between them purer than anything she had known. Enna felt right next to Isi; the fire felt right with the wind.

At the same moment, they both knew the riders had had enough. Enna sucked the heat from the flames, and Isi's wind blew it up into the cold sky. The soldiers gaped, one seeming close to tears. Their horses stamped unhappily.

Enna glared. "I said, run."

Without hesitation, they turned their mounts and galloped north.

Isi laughed. "Well, I know I shouldn't, but I loved that. You are amazing."

"No, you are." Enna laughed from her belly and felt like crowing. The warmth from the fire, the victory, the heat around her ready for a new lighting. The laugh shook her chest. She coughed and bent over, vomiting her breakfast, seeing again the battlefield and men on fire. The memory was so real—vibrant, twisting flames, smells of smoke and burnt hair, the rolling nausea she felt at setting the inside of a man aflame. Slowly she became mindful of Isi standing behind her, rubbing her back.

"I'm sorry." Enna wiped her mouth and straightened. She slowly met Isi's eyes. "I'm so afraid, Isi, of what we'll find in Yasid, of losing this. But I don't want to kill again."

Isi nodded. They mounted the horses and turned south.

Two more weeks of travel did little to improve Enna's fever. She and Isi found themselves unable to converse during the day, both concentrating on staying upright and trying to keep the heat or voice of the wind at bay.

Isi worsened with each day in the open, and the tea worked less and less well. And besides the wind illness, Enna began to sense something else amiss in Isi. The heat from her increased. It was as though Isi had a fire burning in her middle. When Enna asked her, Isi just smiled and said, "I think I'm all right."

One night, like many others, Enna woke in the dark burning from fever. She moaned and rubbed her face, and the heat of her forehead scalded her fingertips. When the fever was this severe, she needed Isi to send a breeze to cool her off, break apart the heat that clung to her skin, and breathe in the cleansing air.

"Isi," Enna whispered.

There was a wash of orange over the dark night. When she closed her eyes, the orange pulsed and spun. The fever dimmed her other senses until only touch felt real—almost too real, sensitive and painful. Her clothes and the blanket seemed as grating as raw stone against her skin. She thought she heard noises outside, though it sounded as though her head were underwater. Sometimes in the night, Enna found Isi curled up on the ground beside Avlado or wandering around the camp, rubbing under her eyes where the dark circles never left.

Enna stumbled out of the tent and called Isi's name again. It was only then she understood that not all the heat she was feeling came from inside her. More choked the air of their camp than the horses and campfire could account for.

She could not see well for the orange fog and dim moonlight, but she spotted shapes gathered around their campsite. On the ground a few paces away from her, she thought she saw the lighter tones of what might be Isi's hair. From that direction a wind blew, brushing away the seeping heat, clearing her vision and hearing. What she saw then made her gasp and choke on the breeze.

Isi was kneeling on the ground. Behind her, a man in tattered Tiran blue held her shoulders and a naked dagger against her throat. Around the campsite stood more men, perhaps twenty, some on horseback, some dismounted. About seven held strung bows, arrows aiming at Enna. Two of the soldiers on foot she recognized as the men she had taunted and told to run. They looked nervous. No one else did.

Fools, she thought. *Why risk their lives for three horses and meager supplies?*

In a moment she could see that she could burn all the bows at once, but not without risk that the arrows would fire anyway and might still find her flesh. She could not burn the man at Isi's back without hurting Isi, but at least she could scald the dagger from his hand. And there would be wind, too, she remembered, and hoped it could take care of all the flying arrows. She had to be clever to avoid burning any more people. Visions of a smoldering battlefield swooped before her and made her shiver as though she could feel hot ash raining on her skin.

Still calculating and eyeing Isi for a clue, she said with some impatience, "Well, what do you want?"

"Just you, Enna."

Sileph stepped from behind the line of horses and into the firelight, standing close enough to Enna to reach her in two strides.

"I came back for you," he said.

is uniform was fraying at the cuffs, and his boots were covered in an inch of dried mud, but his hair was clean and combed and his face smooth shaven, as though he had prepared for their meeting. Standing before his men, she was struck again by how handsome he was and the palpable power of his presence, so unlike that of anyone she had known.

And this incredible man had searched for her, had wanted no one else. His look said that he still needed her, that he would forgive her, that his home would be her home. Her skin ached. Her neck remembered his touch.

"Enna, Enna." A sigh came up from his depths, full of sadness and struggle, and relief. "Enna, at last."

"You've been looking for me?" Her voice squeaked a little higher than normal.

"Yes," he said. "I have been running, mostly, and hoping. I said I would come back for you."

"Enna," said Isi, her voice full of warning.

Enna remembered then that Isi had a dagger against her throat and seven arrows were aimed at her own heart, but she looked back at Sileph, not quite ready to let him go.

"You, you're alive," she said lamely. "I wondered."

"Did you?" He raised his eyebrows. "Thinking of me, were you? Well, many of us did not make it through that one. I do not blame you, Enna, truly. War is brutal. I am just relieved that it is over. No matter now who won. But what has plagued me these past weeks is that you might not know, no matter the outcome, that I still wanted you."

He stepped forward, and she tensed as he put his arms around her shoulders and pulled her in. His smell engulfed her and she felt her knees wobble, but she placed her hands on his chest and pushed him back. He stepped away, though his eyes looked sad.

"Sileph," she said, trying to get an edge back in her voice. "I'm Bayern, and, and whatever you've in mind for us now, it won't work. I burned your army."

"Ah, well, the wisdom goes that what is fair in love is fair in war. We might be even now." He smiled at her. "You do not look battle scarred. You look wonderful."

She blushed and realized she was blushing because her clothes were dirty and her hair was surely a sight. The ridiculousness of that worry stuck in her mind, and as he continued to talk, flattering her looks, her bravery, her power, she found herself unable to be caught up again in the sound of his voice and the longing gaze in his eyes. For a moment she mourned the loss of his enchantment; then she thought about herself mourning it, and it occurred to her that it was all quite funny. So she laughed. Sileph paused midsentence and frowned.

"This is absurd!" She glanced around again, trying to ground herself in the reality of danger and not lose herself to Sileph. There was Isi. With a prickling of her skin, she realized that Isi was not just Isi—she was the queen. They did not know they had the queen of Bayern at their feet. But if they found out? She had to end this now.

"Absurd. What fools are we all. You, there," she said, pointing at one of the archers, "you're a fool, too. Put down the arrows, boys. Enna-girl doesn't want to have to burn you." She spoke with light-heartedness, but her pulse pounded in her throat. *Please, please,* she thought, *please put them down.* They did not move.

"Enna." Sileph's gaze locked hers. His arms reached out for her but dropped when she laughed again.

"You're a pickled plum, aren't you, Captain? I'll bet your nursemaid fell in love with you as soon as you could talk. I'll bet your da beat you out of jealousy over your ma. I'll bet this little persuasion gift of yours hasn't all been a festival, has it? But it worked on me, I'll admit. I'd've followed you to Ingridan and borne your children and bade my heart beat only in time with yours. But now I just feel sorry for you, Sileph, and I don't want to burn you, so please go away. Now."

Sileph smiled his marvelous smile. "I love when you resist."

"Don't," said Enna, her voice snapping with anger. "Don't try to seduce me with all that 'you're so powerful and so am I' nonsense. I've had enough, Sileph. Go away."

Sileph looked at her, and his expression changed from loving to confused to enraged. He shouted once and walked a tight, quick circle as though looking for something to hit. Then he turned suddenly back to her and pointed, his arm extended. "Do not think you can toss me aside, Enna. I have worked too hard to just let you go. You were going to be my answer, and instead, I lost everything."

He dropped his arms and for a moment looked tragic. "Tiedan blamed me for the loss, saying you only used to burn a tent or two, and you never would have broken your fire loose over our army if I had not held you captive for so long."

"Well, what do you know, at last Tiedan and I find common ground—we both blame you."

Sileph raggedly combed his hair with his hand and cast a nervous glance at the men behind him. He smiled and laughed a little. "I just have not explained, then. I want you to be with me. I promised you a house of white stone, three stories up overlooking a river. It was to be you and me, Enna. If it is not, then I just do not know which of us will live through this."

Enna felt a shift of heat. Someone was moving. In her

periphery she saw Avlado, who was never picketed at night, standing much closer to Isi than he had before. Isi closed her eyes as though deep in thought.

"Hmm, let's see, who'll live?" Enna spoke louder and paced a little, hoping to keep their attention. "Your options don't look good tonight, Captain. This just might be a gamble you're destined to lose."

In that moment, Avlado reached over the shoulder of the man holding Isi and sank his great, yellow teeth into the man's hand. The man screamed and dropped the knife. Isi dropped to the ground and rolled away from his grasp as Avlado turned and planted his rear hooves in the soldier's back.

Then there was wind. Enna did not feel as strong a connection with Isi as she had when holding her hand, but even now she could guess what Isi would do, and their wind and fire worked together. Enna targeted the wood of the bows and arrows first, and those arrows that snapped loose flew wild in the gust of wind. One planted itself in the thigh of a soldier. With the flashes of fire, the horses reared and screamed. The soldiers dropped scorched bows and tried to calm their mounts. Others drew swords, which they quickly dropped with shouts of pain. To Enna's relief, she saw that Isi had mounted Avlado. If Enna could not handle these men, if she could not escape without burning them, she hoped Isi would ride straight and safe back to Geric.

Some of the men started to advance on her, swords or no, when Sileph held up his arm. They halted.

"You will not harm her," he shouted. "She is mine."

He met eyes with Enna. He looked fevered, his eyes wet, his face red. He was sweating, and the muscles of his jaw were tight and bulging.

"Do not do this," he said slowly. "Do not make me kill. You know we are for each other. I made you what you are, and you will make me what I am to be. They were necessary lies. Do not let such trifles make you disbelieve that I loved you, Enna."

At his words, Enna felt her heart rip and rage with her blood. He stood before her looking as he ever had, but what she had seen when she loved him had faded, and in its place she glimpsed a desperate, proud, ruthless man. The cracked place in her chest cramped and throbbed, and she felt heat push hard through her entire body. She forced her voice to scrape out of her throat.

"Did you love me most when I was drugged and helpless, Sileph? Did you love me when I was so baffled by the king's-tongue that I actually thought you were a man? You loved a shell, then." Heat seeped out of her, and she let it jump into fire at her sides and back, tearing into the brush around her, the flames clawing at the air. "This's what I am, Sileph. This's what I am! You'd best run or I'll cook you. I'll do it. Run."

"You want me to burn? Then let's do it together."

Sileph leaped forward and pushed Enna to the ground. Before she hit the flames behind her, a quick, hard wind blew through them, sucking the air away and dismissing the flames into ash. Sileph landed on top of her, his hands scrambling for her neck. *Burn him,* came the thought, but he was too close, and she could not bear to do it. Wind battled his head and threw dirt into his eyes. He knelt up, wiping at them. Avlado's hooves knocked him in the chest. When he fell, Enna regained her feet and stumbled back.

Burn him now, came the thought. She hesitated. He stood and made to pounce again.

From behind Enna, from the dark fields to the north, a voice called. Sileph wavered, and Enna turned.

Finn rushed into the camp, straight at Sileph, and knocked him to the ground. He sat on his chest and punched him in the head twice before Sileph caught his breath and kicked Finn off him, sending him sprawling across the ground. When both men gained their feet, they drew their swords. They exchanged one or two blocks and thrusts, but before Finn or Sileph drove a sword home, before heat blistered Sileph's sword from his hand or burned the clothes from his body, before wind knocked him off his feet, something happened that Enna least expected.

A dagger flew into Sileph's back. He looked up, his mouth open silently. Two more daggers pierced his uniform, and he jerked, then fell, quite dead.

They all stood in silence a moment, looking at the body.

Enna stared at the back of his head, breathless, feeling stunned and horrified and relieved at once. A soldier dismounted and took several steps toward the body, his hands up in the air to show he held no weapon. Enna recognized Pol, Sileph's lieutenant.

"Well, that is that," said Pol. Then, gesturing to the body and looking at Enna, he said, "May I?"

She nodded. He took the first dagger from Sileph's back, wiped it off on the dead man's uniform, and slipped it back into his own belt. He drew out the other two.

"I assume from the presence of these two daggers that I was not alone in wishing him gone?" he said.

A few of the soldiers laughed uncomfortably. All glanced around as if trying to figure out who might have been loyal to Sileph and if they would now start a fight in his defense. No one did. Many of the soldiers put away their cooled swords and looked nervously at Enna. Pol cleaned off the remaining daggers as if unaware of the tension.

"We should have done that weeks ago," said a low-voiced soldier, receiving his dagger back from Pol.

"Maybe they will let us back into Ingridan with the captain dead," said another.

"Let us see," said Pol.

They slung Sileph's body over the back of his horse and mounted. Pol bowed stiffly at Enna and said, "I hope we never meet again." They rode northeast.

Finn had not moved. He stood breathing heavily and

looked weathered and tired, but he held his shoulders square and seemed ready to fight again if need arose.

"Hello," he said. He wiped his brow with the back of his sleeve. His eyes did not flick away from hers. He did not try to woo her, to flaunt his greatness, so opposite of all Sileph had been. He was just Finn, just happy to be with her again. That was, to Enna, an astonishing relief.

"Hello, Finn." She smiled and laughed a little because she felt herself starting to cry.

He walked to her, and quite unexpectedly, Enna felt shy. *This is Finn*, she thought. *If this moment happens, we can't ever undo it.* Then she realized, after all that had passed, that the moment had already happened, and she had been too dim to see.

He reached her and put his arms around her, fitting his face into her neck. She pressed the side of her face against his and let herself cry.

"Enna," he said, holding her tighter. Inside Finn's arms, Enna did not feel like the helpless girl shut up in an enemy tent, or the angry, blazing girl who had confronted Sileph. Now she felt she was herself again, just Enna, just who she wanted to be. His touch told her so.

He kissed her cheeks and her hair, his eyes shining as though he could scarcely believe it.

She put her hands on his cheeks to see his face, her thumb covering the scar he had received at Sileph's hand.

"You're so good, Finn. So good."

"I can be better," he said. "You'll see, Enna."

After a few minutes Isi returned, though Enna had not noticed that she had left, bringing Finn's horse in tow. She kept her eyes on the ground until Enna said, "Oh, it's all right, Isi."

Isi looked up and smiled. "Good evening, Finn. How's your mother?"

he going was slow and painful. Enna never felt fully recovered from the struggles with Sileph, and the fever stormed inside her. Sometimes from halfway within a dream, she heard Finn's desperate voice—"Isi, please, she's so hot, you've got to wake up"—and then Enna would feel a breeze help push back the orange haze.

Once she dreamed of Sileph and saw again the moment when fire raged around her and she yelled that he loved a shell. She started awake, breathless, afraid that she was dead. Even in sleep, she was aware of the fever tugging life from her, but awake, she was conscious of Yasid looming on the horizon like a dangerous storm cloud. The fever, and the death it promised in its steamy breath, frightened her as much as the thought that she would live to reach Yasid and be cured. With fire blazing around her, she had said to Sileph, "This is what I am." Without the fire, what would she be?

But relief was palpable when Finn was near. With Enna lost in a fever haze and Isi tormented by wind, Finn became their caretaker. He cooked for them and scouted their path through bogs and stony hills, following as best he could Isi's old map. When Enna was especially sick, he tried to get her talking to take her mind away or asked Isi to tell stories. Or, at the worst moments, he took her in his arms and sang in his dry, low voice silly songs about swimming rabbits and no-tailed squirrels.

Their journey was further slowed by the river Suneast that had obviously swollen since the map had been drawn, and they spent three days looking for a crossing. After the Suneast, they followed a road beside a stream, occasionally meeting travelers with hair nearly as dark as the Bayern and skin the color of polished cherrywood. Finn caught fish and hare and traded some of his meat catches for dark, flat bread.

The other travelers did not speak their northern language. To no surprise to Enna, as often as Isi was well enough to stand and walk she was practicing on the southerners the language of Yasid outlined in her book.

"It takes some listening to figure out how they speak and get the accent down, but I think I've about made it out."

"You would," said Enna. "You're amazing. Here's the extent of my gift of languages: Over there!"

"Over there," Finn shouted without looking up as he cleaned the cookpot.

They laughed, then had to explain the story to Isi, and Enna quickly found in the telling that it was not so funny to her anymore. She stopped speaking and looked away, shunning the various burning images awash in her mind. She had that haunting feeling again that if she just looked over her shoulder, she would see remnants of her handi-work—smoking tunics, blistering faces, mouths open to scream.

"Enna," said Finn.

Enna knew that, though terrible, the memories could not haunt her so fiercely if she did not still harbor the longing to burn. The thought of losing her intimacy with fire hurt almost as much as how it now burned her blood and skin.

Then at last, over two months from leaving the palace, they passed the border of Yasid and into Quapah, the first town. What first appeared to be a stone city wall proved to be built from bricks the color of the sand. The houses and buildings were smooth structures with small, high windows. Everything was pale and brilliant, flashing back at the sunlight and burning the eyes.

Isi asked a woman where to find the *tata-rook*, the fire worshippers. She wrinkled her nose as though she smelled something rotten and pointed beyond the city wall and grazing goats.

They led their horses across the scrubby grasses of the goat pastures, over a rocky ledge, and onto smooth, fine dirt again. Just at the sight of a rambling building, Enna felt her stomach squeeze tighter in dread. It was tidy and well laid. A stacked rock wall surrounded fields of green plants, vegetable fronds sticking their heads up through the pale soil, and rows of corn, cotton plants, and fruit trees with lustrous green leaves. This land was so much warmer and drier, and so much more open to the strikes of sunlight than the forest she knew, Enna marveled that anything grew at all.

Atop a platform in the center of the field, a young man sat cross-legged, his hands on his knees, his eyes closed. A cloth was stretched over his head, shading him from the sun. Enna squinted into the distance and thought she saw similar platforms in the fields on the far side of the house. Enna greeted the man, and Isi asked him a question in the southern tongue, but he did not look their way.

The three scrambled along the rock wall, looking for an opening for their horses to pass. From behind they heard voices. Isi stopped to listen.

Four boys came from the direction of the town. They climbed atop the wall some thirty paces from the travelers. Their hands were full of stones, and they shouted at the man perched on the platform. To Enna, the words sounded harsh and ugly.

"They're saying some words I don't know," said Isi, "but they feel like insults. And they're calling the man 'unbeliever' and asking him why he's so selfish with the rain, only making it fall on their fields."

They heard a loud snap. One of the boys had thrown a rock at the platform. It bounced off a pole.

"Why would they do that?" said Enna. "And why does he let them?"

Isi shouted something at them, but the boys paid her no mind.

Another snap.

"For pity's sake," said Enna.

Finn's hand darted to the sword at his hip. Enna thought, *Good for you.* But Isi put a hand on Finn's arm.

"I don't think even defensive swordplay would be wise in a place where we are the outsiders."

Another stone. This one hit the man on the side of his arm. He flinched but did not open his eyes. The town boys laughed and gathered more rocks.

"Come on, then," said Enna, taking Isi's arm, though she scarcely felt capable of taking another step. "If no one else will stop boys from attacking a defenseless person, we have to." Finn walked beside Enna, his face adopting his wary warrior expression. She faced the boys and raised her voice. "Ho there."

The boys turned to them with amused smiles. Two stones launched in their direction. Finn and Enna remained still, knowing that Isi would deal with it, and indeed, a sudden breeze easily knocked them off their path. One of the boys jabbered something at Enna and threw another stone, this one also missing its mark.

"Just threats," said Isi.

"Tell them the *tata-rook* don't want to hurt them, but that the sun's their father and he'll protect them," said Enna.

Isi translated, pointing up at the sun, and the boys smirked and laughed. Enna took Isi's hand and a felt a little more strength steady her bones. She could sense the heat streaming from their bodies and began to tug, like winding loose yarn into a ball. The action was as satisfying as pulling a barbed thorn from her foot.

"Tell them the sun loves the *tata-rook*, and they must be careful, for when the boys threaten them, the sun takes away its heat."

Isi translated. Enna continued to pull. The loose heat caught, and she yanked harder, pulling living heat from their bodies. It was drawn to her, into her. Without her having to ask, Isi knew to send a wind over her skin, into her mouth.

The boys were no longer laughing. Their confused faces began to show fear, and she saw color fade from their cheeks. One of them lifted his hands to the sun and shouted with a trembling voice.

"He's begging the sun to forgive and let them live."

There's more in there, thought Enna. *If I keep going, I can pull out just a little more.*

Finn touched her shoulder. "That's probably good. Just that."

The wind blew harder. Enna let go of the strings to their life heat and stumbled. Finn caught her under her arms and held her up. The boys relaxed, put arms around themselves, and shivered. After a moment they all raised gestures of thanks to the sun, hopped off the wall, and ran back to the village.

The three turned toward the house and only then noticed a man standing not two paces away. He had dark skin wrinkled with sun and a beard graying around his mouth. For a moment a smile seemed to twitch on his lips, but he stilled it and just stood looking over their faces. As she stood there in the open, the earth felt hotter to Enna than her own skin. She could still feel the sensation of tugging on those boys' life heat. To gather it and let it seep and blow away without lighting fire made her hands twitch as if for a task to perform. She bit her lip and looked at Finn for comfort, but his face swooped in and out of her vision.

At last the man spoke a word. Isi responded in the southern tongue and then translated his response.

"He says that we may've saved that man's life, but it's too dangerous to play with such a force."

Isi and the man continued to speak as he led them closer to the house. A woman appeared and silently led their horses away. The man motioned for them to sit on the cool tiles of a porch. When Enna passed into the shade and yet still seemed to feel the relentless beating of the sun, she knew she was in a bad way.

"Enna," said Isi.

Enna slowly met her look and realized belatedly that Isi

had said her name several times before she responded.

"Enna, this man is Fahil. He is the caretaker of this *roga tata-rook*, this community of fire worshippers."

"Fahil," said Enna.

Fahil thrust his hand against her forehead and pulled it away quickly, then nodded and said something to Isi.

"I'm learning so much, Enna." Isi's voice heightened in excitement, and she spoke the northern tongue to Finn and Enna, occasionally translating further communication from Fahil.

"He says, it's no ugly thing to be a fire worshipper. The sun is the manifestation of the Creator, and fire is the manifestation of the sun. But it is not an easy blessing. That's why they're all here."

"Here in this, uh, *roga tata-rook*? They're all like me?" said Enna.

Isi nodded, looking at Fahil and straining to understand. "He says, some people of the desert lands are born intimate with fire, that when they first show signs of it they come here, or to other *roga tata-rook*." She spoke to the man and got his answer. "Yes, he says he too can pull fire from air, but he won't do it, um, casually. It's not for humans to play like creators. The townspeople, they don't understand, or they fear them. Those boys we stopped were from Quapah. Fahil says they bother the *tata-rook* sometimes, and once townspeople killed a woman as she sat in the field."

Isi spoke for a moment, then translated Fahil's response.

"He is surprised that both you and your brother were taught the skill. He has never known it to be taught, just born in a person after a certain age, and he's never heard of a northerner with the knowledge."

"Why me, then?" asked Enna.

Isi shrugged. "He doesn't know. Maybe you and Leifer had a relative from the south far back, or maybe it can be taught after all and no one ever tried."

"But Isi," said Enna, "Fahil and the others we've seen, they're fine. But there's something wrong with me."

Isi repeated Enna's words, and Fahil looked back at the sky, a crease between his eyes. Then he spoke softly.

Isi hesitated. "He agrees that you are dying."

Finn made a small noise. Enna rubbed at fever chills on her arm. She had wondered for weeks if dying felt like that, the fever burning constant hopelessness. She had thought it was just fear of losing the fire and living in a world void of heat, but it was not just fire she might lose.

Enna felt Fahil watching her. Isi spoke again with much halting, and Fahil seemed reluctant to answer. After a time he pointed to the man on the nearest platform.

"I begged him to tell me how all the *tata-rook* avoid the burning inside that came to you with the fire knowledge," said Isi. "He asks me, do I know why that man sits up there? He's talking to the, uh, water, or the rain and dew. They have a word that means any water that doesn't come out of a well. He can't call the water from the clouds, but what water there is in the air, he can ask it to go to the plants instead of wasted on the sand. Here they grow enough food for everyone in the *roga tata-rook* and much of Quapah. That's how they can produce so much in a desert." Isi turned to Enna, her eyes full of excitement. "They have water-speaking. Isn't that amazing? I've always wondered."

Isi spoke again and listened to Fahil's response. "He says, everyone who comes to a *roga* with fire knowledge is taken in to see if they also know water. It takes years to develop. And in some it never does. . . . He won't say directly, but I think the ones who never develop the water tongue, they go away, or they die. But when a person knows both heat and water, they form a balance. The language of fire doesn't overwhelm them, tempered by the presence of the water, and the water can't consume the person because of the threat of the heat always near. It makes sense, Enna. I often thought that the wind was overcoming me because I didn't speak all languages, as the tales say we once did. But I never thought that balance could come from just knowing two elements that work against each other. I'm going to ask him if he'll teach you rain." She grinned and shook Enna's knee.

Enna wanted to respond, but speaking took too much energy. Everything was slowing down. Fahil spoke, his lips barely moving. His words sounded so strange to her, not like a human tongue at all, more akin to the creaking and moaning of old trees, and she wondered if she was hearing right. He paused and looked up. Enna followed his glance to the blazing sky and felt as though she were falling into the scorching blueness. She tried to grab Finn and stay attached to the earth, but blue changed to black.

nna awoke off and on in a low bed. Often Isi was asleep in another cot, whether the small, high window spoke of night or day. Finn sat on the floor beside her whenever she opened her eyes, and he would proffer corn cakes and sweet water. When she was awake enough to listen, he explained how she had passed out and Isi had gone to bed soon after. Both had been resting for two days. Enna, her voice squeaking, said, "That's all well and good, but as for resting, I don't think I'm quite done."

Another night and day blurred past, and eventually, both Enna and Isi found themselves awake at the same time.

"Sleep well?" said Enna.

Isi laughed.

All that day Enna stayed in bed, listening to the unintelligible conversations between Isi and Fahil that echoed in from the porch. Finn stayed by her side, but she had little energy to speak. Or will. Fahil came in to look at her, feel her face, then left again, frowning. The closer night approached, the more fear seized her. From the sounds of the conversation, something had been decided.

At full night, Isi returned. For a long, aching moment, she did not speak.

"What about learning the rain, and balance and everything?" asked Enna.

"Fahil says rain has never been taught," said Isi. "And it takes years for the *tata-rook* to develop it naturally."

"Oh," said Enna. She could not imagine living in the *roga* for years. "Do you want to leave me here, Isi? Finn can go back with you to Bayern, and I can stay, and try. . . . "

Isi exhaled softly. "Fahil doesn't think you have the time to try . . . and I think he's right."

"Oh, well," said Enna, "that was a lot to hope for, anyway, wasn't it?" She tried to laugh, but it caught in her chest and sent a rip of pain down her spine. A fever chill shook her visibly. Finn wrapped his arms around her.

"Can you walk?" asked Isi. "Fahil says . . . he says you're close to slipping away. He says if you sleep again, you might not wake. There are tales among his people that fire knowledge can be erased from a person who is consumed by it without ever learning the rain. It's . . . tricky, I gather, and it's never been attempted in his life, but we think we should do whatever we can now, tonight. They have a sacred place atop the hill, and he thought it would be a good place to try."

Finn put Enna's arm around his neck and helped her walk away from the building and up the rising hill. Enna felt weary everywhere. She was tired of feeling half-dead all the time, tired of illness making her powerless. But to lose the fire . . . If she survived, she feared the rest of her life would feel like those early weeks in Eylbold, imprisoned in the tent, the king's-tongue deadening every sensation.

At the crest of the rising slope, Fahil waited. He asked Isi a question, and she shook her head.

"What did he say?" asked Enna.

"He wanted to know if I needed a donkey for the climb, and I said I was all right if I could take his arm."

Enna frowned. "Why's he worried, Isi? Are you sicker than you're telling me?"

Isi smiled, bit her lip, and looked down. "He thought that, um, he said, maybe the climb would be easier on a donkey for an expectant mother."

Enna stared blankly at Isi; then understanding rushed through her. "Oh, Isi. Mercy, Isi, I'm a fool. That's the extra heat I was sensing." She glanced at the bulge of Isi's belly. Though her loose tunic hid it well, Enna had to wonder how she had missed it all those weeks.

"What do you think of that, Finn?"

Finn shrugged. "Well, I sort of guessed."

"So, it's just me who's blind." She grabbed Isi's hand and kissed it. "That's wonderful. I'm so happy for you. Do you feel all right?"

Isi nodded. Her smile pushed her cheeks up. "Oh, I've felt better in my life, but I'm certainly happy about it. Geric and I have been wishing for this."

"Geric'll have my hair as it is for keeping you away from him all this time, especially— For pity's sake, Isi, did you know about this when we left Bayern?"

Isi shook her head. "I wasn't sure until we were well on the road. I guess I should've known since I was probably three months along when we left, but my mind was pretty well absorbed in other things."

"So, how long, until—"

"Another three months, I think," said Isi.

Three months. Enna considered how it took them over two months just to get to Yasid from Bayern's capital. And Isi was carrying the future heir of Bayern's throne. And Geric was likely frantic at home in her absence and had no idea she was pregnant. This quest was not all about her. Suddenly so much more was at stake. She felt a new weight pressing her to end it, and a new fear that she would fail. She could not fail Isi again.

It was a difficult climb in the dark, and Enna scraped her hands a couple of times after tripping on jagged rocks.

"Let me carry you," said Finn.

"No." She was through being a burden. Besides, the little pain from the scratches was pleasantly distracting her from the cold dread.

The hilltop was flat and paved with smooth stones.

Benches surrounded a stone pillar the height of a woman. On top, a brazier blazed with fire.

"It's their eternal flame," said Isi. She spoke with Fahil to confirm. "This flame has been burning for over six hundred years."

Another man had been standing beside the altar. He stepped back as Fahil moved forward. Fahil spoke, looking straight at Enna. His sharp, raspy words seemed to burn her even before she understood his meaning. Isi was slow to translate. Enna shivered, waiting for the sting.

"He says he's been talking with the others, and they agree the best option is to try to burn the fire out of you, as quickly as possible."

Enna looked at Fahil. His face was dark, his back to the fire. He was shadow against the light.

"Burn it out," said Enna. "How will he do it?"

Fahil had a pair of metal tongs. He dipped them into the fire and pulled out a burning coal. The flames pulled inside, pulsing like a red heart within the blackness.

"He'll place the coal against the tip of your tongue and then you are to squeeze it in your hands. He'll burn the first word of fire from your tongue and burn away the acts of fire you performed. He believes that then the fire won't remember you anymore."

Enna winced. "But the fire is inside of me. . . . "

"Fahil believes the symbol of this ceremony will cure you," said Isi. Even in the darkness, Enna could see her face was pale. "Enna, I don't think you should. We don't even know if it'll work."

"I'm going to do it," said Enna. "We've got to get you home. You're carrying the heir to Bayern."

Isi took a step toward her. "But if this does nothing but burn your tongue and hands . . . "

"I want to do this, Isi," said Enna. "I'm ready." She did not know if she believed in this ceremony, and the thought of the pain made her queasy, but she wanted to show Isi that she was willing, that she would atone for what she had done. She had caused so much pain—it only felt right that she should have to sacrifice in return.

"Wait, Enna, don't." Finn took her by the shoulders, and she tried not to meet his eyes, afraid to be talked out of her decision. "We can take time, see if you heal on your own. We can."

Enna felt her eyes prick and burn. Finn awoke some of the sadness inside her, and it choked against the dread lodged in her chest. "We've got to get Isi back before the baby comes. And I haven't got time, Finn. I feel that now."

"That fire, it's like it makes you hopeless, Enna, but you can't believe it. You're not going to die."

Enna opened her mouth to protest, then coughed against the rising heat inside her. Her frustration weakened her control, and it rushed through the cracked place in her chest. She wiped her brow and took an unsteady step.

"Isi," she said.

A wind answered, pushing away the searing heat. When she could see clearly again, Fahil was wide-eyed and jabbering at Isi.

"What is it?" Enna asked.

Isi was listening, nodding, her brows high and her look hopeful. "He didn't know until now that I knew the wind-speaking. And he says, wind erases things, like footsteps in the sand. He says, even an immense fire can be like a candle flame in the mouth of a great wind."

"You want to try to blow out the fire in me?" asked Enna.

Isi nodded. "Fahil, he says he'd thought of that, wondered if somehow he could use the rain speech to work against your fire, but that it was too rushed and that he doesn't know you. To work such things on another, he said, requires understanding and intimacy. Enna, I know you. I could try with wind."

"It'll be just like when you send wind to relieve the fever, but . . . "

"But harder, yes," said Isi, finishing Enna's sentence. "Much harder. And different. He says, he's telling me how I might do it. I have to—surrender in a way to the wind. I think I can, Enna. I've felt the temptation before but never knew what would happen."

"Isi, please try," said Finn.

Enna nodded. Hope made her tremble.

Finn let her go and withdrew. Enna and Isi stood facing each other, alone on the paved center of the hilltop. The wind started. At first it was like any of the breezes Isi used to cool the fever, but it swelled so that it tore at Enna's own life heat around her body, pulling it loose and releasing it into the air.

Then it grew stronger.

Her headscarf came loose and her hair whipped around her face. She began to feel a tearing pain. She opened her mouth to scream, but she could not breathe, and the wind rushed into her throat and poured inside her, ripping through her cracked place, gushing through her body. It was taking something away. She felt fear with the pain, afraid that she was losing all of herself. She could not open her eyes, but she reached out and stumbled forward, her hands finding Isi's. She gripped on to her friend, trying to anchor part of herself before the wind took it all.

Surrender. She tried. But each time she began to release her carefully guarded control of the fire, pain burst from her chest. *If it leaves me, I'll die,* she thought, and held on tighter. Her muscles ached and trembled, her chest gushed with heat. She fought and struggled, terrified of losing everything.

Enna became conscious of Isi's hand trembling in hers. She let go and stumbled away, and the wind stopped short like a held breath. Enna gasped to fill her lungs and sat on the ground. Isi sat beside her.

"I'm sorry, Isi," she said. "I can't let it go. I tried. But it hurts, and it seems so wrong, and I'm so afraid there won't be anything left."

Isi took deep breaths, then spoke softly. "What do we do?"

Enna shook her head. She knew only that she did not want to surrender, not as she had with Sileph and not as she had on the battlefield. She glanced at Finn, and the look in his eyes struck her so hard, she felt her body reel. He trusted her. He had complete faith that if she thought the wind was not working, then it was so, and she would find another way.

"I don't deserve you," she said to him.

Surprisingly, he laughed in good humor. "Enna," he said, as though she had told a good joke.

Fahil crouched beside Isi and together they spoke in the southern tongue. It sounded like a desperate conversation conveying little hope.

"I'm sorry, Finn," said Enna. "It might've worked, but for me. Surrender. That's what I'm supposed to do." Her stomach seized at the thought, and she swayed. "I can't surrender anymore. I'm so afraid."

"What are you afraid of?" he asked.

"Dying?" She shook her head. "No, I guess not that. I'm afraid of being the person who let my friends down, of surrendering so that the fire is in charge, the fire that kills, or of surrendering to survive like I did in Eylbold when I was under Sileph's control. Of losing myself again."

Finn held her hand and looked at her palm thoughtfully. "I surrendered in Eylbold. They grabbed Razo. They said they'd cut his throat if I didn't throw down my sword. So I did. That felt right to me." He met her eyes. "Maybe there's more than one kind of surrender."

Another kind. Finn had not given himself away in Eylbold. He had made a choice to save Razo. Fahil's voice rose in concern, and Enna looked toward them. Isi was blinking a lot, and though she held herself straight, Enna could tell her friend was suffering under the heavy voice of the wind.

"Finn," Enna said quietly, "Isi's been bad all this trip, hasn't she?"

Finn nodded.

"As bad as I am?"

"Well," said Finn, looking at their friend, "she doesn't have the fever. I haven't been as worried, you know. But she's not like she used to be. She's been tired, and sad."

Enna felt her cheeks burn hotter in humiliation. In these last months she had scarcely thought of Isi. Her attention was absorbed in herself, in her grand mission that would stop the war, but also in her gift, in the idea that it might make her as special as she hoped to be. And lately, she was taken up in her fever and in her fear of losing what marked her as extraordinary. All this time, why was she not worrying instead about poor, haunted Isi?

As her emotions rose, her control weakened and the heat pushed in, hot hands pressing her from all sides. She did not call to it, did not gather it in, the heat just found her now. She imagined it sensed its language on her skin, the way a blind dog knows its master. It was that unwanted gathering of heat that was so unbearable, as it was the constant touch and speech of the wind that tormented Isi. She stared at Isi as these thoughts pieced together, and she could feel her heart beat harder.

"You learned the wind in one moment, Isi," said Enna. "It only took one word. You know many languages. You can learn another."

Isi looked up and seemed surprised by the energy in Enna's voice.

"What are you thinking, Enna?" asked Finn.

Enna smiled despite the pain. "I can teach her the fire. I thought about it for weeks with Sileph. I think he could've learned, and I know Isi can. We don't need the vellum, I remember everything it said. And fire is a quick language, Isi. It catches onto you and starts to burn."

"But, Enna . . . ," said Isi.

"It makes sense. Wind senses its language on you. That's why it's drawn to you even when you don't call it, right? What you need is something that will keep the voice of the wind a step off. Well, why aren't the *tata-rook* overwhelmed like we are? The rain doesn't completely put out their knowledge of fire. If it did, they'd be bothered by the voice of rain all the time. No, both rain and fire are near them at once, tempering each other. Rain quenches heat, fire burns away water, keeping both their voices away until they call to one or the other. Ask Fahil."

Isi spoke to the older man. "He agrees that this might be so."

"So," said Enna with a smile. "That's fire and rain. Now think of how we work fire and wind together, Isi. Think of that night outside Ostekin when . . . when I sent heat at you, and you just pushed it away with the wind before it became fire. And that night when we camped, when I sent heat to break up your wind and scatter it. They can either build each other bigger or smother each other out. It's not exactly how fire and water work, but I'm thinking that wind and heat affect each other all the same. If you added my fire to your wind, I think both would keep the other at bay. Wind brushes away the heat, heat changes and scatters the wind, and neither voice would be able to get close to you unless you called. Just like with the *tata-rook*."

"Maybe," said Isi. "But what about you?"

Enna brushed off the question with a wave and leaned closer. Excitement made her forget the fever. "Never mind me. I really believe this will work for you, Isi. Add fire knowledge and the wind can't press on you so."

Fahil wondered what Enna had in mind, and when Isi told him, he was quiet a moment, a tender smile on his lips. Enna shook Finn's tunic front.

"It's going to work, Finn. I know it is. Isi's going to be better."

"Enna," said Isi, turning from Fahil, "he says it's a good plan. And he says it could work both ways."

Enna blinked. "How?"

"I described to him how we worked fire and wind together to chase off those two soldiers, and he thinks our friendship, our closeness, will be a bridge, that we can share the elements with each other. I tried long ago to teach Geric the wind, and it didn't work. But you already know one language—maybe you can learn."

Finn sighed with relief. "Good. You should do this, Enna, and no one's going to lick coals."

Enna did not know about learning the wind. It seemed so mysterious to her and something so completely Isi's. But she agreed, determined at least that Isi would profit. The girls sat knee to knee. Fahil stood before the brazier, and Finn sat on a stone watching the girls, his hand on his sword hilt, ready in case there was something to fight.

They began by talking low. Enna wanted Isi to know what she had learned from the vellum. She explained how heat was in the air, where it came from, how she felt it, plucked it, pulled it inside, and the now subconscious gesture of turning the heat into flame inside her chest. Isi tried to explain how the wind felt when it touched her, what it felt like inside when she understood its subtle speech, how she saw and heard and felt the images it carried and yet with a sense that was neither her eyes nor ears nor skin. It was difficult to explain, and after a time Enna realized both had stopped speaking. They held hands, as they had when they faced the soldiers, and Enna became more aware of Isi.

Learn, she urged silently. *Feel the heat. Learn it.*

She focused on the place in her chest that leaked heat, on the swaths of it that hung around her face, and she tried to will it away from her, to make the heat aware of Isi. Strings of heat stretched between Enna and her friend. It was a strange sensation, almost as if Enna touched Isi but not with her fingers. Then she felt a breeze.

It curled off Isi, around their clasped hands, up Enna's wrists. The breeze felt as familiar as a touch from a friend. It had a sense of Isi about it. She seemed to know which direction it would flow before it moved, as she often knew what Isi would say before she finished a sentence. She was tempted to try to pull the breeze inside her, as she did with the heat, but she guessed it would not work that way. Feeling that it might be speaking, she tried to listen, straining with all her senses, with her ears and mind and skin, and with that part of her that could feel heat.

The wind grew stronger, as though it sensed her desperation. It beat Enna's hair against her cheeks. It began to tear at her, and inside the ear-piercing howling there was a kind of silence. She reached out toward the wind again and realized with a start that what she hoped to touch was Leifer. She could see his face so distinctly in memory that it was as though he stood before her, and her heart ached for him. She marveled that at such a moment her thoughts turned to him, and she realized suddenly and with a twisting ache in her heart that she had never wept for his death. The cold rush of the wind made her aware that she was crying now, and her chest thumped with a sob.

All this time, she thought, *I've been clinging to Leifer.* The fire felt like the last tie that bound them together, across life and death.

I can give it up, I can. Inside her, fire raged defensively. Heat stung her skin, leaked from her chest, seemed enough to fill the world. She felt herself slipping again and remembered what Fahil had said: *If she sleeps again, she might not wake.* Enna refused to faint, focused on Isi, and sent all her thoughts toward healing her. Her hands found Isi's bare neck and wrist, hoping that just by touch she could spread the heat. She felt some of the fire sigh from her chest. The heat lessened but slid over everything, so that she could not tell which part of the touch was her own hands or Isi's skin.

The wind did not pause, and Enna knew Isi was sending it at her, insistent. With that place inside her where she kept not only memories of her brother, but the feeling of him, she struggled to listen. The wind thrashed against her skin, and she pushed her senses out toward it, feeling toward it, listening from the inside.

Heat flowed between them. The wind battered them, pushing them closer together. A voice she did not know said, *Enna.*

She gasped. She wanted to scream back, *I'm here! I'm Enna,* but she did not know how. *Enna,* she heard again. The word seemed to enter her where she felt the fire in her chest, then yawn up her throat until it found a place in her mind that understood, that place where she still held Leifer. It was the voice of the wind speaking her name, as cool as a stream bath, soft and plain and easy.

The howling stopped, and the wind slipped into breezes that teased the fine hairs of her skin. Slowly Enna opened her eyes. Something was different. She believed they had been sitting there minutes, or perhaps even hours, but surely not long enough for the seasons to change. Nevertheless, the night felt cooler, like a summer's night in Bayern, rich and fragrant and welcome after a hot day.

Fahil was holding Finn back from going to Enna, but when he saw her look up, he let Finn go. Finn rushed to her side. He smoothed her hair from her brow. His voice was tight with fear.

"Enna, you're all right? Are you?"

"I think so." Dizzily, she leaned into Finn's chest and gripped his tunic. Isi was staring up at a sky prickly with stars. "How are you, Isi? Did it work?"

"I don't know," Isi said. "Everything's so quiet. Did I lose the wind completely?"

Enna closed her eyes and felt around her. The air appeared to be in motion, the heat and the wind moving around each other, swirling together, pushing off, and her sense of them was dimming.

"See if the wind still understands you," said Enna.

A breeze moved across the ground, lifting dust, snaking

up Enna's leg, against her wrist, then touching her cheek.

"Still there, just not so close," said Isi. "A breeze came when I beckoned, but not before. Amazing."

"So, did it work, then? Is it the fire?"

Isi closed her eyes, a line of concentration between her brows. Enna felt like holding her breath. After a few moments, a clump of dead grass on the ground between them sparked with a tiny fire. Isi opened her eyes and laughed.

"And you, Enna? Are you all right?"

The breeze moved through Enna's hair, and she thought she could hear a whisper—no, not hear, feel. She felt its touch and saw an image and understood it as a word. She could not speak to it, could not ask it to go this way or that. She remembered that such control took Isi much time to learn. But if she strained, she could hear its image speech on her skin, how it carried the idea of what it had touched before to each new contact. A cool finger of air against her cheek and a bright thought in her mind. *Enna.* It named her. *Enna, Finn, our lady, the man of fire and water, the air full of dust.*

"I hear it," Enna said stiffly, afraid to move, as though the breeze could be frightened away like a flock of pheasants.

Was the fire gone? No, she could still detect the heat swirling away from Finn, twisting through her fingers and hair, then passing on. It did not stick to her, did not claw at her skin.

Fahil left off speaking happily with the other *tata-rook* to go to Isi. He knelt beside her, asking questions, and Isi responded in light, content tones.

"How do you feel?" said Finn.

Enna thought. She could still draw heat to her, but it did not come unbidden, and for the first time in weeks she breathed air free of heat. She did not feel the heat tease her and gnaw at her, just sensed that it was, but that it could be ignored. She looked inward and felt that the cracked place inside her had not healed, but it no longer leaked rivers of fever heat into her body. It felt now less like the tethered falcon tearing to escape than a sleeping bird, tired and warm.

"Good. Unbelievably good. Isi?"

Isi was leaning against Fahil. "I'm all right." She paused, then smiled broadly. "Yes, I know I am. Everything's so quiet." She sighed. "I'd forgotten what it felt like to be normal. The winds are still there, if I seek them, but they're hushed now and keep to themselves."

"You have . . . ," said Enna.

"Balance," said Isi. "The heat changes and pushes the wind. . . ."

"And the wind takes the breath from the fire."

Isi laughed, happy as a child. "I can scarcely believe we did it, Enna. Both of us. Geric will be so relieved to see me better, he might even think the absence was worth it."

Finn breathed out. "That wasn't so bad, then. And I thought someone was going to have to die before it was over."

"And I'll bet you were hoping it'd be you," said Enna.

Finn looked serious. "Well, I wasn't *wanting* to die, but if it had to be one of the three of us, I hoped I could jump in a fire first or something."

Enna held Finn's cheeks and shook him. "I was kidding! Oh, Finn, you are too good." And she gave him an ardent kiss, a kiss that meant maybe, after all, the world would not burn and everything would be all right.

Enna laughed, feeling as though something had sat on her shoulders for months and just stepped off. She grabbed Finn's hands with the wild notion that she might float away.

Isi laughed, too, and Enna noticed how Isi's belly wobbled with her laugh, so that made her laugh more. And of course Finn could never resist whenever he heard Enna's laugh. Fahil stared at them as though they were crazy, which was, of course, even funnier.

ahil thought they should rest a few more days after the ordeal on the hilltop, but Enna insisted they leave the next morning.

"If I don't get my best friend home soon, she'll pop," said Enna. "Translate that, Isi."

Isi had some gold coins in her saddlebag that they traded to Fahil for supplies. After Isi talked with Fahil about the possibilities of renewing trading between the two lands and much thanking in two languages, the Bayern set on the road for home.

The change in the two girls was immediate, though it seemed even to improve day by day. Enna felt freed from the prison of heat that had been building around her since the first word of fire, and the voice of the wind did not press in. Both were there, but holding each other back, just out of reach. Relief at last from the fever was almost unbearably wonderful, but even better was seeing Isi look around at the world with a forgotten smile on her lips, her face peaceful, at last at rest from the voice of the wind.

Though it was on Enna's mind, they did not speak aloud about how what happened on that hilltop might affect a baby. Enna was relieved to detect a healthy amount of heat from Isi's middle, and Isi said the creature still did flip-flops as much as ever, so they hoped.

There was much time for such thoughts, as the road home was slow. For Isi's sake, they never dared push their horses past a walk. Avlado was good at walking smoothly and slowly for his pregnant rider.

They followed the same path home, keeping to the stream Isi called the Small Suneast for as long as possible. Enna despised the taste of its water and named it the Horse-spittle. Finn always called it Enna's Stream. He tended to refer to most anything as belonging to her— Enna's Meadow, Enna's Mountain. When he referred to Yasid as Enna's Kingdom, she said, "Isn't that your heart?"

Finn smiled and kissed her hand. Isi rolled her eyes.

"Oh, you two are impossible."

Enna laughed. "This coming from the girl who calls her husband 'sweet little bunny boy'?"

Isi blushed. "That was just once."

Isi could not hide her longing for Geric. She observed Finn's affection for Enna, and it seemed to make her both happy and sad. Enna returned once from washing in the stream to find Isi holding her belly, laughing and crying at once and not sure why she was doing either.

Isi's belly doubled in size before they crossed the Bayern border, and so, seemingly, did her aches and complaints. Near the end, they rode half days and then let Isi rest and eat. She alternated between nausea and ravenous hunger.

"How's your back? How's your belly? Are you well?" Enna asked continually.

"Hush up for five minutes, will you?" Isi got grumpier and grumpier and insisted on taking more than her fair share of turns lighting their cookfires as her ability with fire improved. Finn seemed to find Enna's overattentiveness and Isi's mood changes completely delightful.

Enna was anxious to get Isi to Geric and see the baby born healthy, but beyond that, she was hesitant to return to her kingdom and face the consequences of her burning. *Perhaps,* she thought, *Finn and I could see Isi safe home and slip away to the Forest.* The thought was disappointing, because now, with the languages of both fire and wind dwelling inside her, Enna was sure she could serve Bayern well. Her hopes of being useful were extinguished by the heavy certainty that she could not be forgiven.

Once they crossed into Bayern, they followed roads that led them past inns. When Enna could, she sent messages to Geric: "Fourteen days south, Oily Parchment Inn, your wife is expecting"; "Eight days south, the Pinched Nose, Isi is *huge*"; "Five days south, the Silver Hart, I hope you get at least one of these, because you are soon to be a father whether you are here or not."

Enna suggested they just settle into an inn until the baby came, but Isi insisted they ride on each morning, determined to make it to the palace and Geric before the baby came. Then, passing by a village just outside the Forest and two days' ride from the capital, she changed her mind.

"Aah, aaah, ahhh!" She dismounted, grabbed Enna's hand so tightly that she drew blood with her fingernails, walked straight into the nearest cottage, and plopped down on a bed. Enna nodded to the startled cottage dwellers.

"It's the queen, you see," said Enna. "She's going to have a baby in your house. You don't mind?"

When the pains really started, Isi jabbered madly in the language of the south, bird tongue, and some curse words that made the cottage owner blush and his wife laugh. The pains came and went for hours, and Isi was red faced and sweaty and tired, and sometimes she cried a little. Just before sundown, a noise made her stop midholler. From outside came the rumbling rhythm of hoofbeats, then the whinnying of a horse who stopped suddenly. The door flung open. It was Geric.

"Isi, I'm here, I'm here."

And it was, as well, half the court.

Geric rushed to Isi's side, palace physicians gathered around the bed, a birth mistress pushed them all away again, the chief steward took command of the cottage kitchen and fire, a hundred-band was heard to position themselves in a defensive posture all around the building, and voices from outside told them that many more people had gathered. Enna sighed, relieved that at least one of her messages had made it to the capital ahead of them.

When the birth mistress had her way, all but Geric and one capable nurse-mary were shooed from Isi's bed and out the door. Finn took Enna's hand, and they walked into the cutting light of a bright summer evening and the midst of a small crowd. Enna squinted into the setting sun to see what was happening. They were all looking at her.

Several people, some of them Forest dwellers she had long known, pushed some cut logs up by the door and pressed her to step on top of one. She looked up, afraid to see a noose waiting for her. Talone appeared. The crowd quieted their whispering.

"Talone, I'm sorry," she said.

He nodded. "Perhaps this is not the place for such business, but as it is the first time we've seen you for some time, and who knows where you will slip to after this, I have little choice." He raised his voice for the crowd. "Enna of the Forest, for disobeying a war captain and treacherous acts, you are hereby stripped of your title of queen's maiden."

The crowd murmured, and someone shouted angrily. Enna was not sure if it was directed at her. Talone cleared his throat.

"I'm certain this is not the queen's wish, but acts must be accounted for. However, we won't stop there. For stubborn bravery and ingenuity in defense of the kingdom, His Highness bids me make you one of Bayern's Own, a member of the king's personal hundred-band."

"Wait, Talone," she said, "I don't deserve—"

"Don't interrupt, please." He turned back to the crowd. "She fought in secret, she was captured and imprisoned, and she escaped in time to stop Tira's invading force before they could overwhelm our army and invade the capital." He took her hand and held it aloft. "Never has Bayern seen such a warrior."

The crowd did not hesitate when it burst into applause and cheers. More hands pushed Finn up beside her, and she saw someone else step up. Her eyes were bleary now, and she had to blink several times before she could make out his face.

"Razo!"

"You might've waited for me to heal before you went off again," he said. "Though I see Finn found you all right. Hello there, Finn. Well done."

"Hello, Razo. Enna loves me, did you hear?"

Razo laughed. "Of course she does. See, Enna, I told you someday people'd chant our names."

Enna listened to the calls and did not detect any chanting, so began to say quietly, "Razo, Razo." He punched her shoulder.

Enna felt strange atop that stump, the cheers of the people touching her like soft slaps, a combination of aggression and love. The village was not far from the field where she had burned a tenth of the army of Tira. A day from there stood the place where she had dragged Leifer's body to the funeral pyre. The heat from the crowd wafted around her, the breeze that touched her skin told her of clapping hands. So much had changed in a year, she felt stretched and twisted like poorly used cloth. After all this, who would she be? Finn squeezed her hand.

"Go on, Enna-girl," said Razo, "why aren't you smiling? I'd think this would be your scene."

Enna shrugged. "Maybe I've changed."

Razo rolled his eyes. "What a lot of rot." He grabbed her hand and held it up. "For Bayern!"

And the crowd cheered.

As the sun set, villagers joined in the celebration, light-ing fires and warming cider. At last they heard the sharp crack of a baby's first wail. Finn and Enna looked at each other with relief. It was a healthy, loud cry. The birth mis-tress emerged and signaled that Enna could come, with Razo, Talone, and Finn following.

Isi's face was streaked with sweat, but her eyes sparkled. Geric's eyes were wet and cheeks pressed with an unvarying smile, and when he held the baby he seemed completely unable to acknowledge that anyone else existed. At last he relinquished his hold and placed the newborn carefully in Enna's eager arms.

"A boy," said Geric. "After Isi's father—Tusken."

"If it'd been a girl," said Isi, "we were going to call her Enna-Isilee."

"Oh, there'll be others," said Enna.

Geric's eyes widened and he smiled with pure, boylike joy at the thought.

"How does he look to you?" asked Isi.

Enna touched his doe-soft skin. "Perfect. Completely perfect."

She cooed at Tusken, and he looked up at her, almost as if he saw her with his wide, pale eyes. Her heart ached to see such beauty. She touched the healthy folds of skin around the baby's neck, wrists, and thighs, the dark lines crying for life made in his forehead, and thought how people start with wrinkles and end with wrinkles, grow into their skin and then live to grow out of it again.

Just then, Enna felt at home in her own skin, not stretched or sagged or scorched. Everything felt right. Outside, the voice of merriment. Inside, a good fire crackled in the hearth, Geric knelt beside Isi's bed kissing her hands, and a healthy baby stared at his new world.

Enna was glad to have Finn's hand on her own, and that his skin felt right next to hers. She could feel the quiet, good heat in his touch and thought that it was all she would ever need feel. From the Forest, through the window, came a wisp of wind to twine through her hair. She listened to where it touched her neck——*a spring, muddy banks, wasps buzzing, mushrooms climb a pine, a pine needle falls.*

She was home.

The End

Acknowledgments

This work was supported in part by an individual artist grant from the Utah Arts Council. I would also like to acknowledge the following superpeople: Victoria Wells Arms, editor extraordinaire, whose first allegiance is always to the characters; Amy Jameson, my very own Anne Sullivan; and the early readers/editors who give wisdom and hope—Dean Hale, Rosi Hayes, and T. L. Trent.